Praise for t

Playing with Fire

...*Playing With Fire* is an emotional rollercoaster that masterfully captures a journey of healing and self-discovery. The portrayal of trauma and its lasting effects is both poignant and achingly real, resonating with readers who have experienced similar struggles. This story is a testament to the author's ability to craft a story that tugs at the heartstrings, making readers reflect on the power of resilience, love, and the human spirit.

-Shimere A., *NetGalley*

...Beautifully written...I really enjoyed this!

-Kerrie V., *NetGalley*

Training for Love

I'm a big fan of authors who take the time to really develop their characters and both Charlie and Elizabeth were really well written. Both these characters have issues, some based on past experiences, lifestyle, others that are foisted on them. In this story Kabak tackles the sensitive topic of mental health with Charlie being bipolar. The helplessness and the struggle to lead and participate in life is captured extremely well. I also liked the pacing of the book, the titles depicting the training milestones were a nice touch. Charlie's coaching of Elizabeth through her 8-mile run was a particularly good exchange and I really enjoyed it. I do like slow burns and this definitely fell into that category.

-D Booker, *NetGalley*

If you're looking for a book with characters you can't help but like with conflicts that are "real," then this is the book for you. If you want a well-paced book that is also well-written, do not pass on this book.

-Abbott F., *NetGalley*

Ms. Kabak has given us a story about a bipolar woman and an overworked business owner. Strong characters along with a moving plot kept me from putting this book down. Very nice read.

-Bonnie S., *NetGalley*

Changing Her Tune

AMANDA KABAK

Other Bella Books by Amanda Kabak

Playing with Fire
Training for Love

About the Author

Amanda Kabak is the author of the novels *Upended* and *The Mathematics of Change*. She has published stories in *The Massachusetts Review, Tahoma Literary Review, Sequestrum,* and other print and online periodicals. She has been awarded the Lascaux Review fiction award, *Arcturus Review*'s Al-Simāk award for fiction, the Betty Gabehart prize from the Kentucky Women Writer's Conference, and multiple Pushcart Prize nominations. She's lived in Boston, Chicago, and the wilds of Florida, but her home is wherever her wife, Anna, is.

Changing Her Tune

AMANDA KABAK

BELLA
BOOKS

2024

Bella Books, Inc.
P.O. Box 10543
Tallahassee, FL 32302

This is a work of fiction. Names, characters, businesses, places, events and incidents are either the products of the author's imagination or used in a fictitious manner. Any resemblance to actual persons, living or dead, or actual events is purely coincidental. The publisher does not have any control over and does not assume any responsibility for author or third-party websites or their content.

First Edition - 2024

Editor: Medora MacDougall
Cover Designer: Kayla Mancuso

ISBN: 978-1-64247-592-0

PUBLISHER'S NOTE

Acknowledgment

Though I traded music for writing fifteen years ago (there are only so many hours in the day), playing and singing were once the highlights of my week. Disappearing into breath and sound, pitch and rhythm unhooks the mind and turns it around a few times. What's better than that? To be part of a performance, bringing notes on the page to life for other people to hear is a warm rush of satisfaction. Writing about it is the same.

First impressions are both dangerous and necessary. We need to celebrate our differences, not use them to judge and dismiss. This takes time and an open mind, both of which I gave to these characters, but they are often in short supply in real life. We have to remember that we're all just doing our best to make it through; better to do that together instead of on our own.

Enough of the preaching and on with the thanks. To Jessica, Tracie, and the rest of the crew at Bella Books: I wouldn't be here without you. Nancy, your keen editorial eye untangled my sentences and kept me honest throughout. I must've gotten the details of freelance editing down in this book or I surely would have been under your (digital) red pen.

Anna, music helped bind us together in the beginning, and whatever nurtured our start down this life-long love affair is tops in my book. None of this would be the same without you. As always, thank you for being my first reader and biggest champion.

For Anna, because of everything.

CHAPTER ONE

For Cait Durant, editing was a delicate game of excavation. She used a sort-of x-ray vision to trace the sparkling, branching veins of goodness within the bedrock of each manuscript. Almost every time, hiding there, just beneath the surface, was exactly what needed to be exposed to enrich the writing currently on the page—or her screen. The glow of her laptop was a miner's headlamp laying bare every clumsy turn of phrase, heavy-handed characterization, or missed opportunity. She loved to read above all else, and when she'd been young and whimsical, she'd thought she'd grow up to be a writer. The ability to read critically had come slowly at first, but the first time she'd unearthed something not quite right in an essay that had seemed perfect on her first reading, she found her calling with the resonant click of the right path opening before her.

She had been successfully freelancing for the last five years and had turned her home office into a sanctum of thought and productivity, complete with a full-spectrum lamp, a shudderingly expensive sit-stand desk, and a small white-noise machine she'd bought when her neighbor to the left and his girlfriend had gone through a phase so passionate and loud with sex that Cait was equally disturbed and impressed.

The only regular disturbance to her work now was Pancho Villa, her Great Dane. She had adopted Pancho when buffeted by loneliness, so far removed from the act of being intimate with another woman that she couldn't quite remember how it went. While he grew and grew and grew—he now stood chest high to Cait…when he bothered to get out of his cushy bed in the corner—they had provided each other with much-needed affection. Then, as it sometimes went, acquiring this companion had activated the universe's bent toward coupledom, and she'd met Lauren.

Lauren had seemed to like Pancho well enough, even though he was alarmingly large, even as a six-month-old puppy. But a couple of years later, in their final acrimonious weeks together, she'd referred to him as "livestock." Though Cait told herself that was certainly just spite, she had upped the frequency of his baths, something she did outside whenever the weather permitted. Her tub was child-sized, not even big enough for her, let alone a squirming cow of a dog. It didn't fix anything. Pancho now smelled fresh as the proverbial daisy, but the bitter stink of her breakup with Lauren still permeated the apartment.

Lauren had had a lot to say at the end, accusing Cait of being shut down and controlling and of working too much at a job she was never going to be acknowledged for doing. She took issue with the intense training Cait had put Pancho through to make him a model citizen, claiming the dog was now unnaturally behaved. She got on Cait for not introducing her to Cait's family and even for her "obsession" with lifting weights at the gym. But, of course, she'd never complained about the resulting solidness of Cait's body, how fleshy and strong she was, or how completely Cait could cover her in bed, her almost-six-foot frame good for something other than swimming and lifting. No, but she'd spent plenty of time conjecturing why Cait had gotten a dog nearly as big as she was, hinting at some sort of complex when it had just seemed like the most natural thing. Who could picture her with a Chihuahua?

The breakup had taken Cait by surprise, like the unsupported twist ending of an otherwise capable novel. Either Lauren's capacity for vitriol had been stealthy or Cait had been oblivious. It had made her wonder what else she wasn't seeing about her life, but instead of taking a good look around, she did exactly what would have made Lauren roll her eyes in exasperation: she doubled down on work.

She made her living doing contract editing for individual writers as well as for some smaller presses and bigger websites. A good portion of her work came from Grovetree Press, which published a couple of dozen titles a year and accounted for half of her billable hours. Martha Grimes steered the ship over there and threw Cait work with such regularity that the two of them had become friends, trading witty emails and conversation over the thousand miles between Chicago, where Martha lived, and Boston, where Cait had lived since she'd left her hometown in far eastern Tennessee as soon as humanly possible to move into her college's dorms and make her start as a student-athlete.

Though she'd lived all over the city over the last ten years, now she rented a place in North Cambridge, spitting distance from Arlington and neither here nor there, which is what helped make it affordable. She could walk to the T, her gym, a Foodmaster grocery store, and, with a little extra stretch in her step, to Davis Square in Somerville, where she could satisfy her craving for barbeque, tacos, and ice cream, among other things. Though her neighborhood had started succumbing to gentrification, rents were still reliably low, and her side street was quiet and more tree-lined than others. She'd moved into this building two years before and wasn't planning on leaving any time soon.

Through her window, the light on this late-winter day had started to wane, and every time she moved, Pancho raised his head from where he was curled up on his bed, signaling that it was time for his evening perambulation. Being a big dog didn't mean he needed or even wanted big exercise. Great Danes were essentially overgrown lap dogs and were largely content following their owners around the house. Pancho had been an exuberant puppy when she'd rescued him, a big baby forever growing into his paws and head, but now he was dignified in his middle age, having turned three a few months before. In honor of his most recent trip around the sun, Cait had bought him a ridiculously expensive doggie dessert at a boutique pet store a couple of miles down Mass Ave from her apartment. Even though he demolished it in half the time it took for her to unpackage it, it had felt like money well spent.

She turned to him. "One more call, buddy." His tail thumped, but he didn't get up. While she lowered her desk from its standing position, she called Martha about the book she'd just finished reading, the first of two passes she'd make for this developmental editing run. This kind of work was much more exciting than line editing, though she offered both services. Line work was like detailed embroidery compared to development, which operated at the higher level of the fabric itself, examining its warp and weave and the way it was dyed and cut. Story arcs, characterization, motivation, themes, and resonance were why she got up in the morning. She didn't just do this for the money, though that was nice; she truly loved her work and loved the high of accomplishment that solving editorial puzzles left her with.

Martha answered. "You're so good at coming in as the last call of the day."

"You're a creature of habit, and I pay attention." Cait eased herself into her chair. Martha had two kids and a husband—a family with all the trimmings, as Cait thought of it—and she did an admirable job of turning off the publisher side of her identity in the evenings and for most weekends. Better than Cait, according to Lauren.

"Please tell me you're calling about *Put Title Here*."

"I just finished it." Cait took a beat to find the words she should have arranged in her mind before even picking up the phone.

"Whoa, really?"

"I haven't even said anything."

"Your pauses are eloquent. And the tone of your voice."

"Now you sound like my mother." She leaned back in her chair and gazed up at the ceiling, which was "popcorned" with little balls of plaster.

"You didn't like it?"

"I wouldn't put it that way, and it doesn't matter whether I like something or not." Though, of course, it helped if she could balance her intellectual and emotional responses. Besides, if she truly hated the thing, she'd be way more diplomatic about it, given how much of her rent Grovetree paid. "It's just not as far along as I'd think it'd be at this point."

"Fine. Point taken, but it's a great story, and there are some real gems hidden in the sentences."

"I totally agree, but there's a bunch of excavation and restructuring necessary to make it shine the way it should. Consider the character of Dahlia, who's introduced in the first chapter but dropped until the second half of the book. Or the secondary story of the car and its restoration and ownership? Maybe that could serve a purpose, but I'm not sure what it's doing in there right now. It's taking up easily fifteen thousand words, which is a lot of real estate. If it was a boat, it might make more sense because then it would tie in Richard and Ursula even more."

"That's brilliant. All of it, but the boat? I can't see that. Cait, you know I buy more for potential than what's literally on the page, and that'd be a terrible strategy if I didn't have you in our corner."

Cait's neck started to complain at her position, but she didn't move. She still felt the urge to reach up and memorize the textured ceiling's bumps and crevices with her fingertips. She waited, playing phone chicken with Martha, though she knew she was doomed to break first. And she did. "How's the author going to take this feedback? I'm assuming it's a man?" She always read her manuscripts scrubbed clean of identifying information the first pass through so she wouldn't get biased.

"What makes you assume that?"

"It would be a very special woman to know that much about a 1966 BMW 2002. Not impossible but unlikely. And his female characters are a little less developed than the men."

"It took him seven years to find a publisher—"

Probably because the manuscript was still a mess.

"—so he'll do whatever we ask of him as long as we're not talking about substantial changes to the story."

Cait had been around the block enough to know what that really meant and thought about passing on the project. Her contracts always had an out written into them, but even though she and Martha were friendly, refusing something would certainly leave a bad taste in Martha's mouth and could jeopardize future business.

She said, "Okay, but please send out an introductory email or put a meeting together so everyone can be clear on expectations before we start."

"Your wish is my command."

"As if. I still have to read it again, okay? It'll take a couple weeks, but I wanted to give you a heads-up that I think it's going to take some time for the author to make the kind of changes I'm going to be suggesting."

"Noted. Just as long as he stays on the path for publication in eighteen months at most. This will be the featured book for next fall."

Cait couldn't stop a laugh. "Sorry. It's just that the timeline is entirely up to him, as you know." After some ending pleasantries, she hung up and set down her phone, feeling a certain ominous anxiety in the pit of her stomach. This time, when she got up, Pancho followed her lead, his tail sweeping the air behind him, thwacking on the bookshelf to his right. "Out?" she asked, which made him lope to the front door and smell its handle like he'd never been there before.

After making sure no one was in the hallway, she slipped out of the apartment with him and down the stairs, taking a right when they hit the sidewalk. Pancho garnered a lot of attention, especially when he was walking along with his square head held high, sniffing the crook of Cait's elbow. Either people were afraid of him, which Cait could understand, or they were fascinated, remarking on his size, the distinguishing black spots on his gray coat, the set of his eyes, and the length of his muzzle. Sometimes they approached without asking, overcome by their own excitement. Cait let them pet Pancho and look him up and down, giving him his five minutes of fame before urging him along to accomplish the actual aim of their going outside.

She didn't mind the attention because it wasn't really directed at her, but there were times when her purposeful stride was interrupted too often, and she got cranky. Evenings were better, since they arrived at the park after most people had gone home to dinner, two giant specimens of their respective species, moving under the radar in the dark or late evening's light. A matched set. She was always more frustrated than Pancho at the lack of exercise, but their walks were at least a little about her, her needs mattering no less than his. She was the one who kept him in the heap of kibble he required, after all.

He reminded her of the things in her life that made her happy and her own participation in her happiness. His familiar face and lumbering run; a sparkling turn of phrase; the luxurious sheets she'd just purchased; springtime in Boston, which was exuberant with blooms and a pale, robin's egg sky; and the smell of the gym, down to the metallic tang of the bench press bar. She was generally positive about things, especially her ability to craft each day to her own specifications: freedom and self-direction. But then she tripped on the fact that the only one around to share these things with was Pancho.

Sometimes she wondered if he'd be the only match she'd ever have. Even months after the fact, Lauren's parting words still stung, her accusation too close to the truth to be dismissed. "You're always telling people how wrong they are from behind the scenes but never putting yourself out there to be criticized." There'd been more, but her ears had stopped working at some point, turning Lauren into a silent movie of disdain. Had she really thought that? If so, how did they make it over two years together? How much had been an act and how much had been real? If Cait could go back, what would she have to edit to have their story come out differently in the end—or to avoid an end entirely?

She rested her hand on Pancho's back, absorbing the reassuring warmth of him. She didn't tell people what was wrong with them, not really. The only right or wrong in writing could be caught with fact-checking, not what she did. "Wrong" was the wrong word, though she supposed that was more of her nitpicking. She dealt with unearthing potential, in seeing both what wasn't there and what could be changed in what was, in envisioning a more ideal state and some possible paths to get there from where they all started. If people took this as telling them they were wrong, that was their fault.

But, of course, this was exactly what she was afraid of with Martha's new acquisition. Telling someone their book could be great if they only reworked it significantly required a tact she didn't always have the mental fortitude to employ. Maybe that was why Lauren had left. She'd started out loving Cait's bluntness, but Cait knew it could wear thin. Calling it like she saw it was helpful in some ways and harmful in others, and Cait didn't always know the difference.

She goosed Pancho into a more purposeful walk to forestall any more social encounters and rounded the corner that would take them home.

CHAPTER TWO

Allie Coleman tried to make lessons fun for her students. Unfortunately, this didn't keep them from realizing how much work was involved in going from sucking at playing the trumpet to being any good. This progression happened sooner for some, later for others, and the definition of "any good" varied widely across them. For some, being good meant being able to handle the third trumpet part in a John Phillips Sousa march without embarrassing themselves. For others, it meant being as good as Allie.

She was woman enough to admit it: the trumpet wasn't the hardest instrument to nudge past what she called "the suck threshold" to achieve competence. The French horn was way more difficult, with its miles of tubing and tiny, little mouthpiece, and she had no idea how anyone managed the harp. Until you got past the suck threshold with anything—an instrument, drawing, or doing your taxes—the activity just, well, sucked. Getting better was a grind it was her job to help shorten as much as possible for fledgling trumpeters. Of course, that meant she had to listen to a lot of sucky playing across the dozen or so individual lessons she gave every week.

Like this poor kid. Toby was a train wreck and either didn't practice at all between lessons or didn't remember anything she tried to teach him. How he could be so thumb-fingered with only three valves to work with was beyond her, and his cheeks still ballooned out while he played. It was because of this last trait that she'd nicknamed him Dizzy. Other students were Miles, Winston, Louis, Chet, or any of the other great trumpeters of the last century. They were aspirational names, and she played some of their namesakes' music at the beginning of each lesson to get them in the mood.

"Dizzy," she said loudly to interrupt the kid halfway through the current exercise they were working through. He lowered his instrument and looked at Allie. A telltale red ring straddled his lips, the exact size and shape of his mouthpiece. "What dynamic is it there?" She pointed at the italicized "p" on the sheet music in front of them.

"Piano."

"Were you playing softly?"

"I—"

"Let me rephrase that. Do you remember how to play softly?"

He thought for a while, looking down at his dirty tennis shoes. Finally, his head jerked up, and he said, "Use more air. But how come that doesn't make it louder again?"

Allie explained the best she could, not being an expert in physics or anything like it. She talked about energy, about sustaining power, about supporting the diaphragm and breathing from his belly. All the things she'd told him in every lesson for the past month. He nodded and appeared determined. He actually managed some semblance of dynamic shading before they had both had just about enough of each other and he packed up and left.

She checked her watch, closed the door behind him, and cleared spit from her own instrument. Her trumpet was a splotchy, unvarnished version of young Dizzy's flashy, brassy one. In fact, it was more like the original Dizzy's instrument (minus the angled bell). It was nothing much to look at considering that Allie got paid for what came out of it. She wouldn't get paid, though, if she didn't manage to learn the studio piece she was scheduled to record with a small brass band tomorrow. She raised her stand and stood, coming in a couple of inches taller than her usual five-foot-nothing due to her wedges.

Allie liked being a studio musician, which meant she could sleep in her own bed every night and play a variety of music during the day. She'd toured a few times with various shows, once a big-name headliner where they did forty shows in sixty days. The road was not a life she liked. Being a studio musician meant what came out of her bell got recorded on a master—digital or analog—and lived on for posterity while she moved on to the next piece, be it a film score, backing tracks for a pop artist, or the odd commercial.

Taking advantage of an open half hour between lessons, she worked through runs and entrances, using a pencil to mark lurking dynamics and tempo changes. Studio work didn't build in much time for rehearsal, and you likely would never play the music again once the recording sessions were over. It relied more heavily on your ability to get up to speed more quickly than you needed to do in a traditional orchestra, including community orchestras, where she was sometimes brought in as a ringer. Over the last decade, she'd played Beethoven's Ninth Symphony more times than she could count. Oh, and there was Orff's *Carmina Burana*, Mahler's First, and back to Beethoven for his Fifth. She didn't even need sheet music for those anymore.

The practice room she rented was a depressing cinderblock stuck with acoustical foam to kill the worst of the echo. In one corner was the upright piano she used only as a tuning reference for those of her students who played fast and loose with their pitch. Beyond that, she had only two chairs, two stands, and a banged-up filing cabinet she used as a side table for water and snacks—for after lessons, not before. Otherwise, you might blow a chunk of cookie deep into your instrument in your zeal.

Allie had spent a large portion of her life in rooms just like this one. The trumpet was loud and was exceptionally good at disturbing those anywhere near her. It wasn't her fault. The instrument was built to spur soldiers into battle, horses into the hunt, and to rouse people from their beds at ungodly hours of the morning. Loudness was a key feature, not a side effect. Accordingly, she sealed herself away in practice rooms like this one, where she could play her heart out for half the day without alienating anyone.

Being a musician was all she'd wanted since she'd passed the suck threshold back when she was ten, but it was a strange life. While not all musicians had the same experience, for her, it was a life of extremes. She went from hiding away in a practice room to playing shoulder to shoulder with colleagues in a recording studio, to donning a black skirt and white shirt and blowing her way through a classical piece in front of a few hundred people. There was jazz, too, which filled some of her evenings with improvisation and mixed drinks between sets.

Making ends meet was a tap dance, for sure, but she got to do what she loved and had been doing it enough that she no longer worried where her next paycheck would come from, focusing instead on living within her not-very-spectacular means. This practice room was an expense, but a necessary one—and one she got to write off on her taxes every year.

She was interrupted by a knock on the door and a wave of a hand in the narrow window to its side. Miles. Not quite as bad as Dizzy, but he had a long way to go. Good thing she liked teaching well enough, or it would be a nails on a chalkboard experience, for sure. She let him in, and they got started.

Hours later, when it was well past dinnertime, she slipped her trumpet into her black, soft-sided gig bag, slung it over her shoulder, and headed out to freedom and food. On her way, she ran into Carl, a trombone player she saw at studio sessions sometimes. He was carrying an office-paper box in front of him and had his own gig bag, the strap of which slanted over his chest.

He said, "Are you all cleaned out?"

One eyebrow quirked up in a questioning look.

"For tomorrow?"

"What, are they fumigating again? Wasn't that just a few months ago?"

"It was last year, Allie, but no. Didn't you get the memo?"

She laughed. "Do I look like I work in an office?"

He stopped. "Debra was right. You have no idea, do you?"

"What, specifically, don't I know?" She may have been blond, but she wasn't an idiot.

"Renovations start tomorrow. They say it's for aesthetics, but I heard it was for asbestos. We won't be able to get in for months. I thought we'd see you running around like a crazy person today, but I couldn't imagine you didn't know what was going on. They've sent, like, six notices to everyone with leases here."

Asbestos? Months? Allie stood rooted on the spot, not able (or willing) to comprehend what she'd just been told. As painful as this was to admit, this was probably her own damn fault. She had a nasty habit of not checking her mail until it was so crammed into her box she ripped it to shreds trying to get it out. Then it was hit or miss if she actually read it. But…asbestos? Allie couldn't calculate the number of hours she'd spent in her practice space, taking deep breaths and blowing them out through one of her three trumpets, her coronet, or even the flugelhorn she kept mostly for kicks. All those mesothelioma ads she'd seen on TV as a kid before the world went all streaming replayed in her head.

She said, "You knew this and didn't tell me?"

"Honestly, I didn't think you needed a reminder."

"Fine, Debra didn't tell me?"

"You know Debra."

Allie did, indeed, know Debra. She was a drummer in a band that shared a large corner unit with two other groups and came and went at some of the same hours as Allie. Allie dug her cell phone from her purse and called Debra, who started laughing when she answered. "I made a bet about this, and I totally won."

"A bet about what, when the building would be razed as a health hazard?"

"What? No. About when you'd figure out what was happening."

"You knew and didn't tell me?" She slowly started to move through the hallway and to the front door, where, plain as day, there was a notice posted on neon-yellow paper with tomorrow's date featured prominently in large font.

"That would've ruined the fun."

"I see students in that space, Deb."

"Ah. Right, I forgot about that." Her gleeful tone sobered. "Can't you work out of your apartment or something? Or go to your students' houses?"

Allie's prodigious breath control was failing her. "If you get a line on some good temporary space, you'd better tell me. I gotta go make about a hundred calls and figure a way out of this mess. I can't believe no one told me. This is my life you're all screwing with."

"We mostly didn't know you didn't—"

Allie hung up and ducked back into the building to pick up some music and her favorite metronome. Nothing else in there was anything she couldn't live without. Finally, she stepped out onto the sidewalk. It was long since dark, and cars bustled up and down the street, their headlights blinding her. She felt unmoored in her predicament, cast out of her second home, a place she'd had for as long as her actual apartment. How could she be so stupid? How could her friends be so unhelpful? Could she even consider them friends after this? Clearly she was more of a friend to them than they were to her, as usual. Regardless, what in the world was she going to do?

She was a perfectly responsible person, aside from her irrational hatred of mail. She made a living as a musician, which was no walk in the park. Her schedule was brutal and relentless, and she wasn't getting rich any time soon. That said, she got to do what she loved, which made the grind worth it. Though there wasn't much she could do until she was at home with her whole insane calendar in front of her, she started to process this massive change in plans and to work through the cascading domino effect it was about to kick off. It wouldn't affect the studio gigs, but she'd have to practice at home, damn it. Her lessons? She'd have to have them at her apartment, too.

They were mostly after school but still during work hours, so it shouldn't disturb people around her. Trumpets were loud. Kids playing trumpets were loud and terrible. Even as a player herself, it had taken some time for her to get used to the assault of it.

She started walking to her apartment, the wind cutting through her slacks, reminding her that springtime warmth in Boston was often a fleeting aberration. Her stomach growled and her head swam, but all she could do right now was put one foot in front of the other, marking time and distance in a steady rhythm of steps.

Her building was a lemon-yellow monstrosity that was surprisingly nice inside, aside from the wheezy elevator that failed so often it might as well not exist. It was more a slap in the face than anything, especially when someone was moving in. It anchored the bottom of a U of apartments—and the catwalk-style open hallways on the higher floors. Most people used the somewhat grand staircase that crisscrossed its way to the fourth floor on the right side of the atrium and opened up at Allie's doorstep. The building had no amenities, but the apartments had redone hardwood floors and built-ins and kitchens nice enough that she almost felt guilty about not using anything in hers except for the refrigerator and microwave. The windows were original, the walls a boring white, the heat gurgled continuously throughout winter, and the closets were insufficient. Allie loved it, especially since the rent was somewhat reasonable and walking up the stairs to her third-floor unit wasn't a hardship. She'd lived there the last four years and knew most of the other tenants. She'd have to give something to the ones nearest to her as a bribe for putting up with all the noise for the next few months. Wine or baked goods or earplugs. Yes, earplugs for everyone.

She let herself in the building, hoofed it up the two flights of stairs to her apartment just off the landing, and settled in at her small kitchen table, her planner open in front of her. She might suck at reading her mail (and email for that matter), but she was disciplined about her schedule. Each appointment was color-coded, travel time was marked in gray, and buffer space was noted for events that tended to run long. She had it on paper and electronically, a double-entry system that was tedious but had proven its necessity multiple times over the years. She started calling her students.

Forty-five minutes later, she tossed her phone on the coffee table, done with reiterating the semi-true party line a dozen times. It was a good thing she lived so close to her defunct practice space; none of her students' parents had had a problem with shifting the location to her apartment, even with such short notice.

She dug around in her stuffed front closet for the practice mute she kept there and loved to hate. When shoved in the end of her bell, it did just what it said, muted her sound so she could play without disturbing those around her. It let her feel mostly like she was playing at an unimpeded full volume, but it robbed her sound of all its strength. She only used it in emergencies, like when she had to play in a hotel room or when someone was asleep nearby and she couldn't find any place better to practice.

She'd last used it in Kendra's living room before they'd broken up. Had it been six months ago already? The one thing she didn't have called out in her planner was time for a relationship. Only another musician could understand her schedule, but then that person would be involved in the same craziness, and they would be doomed before they even really started.

Allie didn't look like a trumpet player, whatever that meant. She had long honey-blond hair and painted nails. She actually liked skirts and preferred heels when she wasn't going to be on her feet for hours teaching or practicing. She was a few inches short of full-sized (in every direction), which made those heels useful, and she sported two symmetric and equally deep dimples she used to try to smooth right off her face when she was younger. But, oh, she could make her trumpet do some nasty things, squeals and shouts, yips and growls.

Every new place she played, she had to prove herself because of her angelic face and petite frame, which had made her consider herself a fuck-you femme. Fuck you because she insisted on it despite how it made her life more difficult. Fuck you because she liked what she liked, and she wasn't going to apologize for it. Fuck you because that's what the trumpet was, unabashedly loud, leading the charge into battle against all odds.

Too bad that attitude wouldn't get her out of this current jam.

CHAPTER THREE

In college, Cait had spent a lot of her time in the library, not only because that's where all the books were but because it was quiet. Though she had learned to deal with low music or conversation in the background, she never could get used to working with a lot of ambient noise around. One of the very best things about working for herself was that she could stay in her apartment, where the environment was controlled and she could relax into the hum of the refrigerator or the sound of steam in the radiator. Her office was a cocoon of quiet productivity, especially when the rest of the building was a ghost town during the day—or maybe only populated with home-workers like her.

So when a strange and terrible *noise* radiated up from under her feet just after she finished her lunch of a turkey sandwich with a side of carrots and hummus, both she and Pancho raised their heads as if sensing an approaching storm. It stopped and started again, settling into a recognizable pattern of pitches. Cait stiffened, listening, her hand hovering over her laptop, a half-finished sentence ending in a blinking cursor on the screen.

Another pause, but before she could take a breath, it came again, faster and louder than before, moving up and down the scale like a machine gun that fired sound instead of bullets. The notes might as well have been made of metal because she felt pierced by them. Whoever was playing—because it obviously wasn't a recording—was trained, but the sound buzzed and grated against her eardrums. Listening to it was like being faced with a disaster and being unable to turn away from the carnage. She couldn't seem to move at all while the assault continued, couldn't stop listening, couldn't make sense of it all.

When it lagged long enough for Cait to think it might be over, she and Pancho relaxed, and the answer came to her: it had to be coming from the apartment directly downstairs from her, given where the sound had seemed to have come from. This old building's walls were tissue-paper thin, and the floors were no exception. A short, blond woman lived below her, and though Cait avoided idle conversation as a general rule, she knew her neighbor was a musician. Even so, Cait had never heard anything louder than a murmur from below her feet. Maybe this was a total aberration, her showing off for some guy or something. Whatever it was, Cait now knew for certain that the floor and ceiling between them might as well be like the Swiss cheese on her sandwich for all that it was able to block out sound.

A few noises followed but nothing out of the ordinary, and Cait had just about reminded herself of where the sentence she'd been writing was supposed to go when something even worse started.

It was...it was...almost like music? But maybe how music would sound in hell. If she hadn't known before exactly how good her neighbor was at whatever instrument she'd been playing, Cait knew it now. In comparison to what was unfolding beneath Cait's feet, her neighbor was a musical genius. This was like bleating. No, honking from an otherworldly goose. A horrible whining jeer. She catapulted to her feet, jostling her desk and inciting a scrambling answer from Pancho that would have been funny if she'd remotely been in the mood to be entertained.

In a time-lapsed instant, she was down the stairs and in front of Apartment 3B, pounding on the door with the side of her fist, desperate to cut through the noise she was down here to complain about. Of course, it stopped just when she'd hit the shiny wood hard enough to make her hand throb. Adrenaline coursed through her body, making her fingertips tingle. It took all her gumption and indignation not to run away. If there was one thing Cait always tried to avoid, it was confrontation. When the door opened, she said, "It's too loud," in a voice that was itself too loud and shook from the effort of turning flight into fight.

"Oh, hey, just…" The woman ducked back into the apartment. "Hang tight, Maynard, I'll be right there. Just look at passage fourteen. Look, don't play. Try to hear it in your mind." She stepped out into the hall, forcing Cait to move back.

Cait blinked at the unlikely tableau they made: she, a former collegiate swimmer, a smidge short of six feet in her socks, and her neighbor, a real-life pixie, small, blond, blue-eyed, and dimpled, wearing a wraparound skirt and heels. In other circumstances, Cait would find her intolerably adorable, but these weren't other circumstances, not by a long shot.

"I'm trying to work upstairs," Cait said. "You can't just—"

"Yeah, I know, and I'm sorry. The practice space I've been renting for years shut down for renovations today, and I'm in a jam. I swear, all my students aren't this bad, but Maynard is just starting out and doesn't like to practice. Anyway, I only teach part-time, so it shouldn't be too bad. Oh, well, I'll need to practice, too, but that's probably not why you're down here." Her smile, while objectively delightful, made Cait's blood boil.

"Your space closed with no notice?"

"Well, see—"

"There are other people in the building, you know." Cait's arms crossed in front of her chest out of their own volition.

"Yep, I'm aware of that, and we all have to make a living."

"My point exactly."

The neighbor's face hardened in a way Cait couldn't have imagined. "It's outside quiet hours, and I'll be doing what I can to keep the disturbance to a minimum." She turned to go back into her apartment.

This wasn't going how Cait had envisioned it, not that she'd really gotten that far before she'd started whaling on that door. She stuck out her hand. "Can we start over? I'm Cait Durant. I live upstairs in 4B."

The neighbor turned around. "I know. I introduced myself when you moved in. Cute girlfriend, by the way."

Cait, caught off guard, fell back on righteous indignation. "You're saying I just have to deal with this? What's your name again?"

"I'm Allie Coleman. I'm saying I'd appreciate some flexibility while I try to work things out. I'm sorry that we started out with Maynard in there but just, like, pretend it's street construction you have no control over. I have a whole pack of great earplugs you can use if you want."

"I hate wearing those."

"Sucks to be you, then." Allie's smile was no longer warm at all, especially paired with thunderous eyebrows that were several shades darker than her hair. "I need to get back to work," she said and went into her apartment without another word, shutting the door with a firm finality.

Cait stood on the worn, less-than-clean hallway carpeting, noting distractedly that it was a different pattern from the one on her floor. Before she could take a step, "Maynard" started playing again. It was so much worse without the slight muffling provided by the floor, the discordant sound finding every last gap between Allie's door and the rest of the building. Cait fled back upstairs, where she annoyed Pancho by pacing a horseshoe shape from her bedroom, though her living room, into her office, and back again. For a while, he tried to stay at heel, and the two of them jockeyed for position in doorways and around furniture, but he soon tired of this game and watched her from his bed in the office.

This was absolutely impossible. Earplugs? The last thing she wanted was to become a human conch shell, her own bodily creaks and groans amplified inside the canals of her blocked ears. She'd had enough of that as a youth swimmer with an overprotective mother who was sure she was one practice away from going deaf due to swimmer's ear. She'd eschewed the little foam plugs even on those nights when Lauren had overindulged and slept so hard she'd snored like an emphysemic old man. Lauren, right. "Cute girlfriend"? For everything Allie seemed to know, she was out of date on that one.

What commercial space closed like that with no notice? Wasn't that illegal? Had Allie had plenty of time to figure out alternate arrangements and just decided not to? Had she decided that her neighbors could deal with this kind of racket during the day because they were all trying to make a living? Her hubris was astounding. One would never have thought that kind of ballsiness could be contained in such a tidy, attractive package.

It wasn't as if Cait hadn't considered getting a "real" office before, mostly at the prompting of Lauren. According to her, in addition to moving on from having a career telling people how wrong they were, Cait was supposed to get out of the house more. Not that it would make a difference in what she did, Cait thought, or how she saw the world. What was so magical about the world outside her apartment?

Besides, commuting would take time and cost money she didn't want to spend. She was still paranoid about her work drying up even though the last two years had been more than solid and this one was on track to be even better. Part of being successful was keeping her overhead low…and taking pretty much every job that presented itself just in case it was a while before another one came.

Speaking of jobs, her phone buzzed from where her ass was keeping it warm in the back pocket of her 501s, the only jeans she wore: timeless and button fly. She cursed when she saw the name on her screen. Tamara Eaton was one of her individual clients and so needy Cait had blown through her usual flat fee weeks ago. Cait almost dismissed the call, but the specter of a bad review, her professional integrity, and how little she wanted to listen to the voicemail Tamara would leave combined to make her answer. The trumpet playing below her had her scurrying for her bathroom, which was the most insulated place in the apartment.

"Hey, Tamara. What can I do for you?" She closed the solid wood door and leaned back against it.

"I have another question about your critique." Tamara had written a memoir that, just like the latest Grovetree novel she was editing, had moments of extreme competence, but its structure resembled a pretzel, and she had a penchant for the worst kind of purple prose: redundant adjectives, florid cliches, and dream sequences that, honestly, no one did very well. In Cait's opinion, dreams were meant to stay in the realm of slumber and drool.

"Okay, how can I help?"

"About mixed metaphors...they're appropriate sometimes, right? Because with the scene in the swimming pool, I know water and buoyancy and maybe even chlorine are natural pairings, like a strong pinot with a T-bone, but I just can't stop thinking about space and pulling that in somehow. Stars, moons, supernovas."

"See? This is why I'm an editor and not a writer. Those are the kind of creative choices only you can make in your work. Not mixing metaphors is a guideline, but the only real rule in writing is that you can do anything you want as long as it works."

She made a disgusted sound. "Of course you're right, but how am I supposed to know if something works?"

Cait took a couple of steps and sat on her toilet. The trumpet's whine cut through wood and plaster like a heat-seeking missile, and she stuck her finger in one ear and pressed her phone harder to the side of her head. "A lot of writers are part of groups that can give feedback on that kind of thing."

"How many writers do you think are in northern Michigan?"

"You'd be surprised. I've seen writers swarm out of the woodwork at the mere mention of an open mic. Reading books you like or ones you might aspire to can also help refine your eye."

"Am I asking you too many questions?" The woman had gotten several essays published prior to writing this book, and Cait had found her author's page. Not that Cait was at all ageist, but Tamara was the poster child for a late midlife crisis. Graying, curly hair, necklaces made with big beads, and glasses that looked like two saucers connected by an espresso spoon.

"No, really. It's just...it seems like you really want some mentorship. I can recommend a few writers who like to do that kind of thing. You might hit it off with one of them and go on from there." And stop calling Cait in the process.

"How do I know they're going to get my work like you do?"

Her finger was going numb where it pressed against her ear. "Believe me, I don't have special powers. I've just read a lot and have been doing this a long time. You need to develop your own editor's vision. You know, see what's not there and what's hiding the good stuff."

Tamara laughed. "You make it sound so easy."

"Hey, if any of this were easy, everyone would do it."

After a short pause filled on Cait's end with fumbling brass music, Tamara said, "Would you be my mentor?"

"I...my plate's really full now, and I think an experienced writer would be a better bet."

"What if I made it worth your while?" They were both quiet before Tamara blurted, "With money. I meant with money. I just can't wait for the whole next draft to get feedback from you, but you've got that stipulation about reviewing only complete manuscripts, and I think a chapter at a time would work better for me."

Cait closed her eyes and caved. "Let me think about it and get back to you. Maybe we can come up with an arrangement. But you would need to be committed to the process. We'd be on a schedule, and I would expect you to meet the deadlines we both agree to. I can't do something unless I have a plan for how to fit it in around the rest of my work, okay?"

Tamara gushed gratitude for much longer than this "I'll get back to you" approach warranted. Cait didn't know what was worse: the beginner lesson downstairs or Tamara's aggressive thanks. Finally, she hung up and scrunched her face about taking that call in the bathroom. She moved to the living room, incapable of getting anything done in this racket or thinking productively about how to work around it.

She plopped down on the couch with a long-suffering sigh. When Pancho was little, she'd let him get on the furniture— at least until he'd made a game of jumping from the chair to the couch and back, shifting each piece of furniture a foot with every leap. Off they'd gone to obedience school, and now Pancho could avail himself of the floor or one of his two beds, which were both plenty cush. But it left Cait feeling acutely alone on her sofa. Not that she should be sitting there, anyway. If she were really going to take Tamara on (how much could she charge her?), she had work to do.

The lesson appeared to conclude below her, and Cait allowed herself a moment or two to wallow about the lack of Lauren and Pancho on the cushion next to her. "Cute girlfriend"? What had Allie meant by that? Lauren had been good-looking, but "cute"? Allie was the cute one with her sparkly blue eyes—not that Cait had been paying particular attention to things like that. Then again, she had noticed that her dimples had vanished when the conversation had turned sour—or at least differently sour from how Cait had begun it. Either way, being reminded of her ex did nothing for her mood, especially when her loneliness taunted her.

She pried herself off the couch and had just crossed the threshold into her office when the horrible noise started again. Admittedly, it sounded more like an actual instrument than a wounded animal this time, but that didn't make it any less distracting. This was impossible!

The day was a dozen different flavors of annoyance with gaps between them just long enough for Cait to get through only twenty pages of her current project before being interrupted again. Everything took her twice as long, but it had to get done, which meant she ended work well after the day settled down and the evening version of quiet resumed: the murmur of televisions with the occasional blat of death metal or some ultra-violent video game. When she finished, she was drained but still too keyed up to relax, so she got her gym bag from the closet and headed out.

Honestly, she'd liked their dry-land month the best during university swim team training. The satisfaction of throwing weights around was simpler than what came from fighting water. That required a combination of strength and finesse Cait had been good at but had never really loved and had become more dutiful than anything else, her college scholarship being on the line and all. Outside swimming, she'd grown to appreciate the dense solidity that lifting gave to her long frame. Her broad shoulders and toned arms made her physically imposing when added to her height, which was useful when she didn't necessarily feel fully solid inside.

This evening, she took advantage of the fifteen minutes between her building and the gym to get a call in to her momma. Cait had to take her word for it that the woman had actually birthed her and that she hadn't been switched at the hospital (anything could happen in Tennessee). They couldn't be less alike, save for the slight curl to their brown hair and their dark eyes, which, frankly, were a dime a dozen.

As always, her mom answered on the first ring. "Caitie, there you are." Her accent rolled like she had marbles in her mouth. It was familiar and comforting even though Cait had gone to great lengths to get rid of hers when she'd moved north to go to college. Eastern Tennessee was Appalachian country, and though certainly not everyone was stupid there, most people at least sounded it—at least according to folks not from there. The thought made her feel ungrateful and small.

"Here I am, Momma." Cait smiled. "I thought I'd catch you before I work out."

"Well, isn't that right nice. I was just putting the finishing touches on a pie before getting it in the oven."

"What's the theme today?" Cait's momma was the consummate homemaker and the best baker Cait had ever known, though she hadn't known many and was surely biased. As a child, she'd drowned her sorrows about her ungainly height with plenty of pies, cakes, and desserts.

"Easter, though I'm a little early." She went on to describe the filling, which was white-chocolate custard with salted caramel, and the decorations, which featured bunnies in some kind of dance Cait couldn't exactly picture. "You should come home and get a piece while it lasts."

Cait laughed. "I wish I could, but I've got a lot of work to do."

"Yes, I know, but can't you work here? Besides, your work worries me."

"Everything worries you, especially if it has to do with me." While it was touching to be worried over, enough was more than enough.

"You're far away, you work too hard, and I know you say you like to be alone, but it isn't healthy."

"I'm not always alone."

"Well, you're not very settled, now, are you?"

"Momma, I swear that you only have a backbone when it comes to me," Cait said with such force that some of her accent crept back in. "Sorry, but you know that I've been serious about people before, and I'll find someone again."

"How serious could you be? And you're not getting any younger."

"Don't start."

"I just want to see you happy, and I can tell by your voice that you're not happy."

Momma could read her voice like she could read the Bible. "I'm not going to fall into that trap of relying on someone else for my own happiness. I see what happens to you when Daddy's in one of his moods, and I'm not interested."

"You would be if you met the right person."

"And who would that be? Some dumb boy who barely made it out of high school and lives the next holler over?" That outburst was met with the kind of quiet she wished she'd had more of this afternoon but that shamed her now.

Finally, "I didn't raise you to talk to me like that."

"No, ma'am, you didn't. I'm sorry. This is just not a good topic of conversation for us. Why don't you tell me more about that pie?"

They called a truce and went on with more superficial things. Momma knew damn well that Cait was a lesbian, knew it well enough to forbid Cait from talking to her daddy directly about it, given that he would shit a self-righteous, Jesus-shaped brick about it. But Momma worried in a way that felt weaponized, continuing to show a perverse kind of will that she never turned on anyone else, ever. Cait knew it came from love, but that didn't stop it from being infuriating.

With that conversation fueling her, Cait went through her free-weight routine with more vigor than she'd given it in months, using the push and pull against gravity to burn off her frustration at her hometown, her lovely momma, whom she wanted to strangle sometimes, and her neighbor. Allie. Deep-blue eyes notwithstanding, she was maximally infuriating. It felt like everyone but Pancho was out to get Cait. Allie clearly didn't care at all about anyone else and was just telling stories about being dislodged from her studio to feel better about causing such a disruption. Who could deal with hearing such abrasive noise all day, even if it were her job? Editing was a version of teaching, she supposed, but it was a much better version than what Allie did. Thank God she never had to work with beginners anymore—some writing could induce the same headache and nausea as that first student of Allie's had.

It was a legs day, so she puffed her way through squats, calf raises, hamstring curls, adductor and abductor exercises, and more, using a combination of a barbell, dumbbells, and the functional trainer over in this area of the gym. She worked to exhaustion over multiple sets of each exercise, and by the time she'd gotten down to just the core stabilization routine that she did every time she lifted, the majority of her T-shirt was soaked in sweat. She used one sleeve to wipe some from her eyes before starting in on leg lifts, back extensions, and inclined sit-ups. Her abs were shaking by the end, and her whole body had devolved into a quivering, boneless blob that was one of the best things ever. It took all of her effort to make herself work through her stretches, but since she'd turned thirty these two parts of her routine had become critical in the continuing fight not to look like a comma by the time she was fifty.

She was sad that a lot of women wouldn't lift because they thought they'd turn into some steroidal version of themselves. Truth was, it took an enormous amount of focused work for women to build any kind of showy muscle mass, and doing two to three sets of eight hard reps would never cut it. Nor would just lifting a few times a week. Cait had been doing this for years, and she still mostly looked like a swimmer: broad shoulders, narrow hips, and an even distribution of body fat that was meant to keep her insulated in the cool water of the pool. Though she sported more definition in her arms and legs than most women, her power was largely hidden, which was exactly how she liked it. In fact, if she could will herself to be a few inches shorter, she would, just so she would garner less attention. Allie seemed like the kind of person who wanted people to notice her, performing her music and wearing those skirts, but Cait was happy to remain behind the scenes.

Even though she lived within walking distance of the gym—though far enough to give her the time to have a fight with her momma—Cait always used the showers here. The hot water was endless, and the white tiles gleamed with relative newness and a professional cleaning staff. Every shower she took here was one fewer that she had to clean up after at home; besides, she almost always had the locker room to herself this late in the evening. She could languish under the spray, letting the heat soak deep into her body, her hair plastered to her head, the thrumming of water on her skull driving thoughts from her mind. Bliss.

This evening, she added a dip in the whirlpool to the routine and was well and truly relaxed by the time she got back to her apartment. There, in front of her door, she found a gift bag. She bent to pluck out the folded paper that was stuck into the top and opened it to read. It was handwritten in an efficient cursive that somehow surprised Cait, assuming it was from Allie.

Neighbor, it said. *Please accept my heartfelt apologies and these donuts (from Davis Square Donuts) for any trouble you might experience because of my giving lessons out of my apartment for a while. My usual space is under renovation for a few months, and I'm in quite the pickle over it. In addition to the treats, please find a box of my absolute favorite earplugs: soft as silk, and you could sleep through Armageddon with them. Also included are gift cards to Starbucks, Nine Bar, and Diesel Café, all of which have good coffee and workspaces within a mile from here.* Cait found the cards and took a moment to be even more annoyed even though the two local ones were good places, indeed. She went back to the note, which was signed, *The Menace in 3B, Allie.*

Cait peeked into the bag to confirm the rest of its contents and leaned against her door with a sigh. This was happening. Still, it was a kind gesture for Allie to have given her this—or so she thought until she looked around and realized the same package was in front of the doors on either side of hers, too.

CHAPTER FOUR

Some of Allie's students were unexceptional not only musically but in every other way. Even though she sat next to them for thirty or forty-five minutes once a week for months, she was often hard-pressed to remember their names. Well, it wasn't quite that bad, but she relied heavily on her notes to keep them clear in her mind and remember who was working on what. They were mostly dutiful but not excited, and their slow progress would surely end after high school, when they had earned their extracurricular badge for college and would put the instrument aside for something they were actually interested in.

But she had a couple of students who were good and motivated, including Ryan (a.k.a. Winston, though they'd dropped the nickname early on), who stood next to her now working through the Arutiunian trumpet concerto which had been their project since January. While not as popular or well known as the Haydn, it was one of her favorite trumpet pieces, and she'd recommended it to him partly because she liked it so much and partly because Ryan was good enough to handle it—at least for the music contests he was entering and the movement of it that he would play with his high school orchestra in a month.

He rode his bike over from the nearby school over lunch and the next period, which he had free, which was a benefit of being a senior. It meant they could get the lesson in earlier in the day than her other students, which Allie appreciated.

He stopped at the end of the section she'd asked him to play. He dropped his instrument to his side and raised one dark eyebrow. "So? Lay it on me. I can take it."

"Why do you assume I'm going to say something bad?"

"Because you never say anything good."

"Details, details. Seriously, though, it was pretty good. The dynamics could be more dynamic." She smiled. "But your breathing is all wonky."

"Is that the technical term?" Ryan was a small kid and a bit of a smart-ass. She liked him a lot.

"It's just that your phrasing is off, and you're running out of air to support the octave transition properly. You need to get better about sneaking breaths before you really need them. It's called a wind instrument for a reason."

"Ha ha. You're hilarious. Are you going to show me or what?"

"No, I'm not going to show you. We're going to use your magic pencil, mark some breaths, circle that crescendo you totally ignored, and you're going to play it right."

"Yes, ma'am," he said with a pinch too much cheekiness. They wrote a few things on the music, and he licked his lips before bringing his trumpet up and playing again.

Allie knew Ryan had some kind of a crush on her. She wasn't sure how intense it was or if she needed to be worried about it. She indulged him a little bit but also had strict boundaries. He said he learned a lot from hearing her play, but you always learned more by playing yourself. This was his lesson—or at least the lesson his parents paid her for. Everything was fine, she told herself. He was hardly lovesick, and they were seeing steady progress. Allie thought his alleged feelings were mostly because they were kindred spirits.

She had been a band nerd from the day, in fourth grade, when she first got to try the trumpet and had been entranced by the lingering buzzing in her lips after they left that shiny silver mouthpiece. The instrument felt like a gift from some genius anonymous donor and soon grew to be an extension of herself. She played it so much she drove her family insane. She couldn't remember now when she'd been bad, but she believed the stories her mother and brother told, given what she endured with her younger students. But she quickly got proficient, then capable, then good, then notable. When she'd finished high school and enrolled at Berklee College of Music, she'd been as good as Ryan was now, most likely a little better. She'd long ago gotten used to the buzz in her lips resulting from the vibrations they made against the mouthpiece. The process of playing had become so automatic that a note on the page was translated to sound sometimes without even a hint of conscious thought. She still loved it—except when she had a sinus infection and playing felt like her head was being assaulted by a combination between the world's smallest jackhammer and the world's biggest vise.

Ryan finished playing again, and Allie nodded. "Did that feel better?"

"I felt less like I was going to pass out. Is that what you're asking?"

"Hey, this is big-boy stuff you're playing. You'll have excellent chops by the time I'm done with you this year. Have you heard from any of the colleges you applied to?"

"Not yet."

"They really keep you waiting, huh?"

"Someone once told me good things come to those who wait."

She laughed. "I think you mean 'work.'"

"I like wait better, like it's inevitable or something."

"Come on." She clapped him on the shoulder. "It's sweeter if you work for it."

He blushed and looked down at his shoes. Allie cringed. Damn. Sometimes she forgot how much teenaged boys raged with hormones 24/7. Not that she hadn't had her own battles with estrogen growing up, but her struggles had mostly stayed invisible to those around her.

She said, "All right. We have time for you to go through it once more and try to commit those adjustments to memory. Come on, the piece isn't going to play itself."

She got him out the door without incident and pocketed the check he'd handed to her. She wasn't going to worry about it, but she was going to keep her hands to herself during lessons from now on and maybe stand another foot or so away from him. Music was hard enough to master without having to navigate a crush on your teacher as well. He would get there, though. At some point, if he stuck with it like he said he wanted to, so much more of his playing would be as automatic as hers.

Not that she could breeze through every measure of music like she was reading her grocery list. Sometimes, something about a piece made her stop and say, "Wait, what?" and there were too many of those in the one she was now trying to learn in her post-lesson practice session. She didn't know if she was distracted by her mistake with Ryan or what, but she was having a hell of a time wrapping her mind around the music she was supposed to play in the studio tomorrow. Clearly, whoever wrote it wasn't very familiar with the trumpet. Playing it was downright awkward, which she guessed was kind of admirable? It was new, at least, in all sorts of ways. It was the score for an independent movie, and the key signature was so full of sharps she thought she might start bleeding. The melody was…unique, but it wasn't her place to judge. After a couple of hours, though, she got her fingers, brain, and mouth coordinated enough to make it through without flubbing it, though she'd have to revisit it again before the session started in the morning.

After that time practicing, she felt both jazzed (no pun intended) and depleted and pulled on a thin sweater for the walk to Diesel. It was slightly farther away from the apartment than the other coffee shops she frequented, but it was her favorite. Playing always warmed her up, and the day had slowly lost its chill from morning. She slipped her bare feet into a pair of comfortable pumps and left in search of fresh air and caffeine.

As she progressed from Cambridge into Somerville and down to Davis Square, she passed by blocks and blocks of renovated two- and three-family houses that held apartments well out of her price range. Still, at least Davis Square's shops and cafés were within walking distance, even just one stop away on the Red Line if she was too lazy to walk the full distance. She didn't mind living where she did or watching her pennies to a certain extent, but she wasn't immune to the urge to splurge. To circumvent that, she tried to keep her eyes trained on the sidewalk in front of her while she walked past the couple of clothing stores she'd wandered into before—and right back out when she'd seen their prices.

She was barely past Diesel's threshold when she spotted, squished into the middle of the bar seating on the right, the woman she'd taken to calling The Amazon. Allie stepped back outside and frowned. Through the window, Cait looked absolutely miserable behind her laptop, her arms pulled in to try to keep her broad shoulders from brushing against those of her neighbors. Allie had long since noticed her classically attractive profile with a straight nose and high forehead, but she'd had no idea that her arms were so toned. The musculature was obvious under her short sleeves.

On anyone else, Allie would find those guns pretty damn sexy, which, of course, was neither here nor there. Could she go back in and ignore Cait now that she'd seen her? Did she have time to go to Nine Bar, which didn't pull shots nearly as good as those right on the other side of this door? Maybe Cait would be too busy hating having to do her very important work, whatever it was, outside the blessed confines of her apartment to notice Allie coming in and waiting for her cortado.

Allie growled and went in, gaze strictly forward, at least until after she ordered and was waiting for her payment to go through. She broke protocol and glanced over at Cait, who was looking back at her, giving her a stink eye so stinky she could smell it over the strong aroma of ground coffee.

Allie made herself smile and approached. "You picked the right place if you like espresso, though I guess you'd already know that, having lived in the area long enough. I've been told their tea is good, too, if that's what you're into."

"I thought you were back in your apartment busy making too much noise for me to concentrate. Why are you here? Are you putting up fliers for your teaching services or something?" Teaching was put in verbal finger quotes rich with sarcasm.

"I don't advertise like that." She was established enough to work through referrals now, not that she was going to justify herself to this woman.

"Then what are you doing here? I'm only over here because you're"—she made a swirling motion with her hand—"supposedly back home."

"I needed a break to get blood flowing again." Allie did something with her lips to indicate them but realized it might look like a kiss and stopped. "It's all just muscles and air."

"I used to be able to take breaks."

Allie sighed. "Cait, I'm sorry, okay? I know it sucks, but it's temporary, and, seriously, those are the best earplugs. I went through a dozen different brands before I found them. You won't even feel that they're in, and we can both get some relief."

"I can't believe you're making this my problem."

"What about coworking space?" Allie would pay for it at this point even though it would hurt.

"The closest one is at least thirty minutes away by train."

"I'll pay for a ride share."

Cait got up and leaned against her stool, raising puzzled and annoyed glances from her neighbors. "I don't want a coworking space. I want to work in my own apartment that I already pay for."

Even slouched over, she was intimidating. The pose somehow made her look dangerously regal. Allie took a half step back and made her voice low. "I know you do, but I can't make that happen for you right now. Not unless you decide to participate in the situation in some way other than trying to punish me for something out of my control."

Cait looked like she was about to start breathing fire, and Allie thanked all the gods when the barista called her name.

"I've got to go." She turned away before Cait could say anything in response. The urge for this coffee had shriveled up and died under Cait's gaze of disdain, but she took it and hoofed it out of the shop and back to her apartment, where she locked and chained her door as if The Amazon might be in hot pursuit. Cait was kind of magnificent in her anger. And with those arms! If this was the price Allie was paying for not reading her mail, she might just be having a come-to-Jesus moment right now. What else had she missed? She would go down to her box in the front and check it right now if she weren't worried Cait was somewhere close behind.

She kicked off her shoes and wandered around the apartment, sipping her drink, unsure of what to do next. Though she'd really wanted to avoid it, she called a few colleagues from her studio work to see if any of them knew of available space. After leaving messages and rinsing her mouth clean of milk and espresso residue, she picked up her instrument, cast an apologetic glance at the ceiling, and started to play again.

* * *

Allie resettled her gig bag on her shoulder. Inside it, two horns nestled bell-to-lead pipe in their separate padded compartments. She had the C trumpet with her today as well as her regular instrument since she was scheduled to play music in both keys, which was unusual. The score for this independent film was a little too modern and screechy for her taste, but the pay was good, and they were recording on one of the stages at her alma mater, which would provide room to spread out along with good acoustics.

She'd recorded in studios all over the Boston area, from large ones out in the suburbs to literal closets in Back Bay. It could take her well over an hour to get to a gig if she didn't splurge on a ride share or rental and stuck to public transportation. Often, time was the true cost of doing business, as her dad might have said…when he'd been employed and relatively sober. The cost of doing business. The cost of being in a family with him was more like it, not that she had the time or inclination to dredge up old shit like that. Luckily, she arrived at Berklee and slipped back to their assigned auditorium, where she found Maggie Dominico sitting next to an empty chair and applying oil to the valves of her French horn with a squinting look of concentration.

Her dark hair always reminded Allie of her instrument: loops and curls and twists, all kind of held in place with ties and clips and the odd pencil. Allie had thought about playing the French horn when she'd been younger, but, as her band director had so helpfully pointed out, it was as big as she'd been at the time. Good thing she hadn't had a hankering for the euphonium or tuba. Still, she loved the trumpet as much as life itself, so it all worked out in the end.

She set her bag on the empty chair. "Don't spill any," she said to Maggie.

"Funny." Maggie finished and capped the small plastic bottle of oil. "Hey, why didn't you tell me about your practice space?" If you could say one thing about Boston's music scene, it would be that it was small. News and gossip crossed it as fast as Rimsky-Korsakov's "Flight of the Bumblebee."

"I'm in deep denial. Oh, and I feel like an idiot."

"How many notices did you ignore?"

"I didn't—" Allie started too stridently and took a breath. "One too many, apparently."

"I'd offer you my space, but they've gotten really squirrelly about security. I'm waiting for them to install fingerprint scanners or something. Besides, I'm not going to be using it much myself, you know, once we move." Maggie lived in a close-in suburb and was constantly fighting traffic to get to gigs, but now she and her husband were moving even farther out so they could have a yard, of all things. "Thank God, no more apartment living."

"Yeah, yeah, rub it in. I'm pretty sure one of my neighbors wants to lynch me. You know The Amazon, the woman who lives above me? The one with the dog that is clearly genetically engineered?"

"You mean the one you complain about all the time?"

"I think 'all the time' is stretching it. She moves around like a silent fart, sneaking up on you when you're picking your nose because you think you're blissfully alone. Or the way she totally dismissed me when I was all neighborly and introduced myself. Her girlfriend had way more warmth than The Amazon. She's just there and not there in the worst way." Allie slipped music out of her bag and set it on her stand before dipping back in for her instrument and fitting a mouthpiece into its leadpipe. She exercised her valves in a fast finger wave over and over while she talked. "She just sticks out, you know? Monumental and pathologically reserved and always sneaking up on people with freakish stealth. Even her dog is quiet, which, I mean, you have to see this animal."

"You've shown me a picture."

"Right, so you know. At this point, I've kind of resigned myself to teaching out of my apartment until they're done de-cancerifying my regular place. I mean, I guess it's good they're doing it, considering how much time I spend in there, but I need a house like you're getting. Or a building where everyone still goes into work. But, no. The Amazon apparently requires absolute silence to accomplish anything."

"What are you going to do?"

"I gave her earplugs."

Maggie laughed. "How'd that go over?"

Allie stopped fluttering her valves in a palsied rhythm and sat. "About as well as you can imagine. The thing is, I think she's a freelancer, too, so why wouldn't she understand? I'm not sure exactly what she does, but she's always been full of herself, walking through the building with her horse of a dog like she's the one who actually owns the place and the rest of us are just props."

"An Amazon with a horse of a dog. All sorts of mental imagery going on right now."

"It's practically as big as I am. I used to think that maybe she was just shy, but now I'm pretty sure she's a stuck-up bitch. I mean, she is kind of splendid, but she's still a bitch."

Maggie sighed and blew into her instrument without sound. "I kind of miss your vein of drama."

"What vein is that? Tragically annoying?"

"No, adult. From everything I've been told, I'm going to want to trade one of my kidneys for intelligent interaction in about five and a half months." She gave Allie a knowing look that Allie didn't want or even need.

Maggie was pregnant. Allie should be happy for her, she knew, and she was. But she was sad for herself at the same time. This had begun to happen with greater and greater frequency: her friends from the business dropping away, irrepressibly drawn to the siren song of marriage, houses, babies. Sometimes the women made it back into the studio rotation after a year or two, but even then, it wasn't the same. They were always hurrying away to their new biological family instead of hanging with their old musical one. The guys usually didn't take any time off, but if they hadn't hustled for gigs before, they did so now, extra mouth to feed and all.

She and Maggie had been tight for years, since shortly after Allie finished at Berklee, but the writing was on the wall now, given the way Maggie's face was freaking beaming at sharing her news. Allie wanted to blame everyone who had left her, but what if the fault was hers? Was there something hard and unlovable in her that drove people away? Allie found a smile. "Aw, Mags. That's great. I know you guys have been trying. Should I buy it its first trumpet now or wait until after it starts walking?"

"No kid of mine is playing the trumpet, no offense."

"I'm deeply offended." Allie laughed.

"Don't get me wrong, you do well with what you have to work with, but good God, Allie, you must've been a horror when you first started out."

"I know the truth."

"Oh yeah, what's that?"

"You only wish you could match my dulcet tones."

They both laughed. "Dulcet" was not remotely how to describe a trumpet's sound. Allie could coax sweetness out of her horn, but it was made for strident anthems and military marches. It was a brass instrument in every way, whereas the French horn blurred things. Maggie's instrument had a honeyed tone that was both majestic and sometimes edgy. Even though it was metal just like Allie's, it could be found in woodwind quintets next to clarinets and oboes, which was a tiny mind fuck.

One thing was true, though, both instruments could be loud, and Allie and Maggie both loved that. Allie warmed up, feeling her lungs expand and her mouth become supple, muscle memory driving her while her mind wandered. She probably should have waxed more poetic about Maggie's impending new arrival, but what was there to say that a hundred people probably hadn't said already? It told Allie a lot that Maggie was this far along before she told Allie. It was obvious to her yet again that their friendship meant more to Allie than it did to Maggie. There were far too many straight people in music.

She blew through a few scales, thinking about Cait despite herself. Did she really think Cait was a stuck-up bitch? Not even Allie wanted to listen to some of her students play, and Cait wasn't getting paid for the privilege of doing so. Still, she hadn't been exaggerating when she said that Cait moved through the building like it was her own island, not acknowledging anyone around her even with a small nod and smile. What would it hurt to show a little friendliness to folks you'd shared a front door with for a couple of years? What was in her head couldn't be so damn fascinating.

Allie blew spit from her instrument, mirrored by Maggie. "It's not like I want to make things difficult for The Amazon," she said. "Remember that guy who was playing death metal at window-shaking levels when I first moved in?"

"What did you do then?"

"First I complained, then I tried to appreciate it, then I wore earplugs whenever we were both home. He ended up moving out before it went on too long, thank God."

"I think you need to let it go, assuming you've apologized and offered solutions and aren't blowing the shit out of your horn in the middle of the night or anything."

"I don't think she'd mind that. It's a business-hours kind of thing. I saw her at a coffee shop near our place yesterday, trying to work while I was practicing, and she was clearly in abject misery."

Maggie glanced at her, holding her gaze steady while the rest of the ensemble finished getting settled in. "How attractive is this woman?"

"What does that have to do with anything?"

Maggie rolled her eyes.

Yes, okay, Allie knew what Maggie meant. She was a sucker when it came to trying to entangle her life with those of good-looking women. But she wasn't completely driven by her hormones like some teenaged boy. Not that her hormones were all aflutter over Cait. Even though only someone's surface could be taken in initially, attractiveness was more than skin deep. If Allie saw even a peep of ugliness under someone's perfect skin, that was it. Onward and upward. Not that Allie thought Cait was necessarily steeped in inner grotesqueness.

Objectively speaking, Cait was good-looking. Very much so. Fantastic cheekbones and abundantly healthy hair. But she was tall. Man, so tall. And built like... She shied away from the usual crude cliches. Allie just knew that her forearms that radiated don't-mess-with-me strength meant that Cait would have your back if shit went down.

Her wavy hair softened her overall look, falling past her ears to her jawline. Her eyes were nice, too, something Allie had noticed when Cait had faced her directly at the coffee shop. They were a dark brown with lighter flecks nestled within an even darker ring. Those eyes weren't mean even when Cait was clearly angry. They were eyes that maybe had seen some stuff.

The conductor gave the podium a few whacks with her baton, breaking into Allie's thoughts. As she prepared to play, it was Allie's turn to roll her eyes at herself. What in the world was she doing, getting so obsessed about Cait? Face it, she thought. The woman hates you. She needed to get her head in the game or risk tarnishing her reputation, which was just about everything in this business. Being a studio musician meant having to be ready at short notice to pull perfection out of your ass. Rehearsals were scant and recording time expensive, so you had to be punctual and prepared, not to mention versatile, playing moody atmospheric stuff one day and hard-charging, balls-to-the-wall the next. Not that Allie didn't dig Mozart, Brahms, Verdi, and that bunch, but she thrived on variety and pressure, so she'd gone a different way from a lot of people in the industry.

She scrambled to turn to the right page in her music, working as she did to banish some of the errant thoughts that refused to leave as the session started in earnest. Perhaps Cait would mellow after having this day of quiet to reset things, and they could each go about their business the way they used to. Unlikely, she thought, counting the measures to her entrance. She did have nice eyes, though. Friendly despite everything.

Later, walking home through her neighborhood, Allie noticed early crocuses and the swollen leaf buds on bushes lining the sidewalk. Prettily perfect, they were also defenseless, at risk of being clobbered by a late snowstorm or hard freeze. Her sense of foreboding multiplied when she turned the last corner and found her brother, Nick, sitting on the steps of her building. His arms were braced on the concrete on either side of him, and he was looking down the street away from her. She wanted to turn back and disappear around the block. She loved Nick, would always love Nick, but that didn't mean she always liked him, especially when he was intent on crashing at her place. Given the size of the backpack next to him, who knew when she'd ever be able to dislodge him. He'd been imposing on her for years, ever since she was fresh out of college and he had his first decent opportunity to avail himself of her reluctant hospitality.

Things with Nick were complicated, which meant everything and nothing. That was one of the few things Allie and her mother, still back in New Hampshire, could agree on. She guessed they probably also agreed on Allie's father too, that rat bastard. He'd been verbally and physically abusive, but he'd limited his shoves and punches to Nick, probably because Nick had always aggressively gotten himself in the way. He'd consequently been served up a lot of crap for a lot of years, and it had taken its toll on him. Allie and her mother owed him a great debt for his insistent protection, and they loved him for being so stupidly determined. It had cost him dearly, and he struggled with more than his share of demons. While not exactly like their father (Nick had never laid a hand on either of them), he had a simmering temper and a general inability to be a productive member of society. He bounced around between their mother's house, Allie's place, and those of a few friends, a volatile mooch that Allie and her mother couldn't quite say no to. Last Allie knew, he had been back living with their mother, to her great chagrin. Nick was the family hot potato, but given that the family was pretty much just Allie and her mother, it wasn't much of a game, and it wasn't much fun.

All Allie could do was offer him her couch or floor when his roommates got tired of him. Or he lost his job because he didn't bother to show up. Or, once, when the cops were looking for him for something he insisted he hadn't done. She tried to at least see his side if not fully accept it, but thanks to the studio situation, she needed him underfoot right now like she needed another hole in her head. And what about that miraculous day when she was in a real relationship, like Maggie and husband and baby. He'd just have to find some other place to go—unless, of course, she continued to lack all backbone and caved again at his smile and easy explanations.

She took a deep breath and walked on. When she got within easy conversational range, she said, "Everything okay with Mom?" Making him jump satisfied her more than it should have.

The brilliance of his smile told Allie how bad things must've gotten.

"You know her. Doesn't see eye to eye with anyone. It's good to see you, Sissy."

That was a nickname she could do without, but it was useless to try to get Nick to drop it. Contrary was his middle name. "Please tell me the police aren't after you again."

He stood and stretched, laughing. They shared much of the same coloring, including the deep blue of their eyes, but Nick had buzzed his hair, which made it look darker. He had a good eight inches on her—and a paunch that he'd developed over the last couple of years.

"It was one misunderstanding. Don't blow it out of proportion. Your lipstick sure looks nice. Sometimes I can't believe you're a big dyke."

"I'm not wearing any lipstick," she said, ignoring his last comment. She liked lipstick as much as the next woman, but it was incompatible with playing so she didn't often get the opportunity. He just couldn't help himself from trying to get under her skin. It was useless this time, though. Violinists got hickies on their necks, harpists' fingers were covered in callouses, and brass players were saddled with having red rings on their lips the size and shape of their instrument's mouthpieces, which in Allie's case made her resemble a carnival clown.

His smile notched wider. "I think Mom's still waiting for this particular phase of yours to end, but I personally will never forget stumbling on you and Sherry Jacobson liplocked in the basement."

She tried and failed to stop a laugh from erupting. He hadn't "stumbled" on anything but had been caught spying and with an erection he'd done everything in his power to hide from her. "All right. Come on up, but you know there's not much room to get comfortable." While they climbed the stairs, she explained about her rehearsal space. "You'll need to hang in the bedroom during my lessons or leave entirely."

"I've heard that beggars can't be choosers."

"Not that you've ever thought that applied to you."

He laughed. "Well, that's true."

Before Allie could fully grasp that he'd just agreed with her, a flurry of footsteps cascaded from the stairway, both canine and human. A cruise ship of a dog rounded the corner and took a few steps toward Allie and Nick before a sharp snap of Cait's fingers brought him to attention. "Heel, Pancho" Cait said when she made it to the landing behind the dog. "Sorry about that. He's big but harmless."

Allie said, "He didn't do anything." Cait was wearing her usual jeans but paired with a pressed white blouse that had no reason to look so sexy.

Nick put out a hand and approached the King of the Seas. "Allie, this guy's as tall as you are."

"Hilarious."

He got acquainted with Pancho, never asking Cait's permission or anything. While Nick scratched his neck and behind his ears, one of which was black and the other gray, Allie worked hard at shoving the idea of sexy Cait far from her mind. "Were you able to get some work done while I was out today?"

"I didn't know you weren't here. I spent the afternoon at the library surrounded by people, most of whom hadn't showered in quite some time."

"Oh. Yeah, that doesn't sound like my idea of fun. Hey, I'll look at my calendar and tell you the days I'm at the studio and don't have any lessons so you'll know in advance when the coast is clear." Allie hoped her light tone masked any annoyance at Cait's long-suffering tone, which had nothing going for it besides making her a tad less attractive.

"So, this is going to go on for a while?"

"It's safe to assume so."

Allie saw from the corner of her eye that Nick's affection had devolved into roughhousing. She was about to caution him when Pancho let out one echoing bark, startling everyone. Nick thwapped him on the snout and stood stiffly, looking like he wanted to do more despite the incensed look on Cait's face.

"We should go," Cait said in a frosty tone before walking off with Pancho velcroed to her side.

"I'll get that list to you," Allie called after her. She hustled Nick into her apartment, closed the door, and leaned against it. She wasn't sure which side was the frying pan and which was the fire, but Nick was a devil she knew better than any other— well enough to know that criticizing his behavior would be counterproductive.

"You hungry?" she asked, food always being a safe topic since she almost always ended up paying for whatever they got. "I'll order something if you find a movie for us to watch." She wasn't keen on trying to find out what exactly had gone sideways to leave Nick seeking refuge on her couch this time. Especially not after that run-in with Cait. Tomorrow would be soon enough to inveigle some information from him. Tonight, she decided, he could be just her brother and not also her burden. He could help take the sting out of the loneliness that regularly crept up on her after the sun went down.

CHAPTER FIVE

The calendar Allie had slipped under Cait's door was unexpectedly thorough in how it communicated the impending weeks of bad news. A few days were blocked off by teal squares saying "Studio" followed by nonsensical phrases like "fantasy game" or "moody indie." In addition to those words, Allie had written OUT in black pen. Otherwise, the calendar was a patchwork of yellow blocks labeled as "Lessons," expanded upon by what had to be last names, and pink squares denoted as "Practice."

The truth was that while lessons were unbearable, Allie's practice sessions had shifted in Cait's opinion from god-awful to almost tolerable, even though practice sounded very little like actual music. It consisted, instead, of incessantly repeated parts that came across like a skipping record or exercises that rivaled the most strident stutterer imaginable. In her weaker moments, Cait considered using the earplugs, but just the thought of them made her ears itch. She wasn't going to cave and put herself through that insulated discomfort. She had, however, eaten the donuts from the apologetic offering—though she only admitted how delicious they were during unguarded moments in the shower or when watching Pancho gallop through the dog park, a giant among Lilliputians.

But this morning she was not feeling particularly congenial. She had a call scheduled with George Tanenbaum, the author of the troublesome book she'd just finished editing, and Allie was playing without the least care in the world even though her schedule said all should be clear on the downstairs front. With less than ten minutes until the call, she showed no sign of winding down, and Cait squeezed her temples between her fingers and growled, eliciting a muffled half-bark from Pancho. "It's okay, buddy. I just have to go be an asshole again."

Allie surely wouldn't believe it, but Cait hated confrontation. But since she was monumentally alone, if something had to get done, doing it herself was the only option. It took a minute for her to gird herself and make the trip downstairs to Allie's door, where she honestly tried to knock softly but wasn't heard. The clock was ticking, so the next rap left her knuckles stinging. Allie's playing choked off in exactly the way Pancho responded to her snaps of discipline.

Allie opened the door wearing a slim skirt and a sleeveless blouse, though it was a chilly forty degrees out today. The light-blue fabric was soft against her body, hugging her curves without being tight. Cait glanced away and coughed, trying to remember why she was here.

"Hi," Allie said.

"Hi," Cait heard from inside the apartment. The dog-slapping boyfriend, as Cait had started thinking of him after their encounter the week before.

"You're not supposed to be playing now." She brandished the printed schedule like a sword.

"Shit, you're right. Is it okay? I was trying to fit in some practice for a last-minute gig I'm subbing in for."

"No, it's not okay. I have a meeting. I mean I scheduled a meeting now specifically because you weren't supposed to be playing."

Allie held her trumpet away from her like it had gone hot in her hand. "You're right. I'm sorry. I'll stop." Her genuine chagrin undermined Cait's anger—until she said, "Or use the practice mute so it won't bother you."

Everything in Cait went still and stony. "You have a way to play without making a racket, and you aren't using it?"

"Well, yes and no. It's not really a sustainable solution, and I can't use it for lessons, obviously."

Cait felt a storm cloud of frustrated tears brewing behind her eyes. "You just don't care how you're messing up my life, do you? What am I saying? You don't. Obviously." She took a step back, hoping to avoid crying in front of this irritating, pint-sized woman, but Allie clearly didn't take the hint. She followed her out into the hall, closing the door behind her, probably trying to protect some angelic reputation her dog-slapping boyfriend had of her.

Allie said, "Hey, I'm sorry. I do care. I swear. It's just that I'm sure you have tools that you use for your job and need them to work right, and it's the same for me. The practice mute would be like...like..." Her fingers moved up and down her trumpet's valves in a pattern that Cait found both annoying and mesmerizing. "Like...I don't know, reading something on your computer at ten percent brightness. It's not the same as what I need in a significant way."

This explanation was not lessening Cait's urge to cry at all. She took another step back.

"Please. I care. I'll stick to the schedule, and I'll let you know whenever it changes. Believe me, I wish things were different just as much as you do."

"I doubt that," Cait managed to say before hurrying up the stairs, sniffing in hard to make the tears stay put. People tended to make assumptions due to how physically imposing she was, but she tended to cry at every opportunity, shedding tears out of sadness, anger, frustration, and abject confusion. She preferred to do so in private—definitely not in front of Allie Coleman, who was the source of all these knotted emotions. Why did Allie always have to look so put together and like she was friendly. Not to mention actually *act* friendly?

Cait hurried to her desk and took some deep breaths before getting on her call, knowing that she would need to be her most dispassionate and controlled when going over the developmental edits she'd suggested in the five-page memo she'd put together and passed along to the author ten days ago. Editors delivered this kind of feedback in two ways: walking the author through the editorial suggestions in real-time before dumping the documented details on them or leading with the document and giving authors time to overcome their initial knee-jerk reactions and become open to suggestions. She was going with the second option here. She'd found the potentially acrimonious dialog that arose from withholding the document to be not only personally distasteful but not very productive.

Within two minutes of being on the phone with George, Cait wasn't sure either approach would have led to a happy outcome for Grovetree, which, after all, paid her bills. Every writer was wedded to their work, and why not? This book had been nestled right up against George's heart for years already, but writers could get too close, identify too personally with the words they'd written, and George appeared to have a till-death-do-us-part mentality with regard to each scene, character, and even sentence. After a brief introduction, he spent the call refuting every point she'd made in her editorial memo. At least he was calm about it.

Cait let him get it all out of his system before saying, "Wait, you aren't going to take issue with all the things I liked about the book?" When he didn't have a ready response, she went on. "You're a fan of F. Scott Fitzgerald, right?" She continued without waiting for an answer, knowing from his style of writing that he was. "I'm sure you've heard all the stories about how much his editor worked on *The Great Gatsby*. Perkins even coined the 'old boy' affectation that's used throughout the book."

"I'm not Fitzgerald."

"Who is, right?"

"Martha took this book on as-is."

Wait, had she really? No, not if it were on Cait's docket. "No books at Grovetree are published without going through a developmental editing step. Martha doesn't expect the writer to be slavish in response to the feedback they get, but she has used the same stable of editors for years and trusts our judgment. Which titles have you read from the press? If I didn't edit it, I know who did and have heard all about it."

The line between them grew thick with quiet, and Cait waited, holding her breath.

"*Everything is Anything* was my favorite," he said.

Of course. If that weren't a thrown gauntlet, she didn't know what was. That book was sharp, crazy, inventive, and metaphysical. It shifted forms with each chapter, ranging through epistolary emails, dialog-only cell phone conversations, social media posts, and dense expository musings about the cosmos, epigenetics, euthanasia, and the games soap manufacturers play with our emotions. It had been the most challenging book she'd edited, and she'd surfed countless waves of self-doubt during the month it had taken her to work through it. But the author, Michelle Gonzalez, had been receptive to her insight, thankful, even, and the book had gone on to win more awards than any other in the Grovetree catalog.

She said, "In the first version I read, Mack went to the volcano without Lucy. Norman's cancer was more progressive, and he died in the first third of the book instead of the last. Michelle also had a love affair with the passive voice that I could never quite free her from, but she moved the needle a considerable amount over the three drafts we did together."

Pancho had gotten up and was sniffing at her arm, which meant her tone had gotten more strident than she'd intended. Instead of apologizing, she waited.

Finally, George said, "That volcano scene is masterful. I can't imagine it any other way."

"I'm not trying to take your book away from you. I'm trying to help you gain the perspective on it you're probably missing after spending a long time deep in the trenches."

"You want it to be entirely different."

Cait took a deep but inaudible breath, a skill she'd developed over years of these kinds of phone calls and meetings. "I want it to be the best it can be. Any specific ideas I might have mentioned in my memo"—there were three sizable ones—"are irrelevant. You're the one who would know what the best solution is, but I can see that there's a problem. Or a lack. Or something that's not quite up to par with the rest." God! She couldn't believe how much verbal tap-dancing it took to avoid saying that parts of the book were crap.

"Yeah, your ideas were total nonstarters."

"They were just places where you could begin considering changes. I'm not at all thinking you should take them as gospel."

"At least we're on the same page about something."

This guy. "I would prefer if we had a dialog about this feedback. Think of me as your alpha reader. It helps streamline the process. Remember that Michelle and I went through three drafts together."

"I can't write with someone over my shoulder like that. I'll work on it alone from here."

"George, hey, there's no contracted timeline with this, but I'm sure Martha's mentioned wanting to get it out next fall. We don't have much time for multiple rounds of developmental edits."

"Oh," he laughed. "Don't worry, we won't be doing this again. I'll be in touch with Martha directly." He hung up.

It took a long time for Cait to close her mouth and sit back in her chair, inviting Pancho to rest his head against her chest. He huffed while she rubbed his snout and ears, his tail whipping through the air behind him. Processing things made them real, which Cait wanted to avoid like the plague. Maybe if she kept still long enough, that whole conversation would miraculously have gone a different way.

Providence would be smiling if George were right that they were done dealing with each other, but Cait knew better. Martha would likely have a few choice words for him over being an obstruction to his work seeing the light of day, but it would be Cait's responsibility to pilot the editorial ship to the port currently swathed in fog and wreathed in hazards.

She relinquished Pancho and picked up her phone to text Martha but thought better of it after pecking out a few words.

Communicating anything at this point would feel like running to mommy, which was hardly the professional demeanor she wanted to maintain at Grovetree. Martha was a friend, but as with everything, there were limits. She decided to log on to some of her editing groups, where complaints about writers like this were commonplace. It would feel good to vent if nothing else. Some people might chime in with helpful tips, but she was ultimately in this alone. Just like her battle with Allie.

Before she could seek relief in the ether of the Internet, her phone buzzed in her hand, and her computer dinged in front of her. She put a hand to her chest in a very dramatic move and scrolled around to find the source of this interruption. Ah, of course. Tamara. Cait had floated a proposal to her just yesterday with a frankly ridiculous rate for ongoing writer coaching along with a sample schedule of deliverables Cait would be expecting. She couldn't conceive of any writer being willing to work with her terms and rate, but here Tamara was, full of exclamation points and emojis with a signed contract and the first 5,000 words of her revision. What had Cait done? Was she ever going to learn how to say no?

The now-familiar sound of trumpet filtered up through the floorboards, and Cait groaned. She missed Lauren with a tight squeeze of her chest. Not that she didn't love Pancho, but she really needed a salve for this wound of a day, and there was no one here to provide it. Not that Cait had thought of Lauren as a vending machine for warmth and love. No, but if one were on the market, she'd be ordering it right about now—with expedited shipping.

If Lauren hadn't gotten so nasty at the end, Cait realized, she would be hard-pressed not to call her right now. She had been a presence who was on Cait's side absolutely—until she wasn't. Before things had soured, every disagreement had been the other person's fault, every missed deadline had been unavoidable, every new contract had been a cause for celebration. She knew Lauren's view of things during that lovely time hadn't been accurate, but losing a cheerleader like that was hard to recover from.

She winced. The trumpeter of the moment was playing scales clumsily, missing one or two notes in each one and making it through some faster and some more slowly. Clearly not Allie. By now, she always knew when Allie was playing. She had even started to appreciate her finesse with that blunt-edged, blatty instrument. She couldn't quite find a way to forgive her, though, for holding out on a potential solution to this problem, no matter how distasteful Allie might find using a mute.

Allie had been barefoot, Cait remembered suddenly. Not that it mattered. Her feet just seemed so dainty in comparison to Cait's own size 12 flippers. Flippers. For the first time in months, a swim sounded pleasant, the sloshing of water against her ears, the repetitive motion as rhythmic as Allie's scales, which you could set your watch to. She huffed like Pancho at that last thought and got up to rummage through her closet for her suit and goggles. She was looking forward to getting out of her apartment—and to coming back, warm and physically spent, to an evening free of Allie's noise. Assuming she stuck to her schedule from now on as she promised.

She was reeking of chlorine and hollowed out with hunger when she got back to the building, resigned to taking Pancho out to sniff every tree, bush, and fire hydrant within a three-block radius before being able to eat dinner. Swimming always made her ravenous, unlike running, which she hated, or lifting. Visions of steaming tortilla soup from the place down the street were dancing in her mind while she approached her building. She was almost to the front door when Allie appeared from the stairway. She was wearing a slim, black dress and heels and carrying a small purse and larger black bag. She stopped with a stutter step when she saw Cait through the double glass doors but marched ahead, smiling but not widely enough to show off her dimples. Cait had no idea when she'd first noticed Allie's dimples, but now she could picture them in all their dimpled glory even when Allie wasn't right in front of her.

They met just inside the doors, and Cait surprised herself by saying, "You look nice."

Nice was a crying shame of a description, but she wasn't about to edit herself right in the moment. Still, the dress hugged Allie's tidy curves and was cut just low enough to hint at the cleavage hidden beneath. Cait made herself not look away and kept her face neutral.

Allie glanced down at herself. "I have a gig. The one I was practicing for earlier. This is"—she motioned to her dress—"something I wear all the time. Kind of like a uniform." The heels brought her closer to eye level to Cait, though she was still several inches shorter.

"What's the gig?"

Allie's blue eyes narrowed, and Cait couldn't blame her for doubting her interest. She was surprising even herself. "I help out the Brookline Symphony when the repertoire calls for it. All that classical training comes in handy when it's time to pay the bills." She glanced past Cait out the doors. "I need to get going. It takes forever to make it out there on the T. Enjoy your quiet evening. I'm sure I'll annoy you again tomorrow." Then she was gone, leaving Cait strangely disappointed in her absence.

Allie was almost always in a dress or skirt, Cait realized. It was pretty but strange, now that she thought about it. Her wardrobe was unusual compared to Cait's love affair with her 501s and felt clogs, which, while maybe not the height of fashion, were classic. Besides, no one ever saw her, or if they did it was only from the waist up on a computer monitor. That's what the array of white button-down shirts were for: consistency removed distractions. But Cait found herself liking that Allie did things her own way. Forget "nice;" the word she'd been looking for was "gorgeous."

She pushed hair back from her face, catching another strong whiff of chlorine. In college, no matter how much she showered or how well she scrubbed, she had always smelled this way. It had been the background note to the bouquet of those four years, trailing her through the fall and winter, only easing up when leaves and flowers began to bud out and bloom. By the end, she'd been indestructible in the water even though she could only run a few miles on dry land. Her strength and skill had been specialized, not unlike Allie's. Tiny muscles in the woman's mouth and tongue coordinated with her breath to make all that music she played. So much music. She could probably do push-ups with just her lips.

The thought sent a flush through Cait when she realized push-ups weren't exactly what she was imagining. With some difficulty, she brushed off the idea of Allie's mouth doing much more than playing the trumpet and made her way up the stairs to her apartment. After walking and feeding Pancho, she sat down to that soup she'd finally procured and scrolled through emails and texts. A small avalanche of replies to her group post about George made her smile but almost miss something from Martha. She sat up a little straighter when she read it. *Talked with George. Let's touch base tomorrow. I need you to get things under control.*

She swallowed soggy tortilla and beans, the spices heating up her esophagus on their way down. That wasn't at all what she had expected. Martha was always the one who got the writers straightened out and flying right, delivered back to Cait at least paying lip service to the editorial process. Cait shivered despite the chilies in her soup, certain there was something she was missing inside this tangled mess of a book that was apparently so exceptional.

Her dinner suddenly unappetizing, she put her phone face down on the table and wandered back to her office. Pancho raised his head from the floor in the living room but didn't get up to follow her. She pulled up George's novel on her laptop and started reading from the beginning, trying to see it with fresh eyes, kind of like the way Allie had appeared to her downstairs.

CHAPTER SIX

Nick was still sleeping on the couch with fifteen minutes until her first Saturday lesson, and Allie had been tiptoeing around him the whole morning, probably to Cait's great delight upstairs. They had all done this with Allie's father when she was growing up. As she'd gotten older, her mom's deference had burrowed under Allie's skin and proliferated like a cancer. At the same time, she'd found herself sometimes doing it, too— anything to avoid confrontation and to save Nick the danger of coming between a belligerent man and his female relatives. She'd hated her own complicity in the situation when her brother had been staggered by a cuff upside the head, but she'd never insisted on being the one her father hit.

If they were in the same position now, she swore, things would be different. She'd move past her father's sometimes charming façade and confront him. If he hit her, he hit her, but she'd at least stand on her own two feet, without a guardian. She scoffed. Such bravado. Because here she was, being oh so careful not to wake Nick because she wasn't sure which version of him would greet her when he opened his eyes. She tried to convince herself it would be different if she had a girlfriend, that Nick wouldn't come around, that he'd have to behave himself if he did. But nothing had ever stopped her father from being an asshole. Why would Nick be any different?

Her brother had so many shortcomings that she'd stopped counting, and she almost didn't care that they had come from his misguided gallantry. Whatever had gone wrong inside his head made him lazy as shit and satisfied with endless mooching off Allie and their mother. And now he was drooling on one of her nicer pillows. She shook his shoulder, hard. When he only grunted and turned over, she wished she'd gone with her first inclination and woken him with a blast of her trumpet. "Reville" would be just the ticket.

"Hey." She gave him another rough shove. "You have ten minutes to get out of here or deal with the little Dizzy."

"Jesus, Allie." He shot her a squinting look. "Is that the bad one or the really bad one?"

"He's the worst one."

His groan devolved into a cough. "Who names their kid Dizzy?"

Allie laughed long enough to really annoy him. "You haven't noticed?"

"Noticed what?" His face was frozen in scrunched annoyance.

"I name all my young students after famous trumpeters. It kind of lifts them up."

"You are deeply weird."

"Fine. Forget it. But now you only have eight minutes to get out of here or hide in the bedroom and listen to little Dizzy butcher his exercises." She went into the kitchen for no particular reason other than to get away from Nick, who just like their father, was excellent at bursting her bubble.

Nick startled her out of her reverie when he followed her, the stubble on his face and head catching the overhead lights. He said, "Whatever happened to that last babe you were dating?" He was buttoning his jeans, and Allie realized they were the same kind as Cait's. The juxtaposition of those two thoughts was the real deeply weird thing here.

"The last babe?"

"You know, yea high"—he held his hand flat at his chin—"with short, black hair. She went a little overboard on the makeup, but she was definitely a babe. I mean, there's no denying that you have taste."

Okay, so maybe things wouldn't be different at all if she were in a relationship. "That was Rebecca, and we broke up two years ago." They had fizzled more than actively split, both of them too busy and hungry for gigs to spend any time together and sustain a relationship. One day she'd have a better schedule, she told herself without really believing it.

"Excuse me," he said with more syllables than necessary—just like he used to when he was a kid. "You were kind of amazing in high school. You sniffed out willing girls like pigs root out truffles."

"Nice metaphor."

"No, really. It made me wonder if there was some kind of secret handshake or, like, a code phrase that you all learned when you realized you got hot and bothered by girls."

In ways, there had been, but it was more a specific kind of look that told Allie what was only potential in other people was unlocked in this one. "It's called gaydar. And the right kind of conversation. Besides, it was a big school. Odds were at least a little in my favor."

"What is it? One in ten?"

"Theoretically. I haven't really found that to be true, at least in my circles."

"I guess I have no excuse for my poor showing with the ladies."

"Maybe if you got a job and stayed with it for more than a couple months you'd look like a better bet than you do now."

His frown was immediate and as dark as clouds before a tornado. "You're kind of turning into Mom."

"She's more than a martyr, you know." This was meant to convince them both.

It must have given Nick pause because he rubbed his chin with a soft rasping noise. Stubble: Reason Number 472 to be a lesbian. "She did her best, I guess. I'm not saying it was easy for her, but she never helped herself." His quiet seriousness was a pleasant shock to the system. He could be a good person when he was being genuine—or maybe not genuine but a grown-up version of the older brother she'd known when she'd been a girl.

Before Allie could respond to him, which would lead to another of their endless and futile rehashings of their formative years, she was saved by her doorbell. Or maybe foiled, depending on how you looked at things. "That's Dizzy. Are you leaving or staying?"

"Oh, definitely leaving. What's for dinner tonight?"

"I don't know. Why don't you surprise me with something since you'll be out."

He laughed his way to the front door, which he opened and said, "Well, hello, Dizzy. My sister's just chomping at the proverbial bit to get started, God knows why, so go right on in."

She took a deep breath to release her brother and her ex from her mind's eye and put on a smile for Dizzy, who might never get past the suck threshold, no matter how much she helped him. Not for the first time, she wondered if it wasn't her schedule that was holding her back from dating but the fact that she sucked at relationships. How could she be so good at one thing and so terrible at just about everything else?

Allie had always been a bit of a clock watcher, even when she practiced. These days, her schedule and obligations required keeping close track of time, though she loved those few gaps in her calendar when she had nowhere to be and nothing to do and could laze around in blessed ignorance of whether it was 10:30 or 2:15. Her lessons over for the day, she'd scheduled a half hour for some much-needed hydration and downtime before her own practice session and was sitting on the couch with half her attention on her phone, waiting for the time when she could play without surprising any of her neighbors. Okay, without surprising Cait, whose sensitivity might be comical if it didn't affect Allie so directly. Everyone else in the building had been cool with the slight change of plans, though admittedly, they all seemed to be at work during the day.

The other thing that was comical was how Cait had looked at Allie when she'd been dressed up for that concert. Or, more accurately, how she'd so obviously tried *not* to look. It had been endearingly awkward and more than a little flattering. Cait had been rocking her own outfit, too, a T-shirt a little too small that snugged her breasts and biceps, and soft workout pants that hugged some very huggable places. The Amazon was kind of hot, actually, which changed nothing, but it was nonetheless interesting. Cait could be devastating if she wasn't so infuriating. She shook her head at herself. That was a tangent of thought and desire Allie wouldn't be going down again anytime soon.

Nick hadn't returned, which had been something of a blessing, though there really wasn't anything in the house for dinner. Not that Allie had believed for an instant that he would pick up food before coming home. It had only been a couple of weeks, but his welcome had been worn out even before he'd shown up. A while ago, she and her mom had talked about making him fend for himself, but neither of them had the fortitude to close the door in his face and deal with his subsequent anger.

She reached for her phone to text Maggie but stopped before she started. The writing was on the wall with that friendship. Allie had yet to know a woman who didn't fall off the face of the Earth into her fresh and new nuclear family when the first baby showed up screaming but so goddamned adorable. She couldn't blame them, but that didn't stop her from disparaging them relentlessly in her mind anyway. How many times was she going to get dropped like a grace note? She was as independent as the next person, but didn't everyone need friends? Family was one thing: complicated, claustrophobic, disappointing, but friends were supposed to provide an antidote to that. They certainly had when Allie had been growing up, but now that she had tiptoed past thirty, her contact list was the site of a damn massacre.

Allie dropped her head back, but looking at the ceiling only made her wonder if Cait was in the same predicament. She seemed perfectly happy with only her dog for company, and you couldn't miss friends you never had. That was a bit harsh, but Cait hardly seemed to be a magnet for affection, romantic or otherwise. There'd been that woman who had been around for the first year and a half after Cait had moved in, sometimes even coming up and down the stairs solo with Pancho. That had made them seem pretty serious, given how Cait was about that dog. She'd been conspicuously absent for months, though. Allie wondered what had happened, not to mention what Cait would be like in a relationship.

No, she told herself. She most definitely wasn't going to wonder about Cait except to conjecture about what had caused her to have such a gnarly stick up her ass. Maybe not even that. She knew what fueled her own hang-ups and letdowns. That was more than enough information to cause her endless indigestion.

She checked her phone. Just ten more minutes until she could lose herself in practicing, focusing on notes and rhythm, dynamics and tempo. Music was such tangible intangibility, evanescing into the air (and through the ceiling) and disappearing into nothing moments after she played each note, but the playing was as physical as it got.

She was arranging music on her sturdy black stand when the sound of a key in the lock made her stiffen. The slam of the door behind Nick confirmed her worst fears. He was in some kind of a mood, and she wasn't feeling like being very placating. She picked up her trumpet and turned to watch him walk in. Ah, he'd been drinking. She could tell from the shambling looseness in his legs—not to mention that he wore the smell of liquor like a shroud. Great.

"For Christ's sake, Allie, don't you ever do anything else? You and that fucking trumpet. Are you going to try to marry it now? Being able to tie the bondage knot with another girl not enough for you?"

"It's my job, not that you know what one of those is." So much for quickly defusing the situation.

"You don't work. Dad worked, you don't work. Work uses the hands." He brandished a fist in emphasis.

This elevation of their father was new and disturbing. "Dad worked with his hands to make a punching bag out of you."

His lips pressed together into a white line, and a slice of fear gutted Allie, so familiar and tired, yet real. "And why do you think that was, huh? Why would I ever do that to myself?" His tone was musically mocking.

"Can we just cool it?"

"Don't tell me what to do." He was shouting now, and Allie was suddenly exhausted.

"I know, okay? I know how shitty our situation was. I know what you've been through, and I know that you shouldn't be drinking under the best of circumstances."

"I can do whatever the hell I want!"

"You cannot yell at me in my home," she shouted back at him, and they were off, in each other's face, hollering at full volume, so loud that her voice cracked and squeezed. Then his hand gripped her arm, and a horrible blankness came over his face. Allie couldn't stop what was coming next but just hoped her trumpet, which she still held in her right hand, would survive it.

They were interrupted by a pounding at her door, something that would have never stopped their father but that made Nick hesitate and blink. "Hey." The word was muffled by the wood door but still sharp. And recognizable. "Everything okay in there?"

Allie shook herself out of Nick's grip and opened the door to Cait, happy to see her for the first time ever. "Sorry. Everything's fine."

Cait craned her head to the side to peer around her to where Nick was standing, hands balled into fists at his sides. "It didn't sound fine."

"Yeah, well, Nick and I sometimes take sibling rivalry to an unhealthy extreme."

"Sibling? He's not your boyfriend?"

Nick took that opportunity to speak up, of course. "My sister likes pussy. Got more girls than I did in high school."

"For fuck's sake, Nick," Allie said but without much venom.

Cait's face scrunched up, her dark eyebrows pulled together. "I didn't know—" She shook her head. "Maybe use your inside voices to work out your differences?"

Nick laughed, but Allie said, "We'll take that under advisement. Thanks." She slowly closed the door, seeing the look on Cait's face that she'd seen on countless cops when they'd come to her childhood home on domestic disturbance calls. It was the look that said, "Are you sure there isn't anything you want to tell me?" Allie hated herself for keeping her lip buttoned once again and flipping the lock, sealing her and Nick inside to finish what they'd started, only quietly this time.

"Nick," she said.

He sorted through the music on her stand, relaxed but moody. "Forget it. You're such a spoilsport. You take everything so goddamned seriously. You used to be fun. I mean, I remember when you were fun. What happened to you?"

"The same thing that happened to you."

"Yeah, right." He finally gave the music a rest and shoved his hands into his pockets, pushing his jeans low on his hips. They might be the same kind as Cait's, but they wore them so differently. "What's to eat, anyway?"

"I still have some work to do, but you can eat whatever you find in the fridge. I think there's some leftover pasta in the back, but I'm not sure how old it is." She took her stand in her free hand and slipped out the door to the hall, pressing her instrument bell-down on her upturned practice mute on the way. When she was safely outside the apartment, she leaned forward and rested her free hand on her thigh, allowing herself to shake while she breathed deeply in and out, calming herself. What a rotten mess. And having Cait witness any part of it was untenable. The woman already thought she was an ass. A straight ass? Whatever. She sniffed and stood up.

She could call her mom, but what would that accomplish? Misery loved company, but their misery made them unable to do anything for the other. Nick needed help, and neither of them could provide it. Either that or what was wrong in him was too deep to be remedied, woven into his cells like a sinister melody. She knew she needed to stop letting him around her, but she just...couldn't. She remembered too much of when they were young and he was her hero. Besides, getting him to leave wouldn't be remotely straightforward.

Now was the absolute best time to stop thinking about her life, and music was the absolute best way to do it. She leaned back against the wall, settled her practice mute more securely into her bell, and started playing, her sound coming out a fuzzed and quiet version of itself, so subdued not even Cait Durant would find it objectionable. Time passed in an unmeasured blur except for the metronome built into her head, all clock-watching lost to memories of her youth and what just happened. She kept the rhythm steady. Resolute. Anything to feel in control and to keep that door closed between her and Nick.

She played until she was buzzed with oxygen, the magical byproduct of wind instruments. The sheer volume of air she pushed through her trumpet created a coordinating effect with the breath in her lungs, which made it hard to feel upset for too long. Or at least too upset. Everything seemed brighter to her after playing for a while, and the mood persisted, even when she saw Cait and Pancho descend the stairs onto her landing and pause there, Pancho sniffing the air like her music had left a palpable scent.

"Everything okay?" Cait asked again and glanced at the door next to Allie.

"Perfect."

She wore her uniform of jeans and a white shirt—not that Allie was complaining since it looked so good on her. Kind of a business on the top, party on the bottom situation. "Then why are you the one outside your apartment?"

"Everything's fine," she said a little too sharply. The lady was protesting too much, but what else could she do? Cait had no place in her family business, no matter how fresh she looked in that outfit.

"Hey, I'm just trying to help."

"Well, don't."

Cait's eyebrows jerked up before she frowned. "Okay," she said and walked past Allie with Pancho sticking to her leg like he was a blind person and she was the Seeing Eye dog.

Allie waited until she heard the front door close behind them before she brought her horn to her lips again, practicing and soothing herself in equal measure.

CHAPTER SEVEN

Cait was convinced her powers of concentration were what had gotten her out of Tennessee rather than any natural intelligence. They meant she could read more deeply and for longer or focus in the pool on her form for lap after lap. Concentration enabled the accumulation of experience, and that's what made her good at what she did. The millions of words she'd ingested over time were tattooed on her brain by the sheer force of will she'd used when reading them.

Which made what was happening now especially alarming. Her concentration was faltering, and she found herself actually staying home during Allie's scheduled practice sessions and *listening*. What was wrong with her? She had actual work to do, and she was letting herself get pulled away by something that barely qualified as music.

The problem was that after running into her on the landing that night, Cait could now picture Allie playing, the pinch to her mouth that raised the ghost of her dimples, the focus in her eyes, the effortless exercising of her fingers over the three valves.

Not to mention the A-line skirt she'd worn that was a cream color with blue pinstripes—pinstripes that she'd matched with a semi-sheer, short-sleeved blouse. Right, that had nothing to do with it. Now the distraction wasn't just annoying, disembodied sound floating up past the floorboards but something that had become weirdly personal and irresistibly put together. Oh, and gay.

Cait thought she could be excused for this lapse in concentration, though. No one would blame her for keeping an ear metaphorically peeled for sounds of another shouting match like the one that had clearly been headed toward something even worse. She would never have guessed that it was Allie's brother staying with her, the dog slapper. Who did that to someone else's pet? Forget that, who did that to any dog who wasn't actively attacking you? Once Allie had mentioned they were siblings, Cait recognized some of Allie's features in the man's face. He was broad-shouldered like Cait, though, and sported a torso that was half beefy and half paunchy. And he was crude. *My sister likes pussy?* Beyond the surprise part of that nasty revelation (really, she would never have guessed, which spoke volumes about the state of her gaydar), who said something like that? Maybe the same kind of person who would slap Pancho across the snout. Cait didn't like the idea of him down there with Allie, a feeling she tried hard to deny because she was supposed to be hating on everything about her neighbor, not getting all soft. Especially since that easing of hostilities didn't nearly go both ways, her being still persona non grata to Allie.

Cait couldn't afford distraction, literally. She was drowning in freelance work, which was her own damn fault since she was always saying yes to at least one too many projects. Now she was on the hook to Tamara, a commitment that promised to be an avalanche of work she didn't have time for right now. While it meant more money in her bank account, she was also uncomfortably committed to Grovetree and Martha for George's book and had gone as far as printing out the full manuscript and marking it up with a red pen to try to find another way into the writing that wouldn't make George foam at the mouth. Was there something small and unobjectionable she could start over with? Something it would be easy for them to agree on? If she could inch open his slammed door, surely she could break it down entirely with continued gentle pressure.

Who was she kidding? She loved writers, she really did, and she'd even kept many clients as friends. They wrote the best emails and were generally keen observers of the human condition. Most of them knew how to take an editorial punch, especially when delivered as gently as she tried to deliver them. But some of them were fragile little creatures who had a problematic relationship with feedback. They would contort themselves, bending over backward to argue, refute, dismiss, or gaslight, and there was only so much Cait could do about it. You could lead a horse to water and all that... Not that she'd ever liked that idiom very much.

The problem was that Martha expected Cait to make this particular horse drink, and Cait had gotten this far as a freelancer by never ever disappointing anyone in the end. The thought of doing so was more nauseating than the noises that Allie's worst students made. There was nothing to do but give George the best effort she could and hope that something would come of it. This time, she was going into their phone call with different notes from before, notes that she was keeping to herself until they were actually speaking. And she was going to ask questions. Lots of them. Egotistical people just ate up questions.

As she dialed his number, she had to push down flutters of panic and take some deep breaths to try to keep her voice steady. He answered, saying, "George Tanenbaum."

"Hi, George. It's Cait Durant from Grovetree. Is now still a good time to talk?"

"Not if you're going to tell me how shitty my book is again."

"I didn't—I don't think it's shitty. Martha's excited about it, and I understand why," Cait lied. "I wanted to take this time to get to know you a little better and be able to see through the prose to the intentionality behind it." Editorial bullshit. "Can you tell me about the car? Why a 1966 BMW 2002?"

He actually stuttered, which made Cait smile. But then he said, "I know you don't like how I used that car in the book."

"I didn't say that. Can we…I'd just like to know why you chose it and what it means to you."

"My dad had one."

Cait made an encouraging hum, but George didn't take the bait. "Did he restore it himself, like Edgar does in the book?"

"What does it matter?"

"Fine. You're right. It doesn't. Tell me where you learned about sailing. Did you research it for the book or are you a sailor yourself?"

"I know my way around a boat."

Another grand pause. How could this man have such an ego but be so resistant to talking about himself? Cait tried a few other questions to get him going, some about his writing history, some about the settings in the book, some about the dang weather where he lived in sunny Arizona, but the only thing that actually unstuck him was about the previous rejections he'd had and the feedback he'd gotten from them.

"This industry," he said, turning the word into a curse. "What a bunch of narrow-minded idiots. No offense," he said, though he clearly meant every bit of offense in the world. "They all come to work with these ideas of what a book should be, about form and themes and those rules they like to teach in MFA programs that are all such bullshit. Did Pynchon follow the rules? What about Sorrentino? You can't tell me *Everything is Anything* follows the rules. The five-act structure is for plays. Novels can be anything you want them to be. People say that, but when they see something different, they pick it apart and try to make it sanitized and neat. It's all character arcs and plot points, but let me ask you, where's the urgency on the page? That's what I care about. The words should be violently energetic and refuse to be ignored."

Cait snuck in to his soliloquy with her go-to mantra about writing. "I've always thought that the only real rule in writing is that anything goes, as long as it works."

"Well, yeah. People pay that lip service, but what does something working look like? I'm not writing for the lady who's browsing the tabloids in the supermarket checkout line, you know what I mean?"

"Of course. Every book isn't going to appeal to everyone." Finally, something they agreed on.

"Is this art or is this business? Martha and I talked about that. She gets it. But you don't."

Everything came to a screeching halt. "Martha and I agree on a great many things. That's how we've worked together for so long."

"You just don't get it, Cait, and you need to admit it."

"I'm not sure what it is you think I don't 'get.' Do you consider your book to be perfect?"

He laughed. "No book is perfect. Some get closer than others, but you'll never be great if you compromise your vision."

"Tell me what your vision is, and we can start from there. I'm a flexible editor if you give me a chance." She really didn't want to be riding along this cusp of begging, not with this guy.

He sighed but not in a good way. "Like you'll understand. You've already proven you don't with your feedback." She could hear his finger quotes all over that last word.

She spoke before she thought, saying, "If you want to test your own vision out, self-publishing has become a more and more viable way to get your words out there."

"Why would I have worked almost a decade to get this contract if I were the kind of person who wanted to fill the world with uncensored crap?"

She stood up even though she wasn't going anywhere. "Well, George, your book won't see the light of day at Grovetree without going through me first, so take some time to think about that. What would be the difference between what would hit the street if you bypass me and just go ahead and self-publish? I'm not wasting any more of my effort on you until you're ready to behave like a fucking professional." She hung up and dropped her phone like it was on fire. She wished it were, because then she wouldn't have to answer it again and face the fallout that would be coming.

What had she just done? Her hand covered her mouth before slipping down her chin and lying limply at her side. She was as idiotic as George thought the women reading tabloids were. Telling him to be a professional when she made threats she didn't even know if she could back up? What was wrong with her? What would Martha do when she heard about this? Cait couldn't let George get to Martha first.

She snatched up her phone and dialed, Martha's name being at the top of her recent calls list, though it had been days since they'd talked. Martha answered cheerfully. "Cait. I was just thinking of you."

"Uh...good things, I hope?" She felt herself cringe as if awaiting a blow: the editor slapper.

"Of course. I was wondering how things were going with that neighbor of yours."

"What neighbor?"

It was a leap for Martha to jump over her own pause and say, "The trumpet player? What did you call her? A ferociously loud pixie? What an image."

"Oh, yeah. I—"

"It's just so unusual for you to have something going on outside work. Except for that breakup you had, you've been steady Eddie since Mark at *The Appalachian Review* referred you to me."

Cait blew out a long breath and sank back into her chair. "Allie, the neighbor, is fine. She's...fine." Martha and Cait had tiptoed around the line between personal and professional, dipping farther into one side or the other across the years and seasons. Usually, Cait would say something about the practice sessions or the dog-slapping brother, but she choked on those words now, knowing they'd be only a distraction.

"What's going on? You hate the word 'fine.' That and 'nice.' I agree, but you're irrational about it."

"I'm not—" She cut herself off. "I just got off a call with George."

"Ah, good."

"No, not good. I"—she made a disgusted sound—"didn't handle him well. I mean, I tried. Man, I've never tried so hard, but I let him get the best of me and said—" She cast around for the right word but gave up. "Stuff."

"You know how important that book is to our fall lineup next year."

"I know, and he definitely knows. I just, Martha, I don't understand. Sure, there are moments of brilliance in there and some really moving scenes, like Richard and Ursula on their midnight sail, but I can't get past how…how *juvenile* and underdeveloped some of it is. George won't hear criticism of any kind and has dug in his heels about working with me. I can't even get him to have a regular conversation where I'm putting all the focus on him. Doesn't that always work for men?"

"Women, too, darling."

"I do think the whole book could be quite good, but if I can't get him to work with me on the smallest thing, I don't see how that's going to happen. I asked about his intentionality, and he told me I would never understand his vision." She stopped and waited.

Martha took her time. Cait even moved the phone from her ear to make sure they were still connected. "You can't be in this business without getting disaffected. George sees that, which is why we get along. I see the things that are good in something, and you see what isn't. It's our jobs. And our temperaments, I think. It's what makes you so good at what you do. He's also the nephew of our biggest donor, and though I said I'd never compromise my art for business, the fact is that we rely on donations to keep putting out books that need to be read. George's book has real merit, and it could mean whether the future of the press is big or small. That's why I'll take this book away from you if I have to in order to get it published. I've got a business to run, besides the fact that he's under contract."

Cait made a strangled noise that brought Pancho to her side. "Martha."

"Do I have to, Cait? I need to know because we're wasting time as it is. We need to give George a proper opportunity to revise like any other author."

"He's never going to revise. He's going to prima donna his way along until it's too late to ask him to do anything. Or to do anything like what he should do. He'll do just enough to satisfy the participation clause in his contract, but the book won't live up to its potential." She swung her chair around, and Pancho danced along, his nails clicking on the scratched hardwood.

"Then someone needs to get through to him."

"Or give him an ultimatum?"

"I can't. Besides, have you ever seen someone be creative while staring down the barrel of a gun?"

"That's a little hyperbolic."

"Cait, you did such a beautiful job on *Everything is Anything* that I thought this would be a perfect fit for you, but you've got to be honest with me. I'll give it to Terry if you can't see it through."

"Because he's a man?"

"Because he's not you."

"Talk about the barrel of a gun." The headache she'd been keeping at bay bloomed inside her skull, and she closed her eyes, gripping her temples with her free hand.

"George is calling on the other line."

"Please, just wait a minute. He's going to—Just wait." Her fingers pressed harder, and she leaned forward, resting her forehead on her knees. If she passed on this book, Martha might never trust her again, and there went half her income. But if she kept on it and failed, she would definitely lose Martha's trust and half her income. The decision was as impossible as the one in *Sophie's Choice*. Well, okay, not that bad, but bad enough to sour her stomach.

"Cait, I need to know."

"Give me another chance," she said quickly. "I'll figure out a way through his defenses. But try to cut me a little slack when you talk to him. He's persistently difficult, and I didn't handle it well. I'll turn things around, though. I promise."

"Okay, but I reserve the right to yank it from you if you don't fix this situation soon. I need to go call him back. I'm trusting you, Cait."

"I know. I'll deliver. Or I'll get him to deliver. You know what—" And she was talking to a dead line. While she tried to measure the exact dimensions of the hole she'd just dug for herself, playing started up from downstairs. "Fuck!" she yelled. Pancho skittered away, and the playing stopped for a long moment before beginning again.

Even though it was the busy afternoon, she gathered her things for the gym, gave Pancho a kiss, and left him behind. She furiously strode down sidewalks and across streets, getting warmed up for the lifting session she could already feel in her muscles. She'd made the wrong decision; it was clear now. She had her phone with her and could call Martha, tell her she'd changed her mind. Her steps faltered for a beat before her determination made her stupid again. Editors passed on projects all the time, but she'd taken everything Martha had given to her. Maybe it was her pride as much as George's that was dooming them to failure, but she couldn't go back now.

The gym was too crowded, and a couple of the people in the free weight area clearly had no idea what they were doing and were going to hurt themselves, but she didn't care. She made herself take up space, claiming the twenty- and thirty-pound dumbbells as her own and getting to work in front of an open patch of mirror where she could check her form. This was not a beauty contest, as some people seemed to think. She straightened her back and curled the thirty-pound weights slowly up to her shoulders and back down until they were parallel to the ground. She waited a beat and repeated, trying to lose herself in the effort and the pulse of blood in her neck. She lifted to exhaustion, took a break, and did it again, her arms hot and shaking.

She changed weights, leaned forward, and worked her back with bent-over dumbbell rows. Sometimes she did these lying face down on a bench, whether flat or inclined, but she was jumping out of her skin too much today for that. She did two sets, again reaching exhaustion on each one in under ten reps. She cycled through Arnold presses, pausing every rep when the weights were high above her head. People were watching, but she didn't care.

She staked her claim on a bench and began to work her triceps, using it for dumbbell flys, bent-arm pullovers, and declined rotational sit-ups, which left her trembling from her neck to her ass. Sweat darkened her T-shirt around her sports bra, and she was already feeling a lassitude that would overtake her very soon. One more exercise to go, though. She changed position, held both thirty-pound weights against her chest, and went into back extensions, squeezing at the top, moving slowly and completely through the motion.

On the third rep, something went *sprung* in her hip, and she dropped the weights and bit her lip like it was a juicy hamburger. She tasted blood and saw stars and felt around for something that might support her and change things. Her hips, stupid things. Not that her lower back was winning any awards. Hundreds of thousands of yards of breaststroke did things to a body, and she was paying the price. She held herself up with her hands on the support under her hips.

"Are you okay?" someone asked.

She hummed and tentatively moved, making her back spasm now. Her hum turned into a gasp. "Ice."

Even she didn't know if it were a statement of what she was going to do later or a demand for someone to fetch some now. She breathed through the spasm, moving a hand so she could press her thumb into the center of it to convince it to relax itself. It didn't. Apparently, it needed sweet talking, like George, who was the one who'd gotten her into this mess.

Someone who worked at the gym came around and helped her to the mat and on her back, her legs bent and feet planted hip-width apart and near her ass. That at least allowed her to breathe. Then there was ice, which she accepted with closed eyes. This would pass. Some Advil, some careful stretching, a massage or two, and she'd be fine. Unfortunately, that didn't help much at this moment. She opened her eyes to find people hovering around her. "What are you looking at?"

The trainer next to her laughed. It was a woman with platinum-blond hair and a very attractive body she was showing off in just a sports bra and clingy shorts. "People will rubberneck anywhere. We need one of those privacy screens."

Cait laughed and grimaced. "Then they'd get all sorts of ideas of what was going on behind it."

"There also aren't very many women around here who lift like you do."

"Yeah, well maybe they shouldn't, given how it turned out today."

"Are you always this intense, or were you trying to work something out?"

"Believe me, what I have is never going to get worked out." The ice had started to do its job, dulling the pain. She sat up with the woman's help. Her grip was reassuringly tight, and her eyes were the same kind of deep blue as Allie's, though Cait was pretty sure that unlike hers, Allie's hair was her natural color. Lauren had told her that no blondes were really blond, but Lauren had told her a lot of things that ended up not to be true. "Thanks." Cait rose and moved gingerly over to her small pile of things and contemplated them. They seemed really far away from this vantage point, and she almost wished she were smaller.

The trainer was at her side again. "Here." She gathered up Cait's things, handing them to her. "Want me to call a ride for you?"

Cait shook her head. "A walk will keep things from seizing up anymore."

"Ah, so you've had this before?"

"Oh yeah. We're old pals. Thanks again."

The walk back to the apartment was slow and painful, her body shedding the numbing cold with every block. Then, of course, the elevator was out. She stood with her head against it, gathering will, when she heard Allie's playing. Did she have a practice session scheduled now? Cait couldn't remember and didn't really care. All sorts of shitty things were happening right now. Why not that?

She took the stairs one at a time, resting both feet on each one like a toddler. When she made it to Allie's landing, there she was again, playing in the damn hallway. Cait had thought the music was coming from behind her door, but she had that black thing stuffed in her trumpet again. Allie's playing choked off when they looked at each other, each seemingly guilty about their different predicaments.

"Why are you in the hall again?" Cait said.

"Why are you hunched over like that?" Allie countered.

All Cait wanted was to drug herself, lie down, and go to sleep. Pancho, she thought with a twist of her mouth. All these stairs, twice more, to take him out, down and up. Neither of them seemed inclined to answer the other's question, and the quiet stretched out between them. Yes, Allie's hair was natural, and her eyes were kind of mesmerizing, like a deep pool of water that would cradle her aching body.

She broke first, wanting to keep Allie from reading her mind. "I hurt my back at the gym."

"Are you okay?"

"Fine, just"—she motioned up toward her apartment— "dreading taking Pancho out. Do you think he's too big to use a litter box?"

Allie held her thumb and index finger close together. "A smidge." She shifted on her feet, and Cait noticed she was barefoot again, even on this trash heap of a carpet. Allie squinted and said, "I can take him out if you need."

They both froze again. No no no no no. The word cascaded through Cait's brain. This was not happening. There was no room for friendliness between them, even though Allie had her hair up in two pigtails that were objectively cute. "Why are you out in the hall?"

"You know that saying that visitors are like fish? After a few days they stink? I needed some air."

"It is still your apartment, right?"

"So says my rent check every month. Pancho?"

"I'll handle it." Cait moved, but she'd stiffened up standing there, trying not to look at Allie but not being able to stop from comparing her to the trainer at the gym. Allie was prettier, even with that red ring on her mouth. Her cheeks were raw silk. Cait told her mind to shut up but gasped when she moved more and her back seized again. Allie set her trumpet down and was at her side quickly but just kind of hovered her hands around Cait's arm and back.

"I'm afraid touching you will hurt you more, but you clearly need some help."

"I'm fine," Cait said and laughed at the absurdity. "Okay, fine's not the right word. Fine's a terrible word in general."

"Yeah, you're not remotely fine. See, I avoid back pain by never exercising. You could clearly crush me like a fly, but maybe if you put your arm over my shoulders I can be useful in some small way?"

Cait wanted to say no, but even she could admit that she wasn't in a position to. She put one arm over Allie's shoulders but tried to keep as much weight off her as possible. Even so, Allie was more than useful, helping Cait support her torso while she climbed the last flight of stairs and unlocked her door. Pancho was there, gearing up to greet her a little too enthusiastically, and Cait snapped once, loudly. He stopped, but he was in an excited crouch, and his tail was whipping back and forth. Allie was still nestled under her arm, which made Cait a little less angry about her back.

She said, "No, Pancho."

He whined.

Allie said, "There's no way you can take him out. I don't care how well he's trained, which is, like, freakishly well, by the way. Congratulations on that. I'll take him. It's no problem; I needed a break anyway."

Cait really wanted to say no, but Allie was right, as much as it pained Cait to admit. "And by take him out you mean to do his business and not, like, *take him out*, right? Because your brother—"

"Leave my brother out of it." Her words were hard, and she ducked out from under Cait's arm. She smiled a little, though still under the dimple threshold. "Isn't it funny that peeing and pooping are such serious business for our pets? I picture Pancho in a suit and tie, holding his T pass between his teeth."

"Well, it's serious business for owners, at least. Otherwise it's a horrific mess. But, yeah, okay. Please take him out for me if you don't mind. We'll both be forever grateful."

Allie helped her lie down on her couch, looking around with the same interest Cait had felt when interrupting that shouting match. One ice pack later, Allie was gone with Pancho, and Cait counted the seconds until they were back. Was Allie doing this because she felt guilty for being a disruption? Part of Cait wanted her to feel guilty enough for these acts of service, but the rest of her wanted it to be something else. She'd had enough of this feuding and frustration; Allie was in her life in the strangest way, and she was too tired and broken to want to be angry anymore. Not only that, but she wanted to sic Pancho on this dead-fish brother even though the only offensive move Pancho really had was to sit on someone until they relented.

In the quiet, outside of music and schedules and screaming insults, thinking about Allie was a balm for her aches. Her put-together outfits, honey hair, and talented mouth. Maybe Allie would forgive her for being such an ass at the beginning between them and things could be different. Not that it necessarily mattered what she wanted at this point. She'd been such an unrelenting harpy in the beginning that whatever bridge might have been between them had probably been irreparably burned.

Her back was still radiating pulses of pain when she heard the door open and Pancho clatter his way through. "Here," Cait said, and the dog was licking her face the next instant. While she rubbed his ears and neck, she heard Allie hang up his leash before she appeared in the living room, where Cait could see her.

"Should I feed him? He was interested in every discarded wrapper on the walk."

Cait let loose an embarrassingly dramatic sigh and covered her eyes with the inside of her elbow. "He always does that, especially if I'm not around. But feeding him would be great. There's a container of dry food in the kitchen. You can't miss it. One scoop and then get out of the way because he might nibble on your ankles." She dropped her arm to look at Allie.

"Really?" Allie actually looked confused, light eyebrows pulled together over those blue eyes.

"Ha. No. I'm just joking. Clearly I'm delirious with the pain."

Then there was the clatter of kibble, which sent Pancho galloping the ten feet to the kitchen and his food bowl. They were serenaded by his chomping, which now that Cait thought about it, was way more disturbing than Allie's trumpet. He wolfed down the food like he was afraid it was going to get up and walk off.

Allie stood at the end of the couch by Cait's feet, which were still in her gym shoes. God knew when she'd be able to take them off by herself. Allie said, "You okay enough for me to go now? Can I get you anything since you're kind of trapped there?"

"I'm fine." She huffed a frustrated breath at using that stupid word again. "I'll manage. Please don't let me hold you up anymore."

"I won't be able to lock your deadbolt, is that okay?" She motioned toward Cait's front door, which made her blouse pull across her breasts. Cait wished she could blame the pain for her wayward observations tonight.

"Even though it would be right up the alley of this day for me to get beaten to a pulp and robbed, that's acceptable. I'm not worried. Or I have bigger things to worry about."

"Okay…well, bye."

Cait waved until she heard the door close behind Allie. "Great," she said, hissing when Pancho rested his head on her belly like he always did. She scratched behind his ears. "Just great." Now she had some kind of undeniable thing for the ferociously loud pixie?

CHAPTER EIGHT

The day hinted at summer, and Allie slipped out of the apartment to sit on the front steps of the building and make some calls. Nick had settled into her place far too well: it was getting harder and harder for her to dislodge him from the couch when she had students. If she weren't pretty sure someone would shoot her for making such a racket, she'd be considering holding her lessons in the closest park.

He wasn't always hard to be around. They had a good time talking over takeout—almost always about the past, though. They were both painfully aware of his present, and the future looked to be more of the same, so the past it was, digging through layered chords of history. Elementary school, high school, that one epic night they had when he visited her in college. They never talked about their father, rarely talked about their mother, and stayed leagues away from their collective trauma. But the rest of the time, he was moody and at a low simmer Allie was loath to disturb. She had to get rid of him, but he never left until he wanted to. What she needed to do was give him a reason, but she'd never been good at coming up with one.

It was so frustrating, being totally spineless with him when she was so assertive in her professional life. She had to be. Brass sections were still male dominated, though more and more auditions were done blind to try to address this. It started early, with girls getting sold on the merits of the flute or clarinet instead of the trumpet and trombone. Things somewhat evened out through attrition, but they were far from parity. Misogyny didn't stop after you got a job, either, though she'd now been around long enough that most everyone knew and respected her.

It hadn't always been that way, of course. Far from it. For years, she'd had to walk a fine line of presenting the just-right persona that men would respect instead of sexualize. Honestly, this was one part of her life where being a lesbian was a net positive. The guys might still picture her having sex with women, but they also thought she had invisible balls in her somewhere, giving her enough masculinity to fuck another woman. Stupid. Everything was stupid.

After calling a few people who were behind on their lesson payments, she did what she'd been avoiding and dialed her mother.

Instead of hello, her mother said, "He still over there?"

"He's gotten worse. He slapped my neighbor's dog."

"He slapped me."

Allie forgot how to breathe for a minute. Nick had never really touched either one of them, never going further than grabbing one of their arms too hard. "When?"

"The night before he left."

"Why didn't you tell me? I should've known before—"

Her mom's laugh was tired. "Would you have turned him away?"

They sat with that truth for a while.

"It was inevitable, like with your father. It was never if; it was always when."

The sun had lost its friendly warmth and now felt malevolent, making her squint in its glare. "You still should have told me."

"I couldn't bear to." It was a whisper. "But I...I can't do it anymore. All those years with your father and now this? When am I ever going to feel safe in my own home, Allie?"

While Allie had sympathy for her mom, the second-generation wolf wasn't just blowing down her house but was stretched out on Allie's sofa, presumably resting up for his next attack. "You don't want me to kick him out because if I did, he might go back to you."

"Don't make me feel worse than I already do, but I have to do now what I couldn't do then."

"Where am I supposed to land with all this?"

"I was going to see if a restraining order would help at all, but then he left. Don't say anything. I know. I've felt like weak trash my whole life, so why would I think I'd ever be anything different?"

"Mom."

"Do what you have to, Allie. I just can't." She hung up.

Allie sat with her head bowed, her forearms on her thighs, her breath unruly. A restraining order against her brother? He'd slapped their mom? Even though her mom and she walked in the same general direction with respect to Nick, Allie couldn't imagine how much worse this was for her mom than for her. This was her son, and she'd done nothing when her husband regularly laid him out flat. Allie had her own guilt, but she was sure it couldn't hold a candle to her mom's. Now she was alone in this, though, and her chest tightened at the thought. She had a lesson in less than fifteen minutes, and she didn't know how she was going to climb the stairs to her apartment.

The glass door creaked open behind her, but she didn't move even though she was planted directly in the middle of the steps to the sidewalk.

"Hey."

Allie closed her eyes. She felt Cait slip by next to her, her movements slow and exaggerated, making a loud silent statement on Ally's position on the steps. Allie opened her eyes. Cait held on to the railing, and she took the last two steps gingerly. Oh, right. She was injured, not being a jerk, and those jeans looked way better on her than on Nick. Not that there was room in her brain for Cait's ass.

"You have a lesson soon, right?" Cait asked, resettling her backpack on her shoulder in emphasis.

Allie nodded.

"Thanks for your help the other night."

"You're not the only one with problems, Cait." The words were hard and desperate and not remotely what she wanted to say, but not only was there no room in her head for this woman's body, friendliness was off the table. She got up and went inside, not wanting to see Cait's reaction. The two flights to her apartment felt like a death march. Instead of using it to figure out how to oust Nick, she worked on fastening on a mask that said everything was fine, just fucking fine, thank you very much. How in the world had she just become accountable for her mother's safety along with her own? What a righteous mess.

Nick was exactly where she'd left him, on the couch, his feet up on one of the arms, his shoes probably marking up the upholstery. He was reading the latest issue of *Rolling Stone* and didn't look up when he said, "You are so irreparably uncool—at least according to this magazine. Deathly uncool."

It was a joke from their childhood, but she wasn't in the mood. She moved her stand from the corner to the middle of the room and opened up her lesson book on the coffee table. "Chet's coming in a few minutes. He's the loud one if you've forgotten." Chet, in fact, had yet to find a dynamic other than ear-shattering, but they were working on it. No one just starting out believed that you needed more air, not less, to play quietly. How easy would it be if everyone would just trust her now and then? But easy wasn't in the cards for her.

"Maximally uncool," Nick said, but he actually dropped his feet to the floor (probably marking up her rug) and sat up with a groan eerily reminiscent of their father. "Frighteningly uncool. Uncool to a degree never seen before."

Allie smiled despite herself. "Light years uncool."

"Mariana Trench uncool." He rolled up the magazine and shoved it in one back pocket and snugged his wallet into the other, where it settled into a position that matched a worn and frayed outline. Allie wondered if Cait had something like that on her jeans before rolling her eyes at herself and the whole situation. Maybe even every situation out there. "Catch you later, Allie." Then he was gone. More like his old self than she'd seen in weeks. It was like he'd heard the call with their mom and knew he had to smooth things over.

Not that she had time to contemplate it. She was still reviewing her lesson notes when someone buzzed from out front. Chet here for his lesson. She rang him in but stopped on the way to open her door for him. Just because Nick was in a good mood did not mean everything was okay. Nothing was remotely okay, but she'd never been able to fix it before, so how would she ever figure out what to do now? With a sigh, she flung her door open and shouted down the stairway, "Chet!"

How was it that women went from barely pregnant one week to poking your eye out with their inverted belly button the next? Allie wasn't sure how Maggie was managing to hold her horn far enough away from herself to accommodate her suddenly very pregnant belly. Had she known this was going to happen, letting Allie in on the news of the impending bundle of joy at the very last moment before her belly would announce it for her? She pretended not to notice because she'd heard pregnant women were also unpredictable, and she was, as it had been established earlier, uncool and liable to say the wrong thing.

But then Maggie sat back at the end of their recording session and let out a sigh of a size, shape, and duration only possible for someone who spent hours blowing through feet and feet of metal tubing. "Somehow I thought I would skip this part."

"What part, the one where you look like you have a full-term alien in your belly?"

Maggie scrunched up her face.

"Or, you know, an adorable fetus. Or baby. Or almost child." Why couldn't Allie shut up?

"Please tell me you're not planning on becoming a mother."

Allie blew spit from her instrument and slipped it in her gig bag. "God no. I'm far too aware of how parents fuck up their children."

Maggie raised an eyebrow. "Your brother?"

Allie zipped her bag closed. "I don't want to talk about it."

"Fair enough." Maggie turned her horn upside down and pulled out some slides, small sections of tubing out of the larger whole. She tilted each one to drain it of spit.

So much spit all the time with brass instruments. Some people, former girlfriends included, thought it was gross, but, really, it was mostly water. Vapor in her breath condensed on the inside of the tubing and ultimately escaped through the aptly named spit valve and onto whatever floor was beneath her. Maggie had a valve like Allie's, but there were so many loops and curls to her instrument that it sometimes seemed like a wild goose chase for Maggie to find all the lingering deposits of water that otherwise would gurgle like a bad plumbing problem when she played.

Maggie pulled her own soft case from under her chair with some effort. "But you have a gig tonight, right?"

"Yeah, the jazz crew is getting together at Wally's Club for a couple of sets. It's been too long since I could blow off steam like that. If only it paid better..."

"We're all going to have that engraved on our tombstones."

"Speak for yourself. I'm getting cremated and tossed in the Charles."

Maggie zipped her instrument away. "I really need to catch you guys one of these days."

"It's okay. I know jazz isn't your thing." If there was something French horns weren't known for, it was their ability to swing.

"Yeah. I mean, no, that's not it. Trevor's getting a little overprotective these days, and, honestly, I'm just tired by, like, eight at night."

"Don't worry about it. I gotta get going, though. There's always outfit drama before we go to that club."

"You'll look fantastic. You always do."

"Ah yes, but will I sound it?" Allie winked, waved, and slipped out of the studio. She had been going to ask Maggie to grab dinner with her, but Maggie's excuses—and then Allie's deranged idea of an overprotectiveness turned sinister—had made Allie unfit for company.

She hustled to the closest T stop, telling herself no one was following her, that no one was lying in wait. But she couldn't quite block the memory of the last time they'd all seen her father. Drunk and belligerent as always, he'd already bloodied Nick's nose and knocked him into the shelf unit, sending pictures and a flower vase crashing to the floor, shattering into jagged shards of glass.

He wasn't done yet, though, and he turned around to target Allie. He was saying something, shouting something, but Allie couldn't hear. She just saw the tendons sticking out of his neck and the vein pulsing under a thin sheen of sweat on his forehead, a forehead that had gotten bigger and bigger as the years had passed and his hairline had receded. She was going to get hit this time, for sure. There was no escaping it.

Then Nick was hanging on the back of their father, his arm tucked under the stubbled chin. Their father staggered around, clawing at Nick's arm, banging against walls and furniture.

"How do you like it, huh?" Nick repeated over and over until their father dropped to his knees.

Allie felt like she was choking along with him. Was Nick going to kill him? Is that what she wanted? Didn't he deserve it? No, Nick couldn't. Right? But it seemed like he was doing it...until, just as their father's eyes were fluttering closed, Nick released him to fall to the floor, gasping. Then Nick leaned down and said something in the man's ear, and when she'd gotten up in the morning, their father was gone. No one said a word about it, afraid to jinx things and bring him back.

But what had happened to their father had happened to Nick, too. He had been only fourteen then. What a thing for a kid to have to do, and they'd just let him live with it, had been thankful for that savagery. She didn't know what her mother had thought, but she had wished Nick hadn't let go, had just squeezed their father's neck and squeezed it until his arms gave out and the man was dead. Not just gone from their home but wiped from the Earth.

What were any of them supposed to do with any of it?

Maybe she was deeply weird and unfathomably uncool because of her relationship with music, but her trumpet had saved her as much or more than Nick had. If something got in the way, she would take it out, just like Nick had ultimately vanished their father. The thought gave her pause. He hadn't, though, right? There had been no taking out. There had been mercy and quiet instruction and some degree of peace. She hated that her mind even went to the unrealized past where Nick had killed their father with a queasy pleasure, and she forced herself to move on from the sliver of suspicion about what he was ultimately capable of.

True to form, she tried on four different dresses before she was happy with the one she'd chosen for the gig. She settled on a maroon dress with a V-neck and cap sleeves and a pair of black heels—though with only a couple of inches of height in deference to the fact that she'd be on her feet for a few hours. When had everything in her life become such a balancing act? Being pretty but not too sexy. Professional but fun. Removed but encouraging. So many choices and so many ways to get tripped up.

When she finally left her apartment—at a time most people were contemplating the dreaded chores of washing their face and brushing their teeth—she actually felt a lift of happiness that wasn't even diminished by a passing thought of Cait and her back and the sympathy she had felt for her despite herself. Even though their animosity had quieted down to nothing and maybe even reversed a bit, Allie still could feel her lurking upstairs, not wearing the primo earplugs, silently irritated at the noise.

Forget about Cait, she told herself. Forget about Nick and about Maggie's inexorable decrescendo out of her small family of friends. Forget about everything but the music she was going to play, the audience she was going to play it for, and the energy and feeling of cosmic rightness that came from letting herself go and improvising against a known key signature, tone, and tempo. A feeling of mastery came with straying from the written notes and pulling creativity from her highly trained ass.

She listened to Miles on the T, a bluesy soundtrack to the rush of darkness outside the train's windows. Her fingers twitched against her thigh, itching to work the valves of her trumpet. The deep, animal pleasure of air pouring and in and out of her lungs was waiting for her along with the resulting heady buzz of oxygen.

At the club, she hugged her crew, Jennifer on piano, Mike on drums, Antoine on bass, and Patrick on alto sax. Patrick was the newest member of the group, replacing their previous sax player who had moved out of the area for a real job offer he couldn't (and didn't seem to want to) refuse. Jennifer and Mike were married to each other, Antoine played with the Boston Symphony, and Patrick insisted on being a little more handsy with her than their relatively new friendship would justify, his embrace drifting down to her hips when a simple squeeze around her shoulders would have sufficed. Patrick was just being Patrick, but unwanted contact injected a pinprick of annoyance in an otherwise awesome night.

Their first set was a little messy until they got to the third song and clicked the way they always did. They never had much time to rehearse: Mike and Patrick had full-time jobs having nothing to do with music, Antoine taught at the New England Conservatory with regular hours, and Allie and Jennifer's schedules were always a little unpredictable. But they loved jazz and were committed to it as much as they could be, and Allie was fully in the groove by the time they took their break.

Jennifer nudged Allie's shoulder as they found places at the end of the bar. "Antoine's on fire tonight."

"The man can do anything with that instrument. No one would believe that he plays for the BSO."

"This has got to be more fun than orchestral playing."

"It one hundred percent is." She ordered a seltzer water while Jennifer opted for an old-fashioned, which Allie knew would be her only real drink of the night. "Hey, how do you and Mike make things work with your schedule and his job and all?"

Her smile was friendly and warm. "Aw, you're asking me for relationship advice!"

"I'm asking about relationship possibility."

"All I can say is that it helps that we're both pretty independent people and that neither of us wanted kids."

"That's…not very useful."

She took a sip of her drink. "I'm hardly an expert. Every year, I wonder what I got myself into."

"No, you don't."

"No, I don't. Or not about Mike. Sometimes I wouldn't mind having a normal job where I'd be happy bitching about my manager or that loud person two cubicles over."

Allie laughed. "Seriously? You would give this all up?"

"The hustle? The shitty instruments, the boring music, the most Jesus-y shit possible every Sunday? What's there to complain about? Oh, right, the ridiculous pay? Don't get me started on this country and the arts."

Allie's glass was frozen halfway to her mouth. "Wow."

"I'm fine," Jennifer said but took another long swallow of her drink. "I can't not do it, so I shouldn't complain about it."

"You can complain to me anytime. We're in the exact same boat, but I don't have someone like Mike in my life."

Patrick appeared out of nowhere. "Just say the word. I'm happy to step in."

Jennifer said, "You're not her type, Pat."

"Hey," he said, "don't knock the Patrick train before you try it." He punctuated that with a squeeze of his hand at Allie's waist.

She said, "Patrick, please."

He smiled. "See, she's already asking for it."

Jennifer said, "Knock it off. How much have you had to drink?"

"I can still blow a straight scale."

Allie gripped the edge of the bar and avoided Patrick's gaze, but she said, "Don't do this. Why would you fuck around with the group?"

"It's not the group I'd like to fuck around with." This time his squeeze was on her ass, and she jumped away from him.

"Don't touch me!" The words came out at full volume, and she could feel the gazes of everyone else in the club. Even so, she couldn't temper her voice. "I don't want your hands on me. I don't want any man's hands on me. I fucking like pussy, you dumbass."

If a club could ever be silent, this one got there, and dread loosened her knees and tightened her chest. She ran from the bar, past the stage, and out the back door, which opened into an alley perfumed by several dumpsters. Antoine was there, leaning against the building and smoking.

"Hey," he said.

She'd had more than her share of words already, so she just turned away from him and hurried down the alley into the darkness away from the club. Not that anywhere in Boston got truly dark, but this would qualify as a probably-not-safe-for-a-woman location. What the fuck? She was sick of the world's shit. There wasn't a corner of it that didn't stink to high heaven. What was wrong with everyone? Patrick succumbing to his hormones like some 'roided out dude. All her students' parents who forced years of lessons on kids who hated playing. Cait, who couldn't be bothered to wear a simple pair of earplugs. Maggie, who was going to dump her any month now. And fucking everyone who couldn't conceive of a feminine woman being a stone-cold lesbian.

And herself, Allie guessed. What had she been thinking, echoing Nick's words like that, at full volume, in front of total strangers? She needed to get a grip, but her edges were so frayed her middle was threatening to unravel, too, and she didn't know what she would do if that happened.

"Allie?" The word sounded loud in the shelter of the alley. Jennifer.

Allie considered keeping on walking, but she loved Jennifer. Besides, her instrument was back on stage at the club. She stopped. "I don't want to talk about it."

"I wouldn't, either. He's gone. Or he will be gone. Mark and Antoine are taking care of it."

"I can't go back in there."

Jennifer was next to her, arms crossed in front of her chest in the night's chill. "You were totally justified."

"I told everyone that I like pussy."

"I think there are two or three women in there who might be interested."

Allie's laugh was a blurt. "Good luck to them. I'm a handful." She gazed up at the sky, all stars obscured by the streetlights. "I don't understand it. Did I do something? I feel like I must've done something. Why tonight, after the months we've played together?" Was this feeling of culpability appropriate or had it just gotten ground into her sense of self early with her father?

Jennifer shook her head. "I have no idea. Maybe he was on something. I've wondered about that before."

"I know better than to get so worked up. The only way out of those situations is to defuse it if you can or leave if you can't."

"Hey," Jennifer said and grasped her arm, which made Allie flinch away. "Sorry." She dropped her hand but frowned. "It's not your fault when someone assaults you like that."

"He didn't—"

"He absolutely did. You didn't want his advances, you specifically told him you weren't interested, and he still touched you."

"Yeah, but—"

"Allie, stop. I know you know this. You can't be in the industry without knowing it. Men are fucking pigs, and we can't be responsible for their behavior. Not even if we wear dresses and makeup and look beautiful and tempting."

"Maybe if I'd been clearer," Allie said.

"Come on. I never thought you'd put yourself in the victim's role."

"You don't know anything about me." Her tone was hard, but even though Jennifer took a step back, Allie didn't know if she regretted it.

They stood quietly, a siren blaring on the street they were behind, red lights strobing around them. When it passed, Jennifer grinned and said, "Except that you like pussy."

Allie's laugh broke her open. "I do. I really do. Not that I've been getting any lately."

Jennifer said, "Can I hug you, or will you rip me a new one?"

"I can't promise anything."

Their hug was fierce and long. When Jennifer pulled back, she said, "None of this is your fault. But we do need to figure out how to make things work in our next set without a saxophone. Ready to come back?"

Allie wasn't, but she followed Jennifer inside. The show must go on, but her nerves jangled and her lungs still felt constricted. She was already looking forward to finishing this night and curling up in bed to try to put it behind her. Then she remembered Nick and felt a twist in her gut that left her queasy. She was going to have to do something about him, but fixing that felt as impossible as everything else.

CHAPTER NINE

Cait woke with either the most brilliant or the most harebrained idea ever. She was still half asleep when she texted one of her writer clients and asked him to call when he had a minute. She and Daniel had worked on a couple of books together, and their respective dry senses of humor had lit an intellectual fire between them. Daniel had a wife, three kids, and a mortgage, but inside his suburban existence lurked a renegade.

Her subconscious must've been working overtime, trying to solve the problem of George and *Put Title Here*. Since they'd last spoken, she'd called him twice and been greeted by the impersonal stock message of his voicemail. She'd also emailed twice a week, each one recommending a book she thought George would like and that also elegantly solved one or more of the problems that she had brought up multiple times. Each note focused on the book recommendation itself and some specific sections that might interest him and said nothing about how it related to his work. His response to all of that? Either a clipped, dismissive note about how little she got his vision or crickets, which Cait had come to prefer.

A few seconds later, Cait's phone rang. Jackpot. She answered and lay back in bed, her T-shirt and shorts still twisted and riding up from the night. She was, to put it nicely, an active sleeper. Pancho nuzzled her unoccupied ear, and she said, "Are you calling so quickly because you're bored or just blocked?"

"Does it have to be one or the other?" His voice was a reedy tenor that was oddly comforting.

"I guess not. Would you be willing to do me a huge favor that shouldn't be boring at all?"

"If you're looking for people to help you move, just remember that I'm technically in the next state." He lived out west, just over the border in Vermont. "Oh, and I'm practically a ninety-pound weakling. Not to mention that I really don't want to, especially considering how many books I'm sure you have."

"How much coffee have you had today?"

"Not nearly enough. I've already had candy, too, which is proof that working from home is terrible for everyone. Are you going to tell me what this favor is? Because my brain's going absolutely everywhere."

Keeping George's identity out of it, Cait told Daniel about his manuscript and the challenges she'd had getting him to participate in the editorial process. Those were the words she used, knowing from previous conversations that Daniel would read between the lines and understand the full extent of her predicament.

In fact, he said, "So you want me to rough the idiot up? Does he know how good you are?"

She ignored his second sentence and tackled the first. "I thought you were a ninety-pound weakling."

"Remember that mugging scene I wrote in the last book? There are ways other than brute strength."

She rubbed her lips with her fingers, feeling their scratchy dryness. Funny that lips got chapped while all her other skin went dry, especially after she spent any time in the pool. "I have something else in mind. Tell me if you think it's a dumb idea, though. Be my editor in this."

"You're upending our whole power dynamic, but okay, if you insist."

"If you were this clever in your writing, I wouldn't have to work you so hard."

"I know. All my wit goes out the window when I try to put it on the page. That's why I write deadly serious thrillers. Are you going to tell me this idea already?"

She did, and it sounded increasingly harebrained the more of it she released out into the humming cell network between them. Her thought was that if she could maybe present George with a more concrete version of her notes, he might be able to see more clearly how the book could be improved. It was contingent on him seeing his own voice in the rewritten segment, to have it appear as if he'd done it himself, and Daniel was really good at writing mimicry—so good, in fact, that it was sometimes hard for him to let his own voice show through. Cait was sure that he could take the original manuscript and her notes and come up with at least one scene that would do the trick. If any trick would do it. What self-involved writer wouldn't like seeing a piece done in his own image?

When she finished outlining the plan, she held her phone to her ear and waited, gently pushing Pancho's head away from her with her forearm. It had better work since over the weeks since she had been told in no uncertain terms to fix the situation, it hadn't gotten any better. She heard a hum from Daniel but nothing more. "Really? That bad?"

"No. It's an inventive idea, and I'd love to do it, but what do you think the odds are that it'll actually work?"

"I figure I either have excellent odds or nonexistent ones. Unfortunately, I don't have any other ideas right now that would be a better bet."

"I'm your man, then. Edith is going to kill me for taking it on, but it keeps the spice in our marriage." He laughed.

"I can't be a party to endangering someone else's relationship."

"Cait. You've got to get out more. Loving your partner's faults is most of the work of loving them at all. What would happen if I didn't give Edith ample material to work with?"

She huffed out something that sounded less like a laugh and more like a Pancho vocalization. "I'll keep it in mind. Maybe I'll use it in my next dating profile. That should have women flocking to me."

"Don't lose hope. It's always when you least expect it, as cliched as that sounds. Send me the materials and your notes. When do you need something back from me?"

"As soon as you can without putting yourself out too much."

"Aye aye, Captain. I'll start on it tonight and let you know if I run into any snags."

"Oh, and, Daniel? This is super confidential because the work is under contract. Keep it on the down-low, okay?"

"This is the most cloak and dagger I've had in my life since we were trying to keep Edith's first pregnancy from our parents. Mum's the word, I promise."

After a few more pleasantries, they hung up. Cait was disappointed that taking some action didn't make her feel better at all. Maybe it was all that talk about relationships. The problem with cliches, aside from them being tired and unimaginative, was that their supposed truths were immediately unhelpful. How was she supposed to stop looking or keep from expecting? Had she even started in the first place? Or had she promptly succumbed to all her natural instincts when Lauren left and burrowed into her aloneness ever since?

She sat up, mirrored by Pancho, who was on her like white on rice. She pulled on some sweatpants and a light jacket and took him out, all business for this morning's business. She recalled Allie's playful idea of Pancho all dressed up, trotting down the sidewalk in a three-piece suit. It had been generous of her to help Cait out the other evening. Too bad about that brother of hers. He seemed like a catastrophe waiting to happen. That fight of theirs had been scary. She shrugged. Everyone had their own problems. It's just that hers were quiet and internal.

Pancho's leash hung loosely from her pinkie finger. Something extraordinary (maybe aliens landing) would have to happen to make him stray from his heel, but with a dog that big, the appearance of active control was important. What people thought they saw bore only a passing resemblance to what actually was. They placed so much weight on what their eyes perceived, not recognizing that sight was nothing without interpretation, and interpretation engaged all sorts of gnarly pathways in the brain. Take the two of them, she thought, as her legs ate up sidewalk and Pancho's tongue lolled out the side of his mouth. They looked formidable together, which was impossible to avoid. A smile might help to soften their image, but one wasn't forthcoming this morning—or most mornings, to be honest.

She wasn't mean, right? She wasn't, no matter how Allie looked at her, no matter how George reacted to her just doing her damn job, no matter that too many people shied away to the other edge of the sidewalk when she and Pancho were approaching. She just triggered the wrong synapses in people's brains and then sometimes refused to try to untrigger them later.

On her way back up to her apartment, she lingered outside Allie's door, listening for anything inside, music or shouting. Not that it was her business. Allie had made that abundantly clear. So why did Cait spend so much time listening to what was going on downstairs from her? No good reason, she told herself, taking the steps up to her apartment two at a time.

Of course, once she sat down at her computer to send Daniel what he needed, she wished she'd taken her time with a shower, maybe a mug of tea and a bowl of cereal before facing her inbox. Tamara had dropped five messages to her in the last twelve hours, and even though Cait told herself not to, she clicked on each in turn and read them. The good news was that Tamara was better at editing her own prose than her emails; the bad news was that Tamara was better at editing her own prose than her emails. Each one was a small avalanche of words containing just one or two nuggets of real information. They were hyperactivity on the page, and Cait felt jittery after reading them.

The gist, after all that, was that Tamara wanted to rework the first chapter again "until she got it right" and apologized for being "a disappointment of a client," swearing that she would "get her head out of her ass." God, everything was exhausting and yet she somehow was living the most damn blessed life, ever.

She shucked off her sweatpants and jacket, fed Pancho, and crawled back in bed, which was massively confusing for the dog, who stood next to her and stared at her as if he expected something magical to happen—or at least some extra food to appear after the breakfast he'd just inhaled. When Lauren had slept over, Cait would curl around her in the mornings and they'd whisper to each other, hoping Pancho wouldn't hear and they could lay in their cocooned warmth a little while longer. It rarely worked. Cait could still feel the curves of Lauren's body and the brush of her breath against Cait's arm where it curled under her neck. She could feel the rise and fall of her rib cage. God, she missed that, she thought, her throat tightening.

Right now, she even missed Lauren forcing her to get out of her head and do something with her: a book reading, an easy meal in Davis Square, a walk that didn't include Pancho, even getting sweaty on the dance floor at a ladies' night somewhere and feeling the sweet release of energy through her thighs as she moved and grooved. She could do these things alone, but she didn't. Was she subconsciously waiting for someone to show up and fill these holes in her life? If so, she was well and truly screwed. That was impossible given the way she lived every day so much inside herself and her apartment.

The sound of trumpet music filtered up through the floorboards, and Cait closed her eyes and turned over away from Pancho. Could everything just stop for a minute? Could only the right people need things from her and the rest leave her alone? It was clearly Allie practicing downstairs, but it was too early, and she didn't want to hear it or to have to go somewhere and face the unwashed hordes outside.

She fumbled in her nightstand drawer for the earplugs that had accompanied Allie's bribe of the delicious donuts, the spoonful of sugar to balance this foam medicine. They were hot pink and squished easily between her fingers. The last time she'd worn earplugs had been her final season in high school. They'd been a waxy brown plastic intended to protect her ear canals from infection, and after the last meet, she'd ceremoniously burned her entire supply with the help of a friend's lighter. The flame had been small and sputtery but deeply satisfying, though it didn't make up for the previous five years during which, at her mother's insistence, she'd spent hours of practice closed off from the other swimmers, the water, and her coaches, all in the name of avoiding swimmer's ear. Her teammates did just fine avoiding the malady without having to say "What?" to every little thing. For years, she'd worked on her mom tirelessly to get her to change her mind, pounding the drum of unfairness loud enough for the neighbors to hear.

Finally, her mom decided she was old enough to deal with the consequences herself and relented. She pretty much had to. Cait had left for college and could no longer be monitored. The resulting freedom was a revelation. The soft sound of water as she broke through the surface before submerging again. The cheering that accompanied her during races, growing loud with each breath and then muted again. She had finally felt fully a part of it all. She never wanted to go back to the isolation that those ugly brown plugs had imposed, but desperate times called for desperate measures.

Allie's scales were tick-tocking along, remaining an impediment to sleep. Cait rolled one of the earplugs between her fingers into a tight cylinder and nestled it in her ear, waiting for the foam to expand and fill her canal. She did the same to her other ear and lay back, blinking at the ceiling. The world went quiet. Gone was Pancho's breathing, gone were Allie's scales, gone was the wheeze of her refrigerator. The quiet was beautiful, and the pink earplugs were as comfortable as Allie had claimed. She curled around a pillow and willed herself back to sleep.

The shouting must've started after Allie's last lesson. It was already raging when Cait finally took out the earplugs. Six straight hours of productivity had set her right, elevating her from the morning's funk like a fat sun over a steaming lake. Yes, her eyes felt like they were covered in sand and her back ached in a last gasp of her lifting injury, but this had been the best day's work she'd had in weeks.

Allie and her dog-slapping brother were going at it again. Hard. She picked up the earplugs, preparing to reinsert them, but paused before slipping them back in. The words were muffled beyond comprehension, but the tones came through: sharp as a buzz saw both in the brother's lower register and in Allie's higher one.

It was none of her business, she reminded herself. Allie had made that clear last time she'd intervened. Sibling rivalry. Right.

She put in one earplug but hesitated with the second one, listening to the argument more attentively than she should. She didn't have siblings, but this seemed like above and beyond any normal familial acrimony. What did she know, though? She talked to her momma weekly and to her father only through her momma. Cait made a point of not visiting her parents or her hometown. She'd been too odd for that place, maybe even for that whole state, and no one had stopped themselves from telling her so.

A crash downstairs made her jump, and she was at her front door before she fully recognized what she was doing. She put her hand on its handle and waited, hyperalert to the exact nature of the sounds coming from downstairs. It wasn't her business. Allie didn't need Cait to save her. What was she thinking, standing here, poised to dash downstairs like a knight in shining armor? Really, what was she thinking?

Another crash, and she wasn't thinking anymore but leaping down the stairs four at a time to the floor below and pounding on Allie's door like knocking was going out of style. This time, the fight didn't stop at her interruption, and she had to keep at it until the impact threatened to bruise the side of her hand. She almost fell into the apartment when Allie jerked the door open.

"What?" It was a vicious shout.

"I—" But before she could say anything more, Allie was shoved out of the way, and the brother was in her face, a couple of inches shorter than she was but far too close for comfort.

"You want a piece of this? Is that what this is?"

It would have been funny if it hadn't been so menacing. She held her hands up like the brother was a growling dog. "I think you guys should stop before things get out of hand."

This time, Allie pushed Nick, but instead of yielding, he reared back and hit her in the face, the tight knot of his right fist connecting with her left eye. Cait hadn't expected to be able to hear the impact from that contact, but she did. It was hard sounding, with the worst kind of fleshy overtone, and it left her feeling like she'd had the wind knocked out of her. Gasping for breath, she took a half step toward Allie, who was covering her face with both of her hands. Nick yelled, "Mind your own business." He made to close the door between them, but Cait instinctively stuck her foot out to stop it. Stupid move. She wasn't wearing shoes, and the door stripped a layer of skin off her toes before it skidded to a stop a couple of inches farther back.

She grimaced and gritted out, "I think you should leave right now."

"If I wanted your opinion, I'd give it to you."

This all would have seemed like a bad movie if Allie weren't cowering there, her fingertips going white where they were pressed against her forehead.

"Allie, come with me."

"I can't—"

Cait held out her hand. "Please."

Nick said, "Don't even think about it."

"Fuck you," Allie mumbled. She dropped her hands, revealing angry red skin, and, giving Cait a wide berth, she moved out into the hall and started upstairs.

Nick said, "This has nothing to do with you."

"Don't come looking for her, or I'll call the police."

He slammed the door in her face, missing her nose by mere inches. Cait trotted upstairs, her foot smarting where it was minus a wide strip of skin. Pinpricks of blood had started to spot the wound, and it was only going to hurt more when her nerves got over the assault and transmitted the full extent of the pain.

Allie stood in front of Cait's door, her shoulders shaking, hands pressed to her face again. Cait touched her shoulder on her way to opening the door, and Allie flinched. "Sorry. I'll just—Let me go in first so I can make sure Pancho doesn't bother you."

"You really shouldn't have come down there." Her hand muffled the words like that black mute robbed her trumpet of all its power when she practiced in the hallway.

"Well, I did." Cait stepped inside, snapped when she saw Pancho, and said, "Sit." He sat, taking up half the hallway. He was still except for his tail, which swept the wood floor behind him. "Stay," she said for good measure before opening the door wider and motioning Allie inside. "Come on in."

The smaller woman inched her way past Pancho, one hand still clasped to her face. Cait realized she'd never actually seen someone get punched in real life. Plenty of books featured that kind of violence, but her imagination had really missed the boat when reading them. This had been both faster and more shocking than any passage she'd ever read. There wasn't any visible blood, but she found herself fearing there wasn't an eye left under that protective cover.

She went to Allie, being careful not to touch her. "Here." She indicated the armchair. "Sit down, and I'll get some ice for your face. That's appropriate, right?"

Allie sat but offered no response.

"Okay, back in a minute." She locked and chained the door and went into the kitchen, motioning Pancho to come with her. Since there was always the possibility of food in this room, he stuck right next to her, underfoot in every way as she pulled one of her ice packs from the freezer and massaged it with her hands to get it a little more flexible. "Not yet, buddy." She turned toward the living room and said, "Be nice," to Pancho.

Cait knelt next to Allie, whose unscathed eye was closed. "Hey. Will you let me take a good look at what the damage is?"

"It's nothing. It only matters that he didn't punch me in my mouth. I knew I should insure my lips."

"I feel like that side of your face is the crown jewels for as tight as the security is right now."

"You think you're smarter than everyone."

"I just saw your brother hit you, and I'm pretty freaked out. Overcompensation, I guess. Has he done that before?"

Instead of answering, Allie lowered her hands and laid a defiant stare on Cait. Her left eye was hidden behind a sheen of tears through which Cait could see some burst capillaries. A cut split the top of her cheekbone, and, though it was too soon for the swelling to start, Cait figured it would be as extensive as the bruising would be.

She said, "You might need a couple of stitches."

"I'm fine." Allie took the ice pack from Cait. She pressed it to her face and sat back, letting out a bottomless sigh. "If I was a few inches taller, he could have really messed up my career for a while. Shit, listen to me, being fucking grateful right now. Ridiculous."

Cait hovered to her side. "It's not ridiculous, but I do think we should call the police."

"Nick was right. This isn't your business."

"Has he done that before?"

"Don't try to understand my family."

Cait sat on the rug, Pancho lying down next to her. "I'm not trying to understand your family. I'm trying to understand what just happened right in front of me."

"It's complicated."

"Actually, even though it's not my business, I think it's rather simple."

"Believe me, it's not." Allie breathed quietly for a while before swearing. "He's down there with my instruments."

"You think he'd do something to them?"

"Yesterday, I would have said no, but at this point, I don't know."

"I can—"

But Allie cut her off. "You've done enough. If you hadn't been there in the first place…"

"You guys were screaming at each other, and multiple things broke."

"He didn't want to hit me. He didn't mean to."

Cait couldn't think of a single thing to say to that. "Is there anything I can do for you?"

"I need three Advil. Or Tylenol. Whatever you have lying around."

"Coming right up."

After Allie swallowed the Advil with a gulp of water, they sat in quiet for a while. Water condensing on the ice pack was dripping down Allie's face and neck, darkening the blouse she wore, which, now that Cait looked closely, sported a few drops of blood from that cut on her cheek.

Allie said, "Have you ever been messed with? By a guy, I mean."

Cait leaned forward across her crossed legs. Allie's head was tilted back, the ice pack resting on her face with no support, which left her hands free to grip each other, their knuckles in stark relief. "You mean harassed? Or assaulted?"

"Whatever. I'm not in the mood to split hairs."

Cait considered her own personal history, putting her experience under a magnifying glass she'd never used before. "No, not really. Nothing beyond the regular background level of jerkiness you get from men in general." Worried that might make Allie feel unfairly targeted, Cait went on. "Guys apparently find me intimidating."

"No shit. I'll bet you can make someone's face look way worse than mine. Nick's arms are noodles compared to yours."

"I prefer to use my size and strength for good."

"Like rescuing neighbors in distress?"

Cait frowned. "I didn't say that."

"I didn't need rescuing."

"I didn't say that you did."

"Well, you certainly thought it. Why else would you have put yourself in the middle of it?" Allie sat up, catching the ice pack as it slid from her face. Despite the ice, swelling had already started, and the cut on her cheek was oozing.

"Will you at least let me put a bandage on that cut? I'd hate for you to have a scar if you don't need to."

"So, you're a doctor now?" Her tone had turned more tired than antagonistic, though it was still cutting.

"I've read a lot of books." Cait got up, which made Pancho follow her. They went back to the bathroom, where Cait dug around under the vanity for her bandages. She took a pair of scissors to a small one to make three tiny strips, like she'd seen in the movies. Resting in her palm, they made her fingers look monstrous. She hesitated before going back out, her free hand thumping Pancho's side. She wasn't entirely sure what was going on. It's not like she expected a ticker-tape parade, but having such animosity be the response to her helpfulness was downright confusing.

Was part of it the fact that Cait had gotten by without bearing the brunt of a guy's harassment? Allie's question made Cait wonder what had happened to her before this. Was it just being hit on in a clumsy way or was it worse? Had she been hit before? Had she been sexually assaulted? Cait knew nothing about her life. Why would she? They were just neighbors. They had no history. Until very recently, in fact, Allie had been one of her least favorite people, and surely the reverse had been true as well. Cait wasn't sure why she thought this would change things, but she had.

She gave Pancho one more thump on his rib cage and walked out into the living room, where Allie still held the ice pack in her hands. "Okay, can I…Do you mind if I literally get right in your face?"

"Why not. Everyone else has gotten comfortable all up in there today."

Cait perched on one arm of the chair, dabbed at the cut with some tissues she'd gotten in the bathroom, and doused it with peroxide, which made Allie hiss and grab at the arms of the chair. She leaned in with the first bandage, squeezing the cut together as gently as she could before using the adhesive to keep it in place. She could feel Allie trying not to move, her breathing growing a notch more rapid and shallow as Cait worked. "Sorry," she said, but Allie didn't reply. She repeated the process with the second and third strips and surveyed her handiwork. She covered it with a larger bandage before getting up and sitting on the couch, as far away from Allie as the furniture would allow.

"Thanks," Allie said. "I should go."

"I don't think it's a good idea for you to go back to your apartment if Nick's around."

"He probably ran off after that."

"Can I at least check first?"

Allie frowned, wincing at the motion. "What makes you think I want or need yet another person trying to control me?"

"I don't, and I'm not trying to do that at all. But I think you should consider calling the police."

"They won't do anything."

"But—"

"I said no! What, are you deaf and dumb?" Her voice, loud and strained, made Pancho raise his head with a jangle of his tags.

"I'm sorry," Cait said. "I guess what I'm trying to say in a really roundabout and ineffectual way is that you're welcome to stay here for as long as you want."

Allie dropped her head back again. Her laugh was weak but caused a small jump in her chest that Cait noticed acutely. "I bet you never imagined I'd be sitting in your living room right now. Or ever, I guess."

"I don't know. It's kind of like karma. You helped me out before with my back, even getting me an ice pack, and now I've returned the favor, even though you didn't need any help. You had everything under control."

"I never said that." Her words were quiet. "But it was a chaos I understood. I could really use a drink if you've got anything. It's okay if not. I probably shouldn't. No, I definitely shouldn't, so never mind."

"Okay," Cait said, not seeing the point of telling Allie that she was pretty much a teetotaler and had nothing in the house but water and some strong, black iced tea she used as a pick-me-up in the afternoons. "You're probably right."

Allie explained. Sort of. "My dad used to use Nick as a punching bag. He took the brunt of it for years instead of me and my mom. So, yeah, it's complicated."

The words were directed at the ceiling but struck Cait right in the chest. She sat still, her heart thumping. Suddenly, supplying Allie with a little ice and some Advil seemed woefully inadequate.

CHAPTER TEN

Allie tolerated being in Cait's apartment for as long as she could before making a bid for freedom. The apartment itself was pleasant, if not a touch austere, books being the primary decoration. Cait had a second bedroom that was somehow new to Allie despite her brief introduction to the space when Cait had hurt her back. Even Cait had been mostly fine. Thankfully quiet if not several notches too helpful for Allie's taste. Pancho was extraordinarily well behaved, but Allie was sure Cait had been seconds away from ripping through the knees of her jeans given how often she'd rubbed her hands across the faded fabric. Her awkwardness would have been endearing in other circumstances, especially when contrasted with such an imposing body, but that was neither here nor there. The bottom line was that Cait had no business in this part of Allie's business. They were far from friends, and Allie couldn't deal with what had happened in front of a neighbor.

Her head was still aching when she slipped out of Cait's place with only a little more fanfare from her host than she would have preferred. Cait and Pancho watched her make her way slowly down the stairs to her floor, where she stood in front of her apartment, steeling herself for another encounter with Nick even though she didn't know who she'd find when she opened the door. Would it be the chip off the old block who had just rearranged her face or would it be the more remorseful, gentle version of her brother? She had no desire to deal with either right now, but what else was there for her to do?

The door was unlocked when she tried it, but she could tell right away that the apartment was empty. "Nick," she called out just in case, not wanting to surprise him sleeping on her own damn bed or something. When she got no answer, she locked the deadbolt and walked further in, bringing the whole living room into view. It was trashed. Music was everywhere, her stand was overturned, one pillow had split open and was puking up feathers, and her trumpet lay on the floor half under the coffee table.

She went to the instrument first, landing on her knees next to it but not touching anything—as if it were a person with a potential spinal injury at an accident scene. Finally, she picked it up, exercising the valves while she inspected it from mouthpiece to bell, where she found the damage. The edge of the bell must've connected with the floor when Nick knocked it out of her hand, and there was a crease and a flattened part of the curve on the left side of the bell. It wouldn't affect her sound much, if at all, but she shook with fury.

Their fight had been utterly predictable, with Nick getting on her case about her playing. He had turned into Cait that way, dripping with judgment and dismissal. Why was she practicing so much instead of entertaining him or at least going out and getting into trouble with him? She hadn't missed her practice space as much as she had when he'd gotten in her face, swiping at her instrument. If only she'd been playing there instead of here, none of this would have happened. Maybe he would have eaten everything in her fridge or ordered porn on her TV, but her music would have been off the stage of his attention. Maybe they wouldn't have fought at all. Maybe they would be sitting on this couch now, watching a movie, laughing at the same jokes and splitting a pizza. Maybe he would remember that he could be easy with her and not be a lazy prick all the time.

But Allie knew that "maybe" was the stuff of dreams. Maybe never happened. Maybe was downright poison, a wishful thinking that kept her from accepting reality. Nick had gone after her instrument right before he'd gone after her. How did they walk back from this?

She locked her trumpet in its hard case and went to the bathroom. She turned on the light and let her eyes adjust before leaning across the sink to examine herself in the mirror. Shit. The cut on her cheek was still oozing into the larger bandage, and Cait had been right that it probably could use a few stitches. Her eye was swollen half shut, and the bruising had already started, spreading out from her cheek to her temple and up past her eye and over to her nose. She let out a long exhale. Double shit.

For the first time, she actually considered involving the police. Her skin got cold at the thought, and her breath caught in her lungs. Panic, she thought. She used to feel this way before auditions or big concerts, a crawling dread and deepening premonition of doom. It felt like a wholly physical version of the word "no," but despite how urgent and undeniable it appeared to be, it couldn't be trusted and should mostly be taken with the hugest grain of salt possible. It always, every single time, passed. This kind of emotion came from her deep, lizard brain. It existed outside of reason and, often, reality. But it existed, and that made it impossible for her to call the police or even go to the hospital to get those stitches. They asked questions at the hospital, and Allie wasn't sure how she'd answer them. Who would she end up protecting?

She picked up her phone, took a picture of herself, and sent it to her mother. Though it was getting late, the phone rang in her hand almost immediately.

Her mom said, "That's enough, Allie. A slap wasn't, not yet, but he did that?"

Allie sank onto her couch but sprang up again when she realized her door wasn't chained and that Nick could waltz back in any minute. "I don't know what's going through his head anymore."

"I let it happen."

She chained the door for good measure and slid down to sit with her back to it. "What, the slap? No, he did that all on his own."

"No, with your father. I let him beat on Nick instead of either of us. I was an adult, and I let my son take that abuse instead of me."

Now Allie remembered why she didn't often talk to her mother. Here was the old refrain of guilt. What was she supposed to do with that? What had happened, happened. Besides, she wasn't remotely in a position to comfort her. Even so, she said, "Dad was a thug and a bully, and I still can't believe he did as little to you and me as he did. And Nick had this savior complex that always felt a little like a death wish. We were all abused." She drew upon something she'd learned in expensive but priceless therapy over the years. "We all have to take responsibility for what we did and didn't do."

"That's easy for you to say. You were a kid. You have nothing to take responsibility for."

"I knew Nick was going to hit me before he actually did." She hadn't known that was true until she said it out loud. At the time, it had been a crushing surprise, but it now felt like it was inevitable given how she'd refused to step back from their screaming match. What a shitty little family. Allie had lain awake more than one night wondering what she would prove capable of over time. "How come you never called the police back then?"

"It would have just made things worse."

The old party line. "Then why didn't you take us and run?"

"Where would we go? I had nothing without him, just you kids."

Right, and kids were far from an asset. Kids were always eating and needing new clothes. All Allie and Nick had had to do was breathe funny to get their father going about what little leeches they were. "I don't know, Mom. What about a shelter?"

"How would that have been better for us than being at home?"

Allie grabbed a fistful of hair and pulled on it, hard. She'd given herself bald patches when she was little, but she hadn't done this in years. She made herself loosen her grip, taking a deep breath and standing up. "This is ridiculous. Enough rehashing the past. What's done is done." Though that, of course, was a fallacy of the highest order. Not only was physical abuse woven into her cells and the deranged patterns of thought in her brain, it was happening again.

"What are you going to do?"

"I don't know. But I have to get some sleep before I decide anything."

"Do you have some place to go?"

Allie laughed, which aggravated her head. "If he thinks he can run me out of my own apartment, he's got another think coming."

Her mother's sigh made Allie think of a deflated balloon. "Be careful."

"Goodbye, Mom." She hung up. In the bedroom, she changed into pajamas—and found two drops of blood on the chest of her blouse. One of her favorites. She went back to the bathroom to try to wash them out, but before she turned on the tap, she heard something and froze. A jingle, a snick, and the thunk of the chain getting pulled taut across the partly open door. Adrenaline surged in her, making her lightheaded.

"Allie?" Nick said. His voice was calm. "Are you okay?"

Allie pressed the back of her hand against her mouth.

"Allie, come on. You know I didn't mean it. I just got stir crazy. Let me in, and we can talk about it."

"There's nothing to talk about," she called from the bathroom. "You need to leave."

"So I only get one chance?"

"I heard what you did to Mom."

He laughed. "You know Mom. She was driving me crazy. She practically walked into my hand anyway."

Her stomach cramped at that assessment; it sounded *just* like their father. "You need to leave." The power she'd put into her previous words was fading, and these came out unsteady and weak.

"Where am I supposed to go?"

"I don't know, but I'm sure you can figure it out."

A quiet thump that followed sounded like the bump of Nick's head against her door. She wondered if he was trying to see inside through the gap the chain made. She stayed in the bathroom, out of sight.

"We still need to talk."

"Not here and not now. I'll tell you when I'm ready."

"Allie." Her name was sharp and was followed by another thump. "I know I screwed up, okay? You really should let me come in."

"Goodbye, Nick. I promise we'll talk. I promise, okay?"

"Why is everything on your terms?" he said and slammed the door shut as hard as he could manage with a gap so little. The impact was enough to shake the pictures on her wall. She relinquished the grip on her blouse and took a shaky breath. After counting up to one hundred and back down again, she felt marginally sure that he had left and wasn't contemplating breaking the door open. He totally could. Those chain locks were flimsy.

She peeked into the living room. It was disheveled but quiet. Exhaustion flowed in as her adrenaline ebbed, and she knew both that she wouldn't be able to sleep with the room like this and that she didn't have the fortitude to clean it up and face memories of their argument. She retreated, closed the door to her bedroom, and sat on the end of the bed, apparently waiting for a sign from the universe that had no intention of showing up. Her cheek pulsed with her heartbeat, and it was hard not to press against the cut and into the sweetness of pain.

Finally, she got up, pulled on some jeans and a sweatshirt, and made a beeline for where her trumpets were stacked up in a corner of the living room: Bb now with the creased bell, C, flugelhorn, piccolo trumpet, and a bugle she'd gotten on a lark at a yard sale some years back. Shit, there was the cornet, too. She filled her gig bag, tucked a case under each arm, and picked up her main instrument, leaving only the bugle behind. After barely managing to use her nose to unhook the chain from her door, she admitted defeat and put down some of her load in order to open the door, close it behind her, and lock it. She made her way upstairs, cursing herself for her collection and this new madness until she stood outside Cait's door, stuck in the world's longest fermata.

Before she could decide to knock or to go back downstairs, she heard Cait's voice from inside her apartment. "Sit. Down." Then the chunk of the deadbolt and a squeak in the hinges that rang in at a high A. Cait's eyebrows raised a fraction at what probably looked like Allie wanting to move in.

Allie pushed past the messy flurry of emotions that took her by the throat. "I know I just made a big deal of needing to leave here, but I don't want them damaged."

"Okay. Are you dropping them off, or…?"

Why did this woman make Allie work for every little thing? She understood a bit better Nick's frustration at everything supposedly being on her terms. "We're a package deal, but just for tonight, if that's okay."

Cait stepped back and snapped and pointed for Pancho to skedaddle. "Come on in. I hope you don't mind the couch because I'm too tall for it."

"Believe me, I'm not picky. Even the floor sounds good right now."

Cait closed the door, locked and chained it, and took the cases from under Allie's arms. She stacked them in the entryway under a slim table and motioned her hands for the rest of Allie's things. "Let me get you a pillow and some sheets. I imagine you want to sack out right away?"

Allie wasn't sure she'd sleep again, ever. She could feel the disarray of her living room from all the way up here, but Cait was in soft shorts and a long-sleeve T-shirt, hair already sleep disheveled, which meant sleep might be possible here. "Yeah, of course." When Cait disappeared into the bathroom, Allie went on. "Thanks for this. I just can't be there right now."

"Did he come back? Is that what you're afraid of?"

"I didn't say I was afraid." No, she hadn't, but she had enough experience to know that she was traumatized. "Can we skip the inquisition? I need a bed, not psychotherapy." Harsh, but what was that stupid saying? "Hurt people hurt people"? Maybe Cait didn't care about Allie enough for this minor verbal warfare to hurt her. Allie hoped so because she clearly couldn't stop herself.

Cait came back with folded bedclothes on top of which rested a fluffy pillow in a snow-white case. "Sorry for prying. I'll knock it off." She set the bedding at the end of the couch, and Pancho got busy sniffing it. "Pancho, come on." The dog let off even without one of the sharp snaps that Allie was beginning to think she'd probably obey if push came to shove. "You know where the bathroom is, and there's cold water in the fridge, books on the shelves, but nothing alcoholic in case you've changed your stance from earlier."

Allie waved her off. "Don't worry. Drinking should never be combined with any of this, though it usually is."

"Well." Cait rubbed her hands down her hips. The move was nervous, which, again was endearing when showcased in that Amazonian body. "I'll leave you alone, then?" When Allie said nothing, Cait retreated.

Her bedroom door was half closed when Allie felt panic rise into her throat and push out an unanticipated word. "Wait."

Cait stopped.

"Can you leave it open?"

Cait's mouth twisted to the side in a move that wasn't quite a smile but wasn't not a smile, either. "Sure thing." She flipped off the lights and retreated to her room.

Allie heard her get into bed and Pancho settle down near her with a deep, huffy sigh. She sat on the couch and wondered what she'd done. Not just in coming back here but in tolerating Nick for so long, in not spending the time and money to get new rehearsal space, in not getting far enough away from her mom in the first place. Hell, people commuted to work here from towns in New Hampshire that weren't far from where she'd grown up. She should have sought her fortune in Chicago, not just down the road. Her life suddenly seemed like one cascading series of foibles, and she wasn't sure how to step any of it back.

With her head cradled by the pillow, she stared at the darkened ceiling, which had the same moonscape popcorn texture as her own downstairs. Their apartments were exactly the same except for Cait's extra bedroom, which must be allocated to Allie's neighbor downstairs, but they couldn't be less similar. Cait's soft gray walls that looked ghostly now were adorned with books and photos of cityscapes from around the world. Everything was excessively tidy and put together. Even the sheet she pulled over herself had been folded into a perfect, creased rectangle. While it was definitely more restful than Allie's apartment, it was also strangely sterile.

Just yesterday this wouldn't have surprised Allie in the slightest, but even though she hadn't wanted to admit it, beneath Cait's intense awkwardness was someone warm and generous. Her legs in those shorts had been unexpectedly impressive, too, a thought that had no place except in the most addled of brains. Which, Allie supposed, hers qualified as tonight.

She fell asleep in the middle of thinking of all the reasons she wouldn't be able to: the shakiness from depleted adrenaline, Cait right there in the next room, her apartment still open to Nick's key, the tired rage at the damage to her instrument. The open door between her and Cait was ultimately a silent balm to her nerves.

She woke to the sound of quiet typing and the smell of coffee. She picked up her phone from the table behind her head and held it in front of her face, squinting at the stupid analog clock she insisted on having on her lock screen. Almost nine thirty. Waking at this time felt like that punch had knocked her unconscious in a sort of delayed reaction. She turned over, and Pancho's nose was in her face before she could even push her hair back behind her ears. "Hi," she whispered and gave him two neck scratches before gently guiding him away from her and rubbing her eyes, wincing at the pain that ignited in the left one and surely doing a bang-up job of racooning the makeup she hadn't removed the night before. She pressed lightly on the bandage on her split-open cheek and hissed.

"Hey. Good morning." Cait stood in the doorway of the second bedroom, hands in the pockets of her jeans.

Allie sat up unsteadily. "Sorry. I'll get out of here right away. I have no idea how I managed to sleep like that."

"I think it's something like adrenaline exhaustion, and there's no rush. I checked your schedule, and it looked like you only had a practice session before your noon lesson, so it didn't make sense to wake you. Have some coffee if you want. I made extra, and the mugs are in the cabinet above the machine."

It took a while for Allie's brain to churn through all of that, forgetting for a minute that she'd been the one to give Cait her schedule and getting angry at that lack of privacy. She marshalled her scant resources for a quick attitude adjustment. "I'm the one that crashed at your place. You don't have to play hostess with the mostess or anything."

Cait frowned. "I'm…not? I mean, I think anyone would do this, not that there's a rulebook for it or anything."

"Yeah, but the blanket." Allie motioned at it on her lap, something she was sure hadn't been there when she'd drifted off the night before. "And now coffee? I know you hate me, so, really, don't put yourself out."

"Allie, I wanted to help. Coffee is nothing. I just put in an extra scoop of grounds and some more water. I'll drink it if you don't want it. I don't—" she started but shook her head instead of going on more gently than Allie deserved. "I'm just in here working, so take your time getting yourself together." She melted back through the doorway.

Allie pressed the heel of her hand against her mouth until the pressure of its flesh against her teeth approached the edge of pain. Everything felt wrong, and her mouth tasted like shit. She dragged herself to Cait's bathroom, which, of course, looked exactly like her own, down to the hexagonal black and white tiles on the floor, though minus the blouse she'd been about to scrub when Nick had returned last night. She wrote it off as a casualty of war and took a closer look at herself in the mirror. She looked like roadkill, with bruising seeping out across much of one side of her face. Her father had given Nick plenty of split lips, and she remembered to be thankful again that all her damage was higher up. Still, it was damage, and, really, there was nothing to do about it besides make it look worse with foundation. Even with her extensive experience, it was hard not to be astounded at how much damage one punch could do. She couldn't count how many punches Nick had taken on her behalf. She didn't want to think about that. Not now.

Splashing water on her face would do more damage than good at this point, but Cait's mouthwash was on the sink, and Allie tilted her head back and poured some in her mouth without touching the bottle to her lips. After swishing and gargling, she felt less like something that had crawled out of the deep, which was probably the best she could hope for. She started untangling her hair with her fingers but gave up quickly, knowing that shortly she would be headed directly to her own shower. What did she care what she looked like between here and there? Besides, Cait had already seen her at her beaten, bloodied worst.

Wasn't that part of the strangeness of this all? Or the strangest part? Anyone with two eyes and half a brain could have seen what happened last night coming. It was never a question of if, but always one of when. But Allie never would have guessed that Cait's inability to deal with any kind of noise would lead to her becoming Allie's unlikely savior and offeror of a safe haven. At least until Allie had gone and spoiled it. She should be thanking Cait instead of second-guessing her help.

After emptying her bladder and washing flop sweat and Pancho slobber from her hands, she stood in the doorway of Cait's office but hesitated before knocking. Cait was standing at her desk, her head and broad shoulders blocking part of a large monitor mounted on something in front of her. Her posture was admirable, her feet bare on a squishy mat. While Allie watched from behind her, Cait murmured something low and indistinguishable and followed it with a short but rapid clatter of typing.

Allie cleared her throat, and Cait turned around. "Thank you again. I'll get out of your hair. And I don't think I'll be practicing before my first lesson if that makes things easier for you."

"I don't hate you, Allie." It sounded genuine enough, but by this point Cait surely was pitying Allie, which might be worse. "You don't deserve to go through something like this."

"Deserve doesn't mean shit, but thanks anyway. Can I leave a few of my instruments up here for now until I figure out what's happening?"

"Of course. Listen, it might not seem like it, but I'm not..." She motioned to her chest before dropping her hand against her hip with a soft slap. "What you think I am, I guess." She tilted her head up and to the side as if she were rolling her eyes at herself.

"What do I think you are?"

"Nothing. Never mind. Leave whatever you want. I'll be around if you need anything."

Even though that last bit cried out to be acknowledged, Allie just nodded and left the apartment, taking her regular instrument as she went. Her apartment was just as she'd left it, and she set about restoring order to her living room once she'd chained the door behind her. Music had been scattered all over the place, feathers drifted across the floor, her heavy metal stand had punched a sharp crease in one wall, and two different thick-bottomed glasses had first dented the floor and then shattered across it.

As she started cleaning up the mess, she found herself hoping that Nick would move on, for a while at least. She needed some time to decide how she wanted to deal with him. She could practically hear Cait advising her to let the authorities handle it, but Cait didn't know anything about these sordid matters. No one knew anything about it unless they'd been through something similar. The situation with her brother and to some extent her mother left her feeling a claustrophobic terribleness, something tight and infected like an angry boil. But ridding herself of its poison was going to require more than a simple lancing.

No way could Cait understand that. Still, Allie regretted having prompted the sad statement Cait had made earlier about the presumptions she thought Allie had about her. Did Cait really think that was all that Allie thought of her?

Ah, hell. What did it matter, anyway?

Stooping to sweep up shattered glass, she examined the behavior Cait was basing her opinion on. Could it be true that she had the woman all wrong? Everything Cait had done— from the imperious way she and Pancho walked through the building to her complete lack of sympathy for Allie's practice space plight—indicated she was arrogant, self-absorbed, and unsociable. Allie didn't blame herself for reacting as she had. Not really.

But then Cait had surprised her by choosing to get in Nick's face not once, but twice, in her defense and by making a fuss-free offer of comfort and safety. She had to admit, it really had felt safe having her and Pancho right in the next room last night. So perhaps her ideas about Cait were wide of the mark, and that awkwardness Allie had delighted at seeing was simply a manifestation of shyness.

Which kind of changed everything.

Or changed nothing, since it didn't matter. She dumped the last few glass shards in the garbage can. So many things that had mattered no longer did. She had to stay focused on protecting herself and figuring out a way to get Nick out of her life. Cait's calm competence had nothing to do with anything, especially since she couldn't understand how problematic calling the police was in these situations. Despite Nick wanting to talk last night outside her door, she couldn't completely buy the possibility of actual remorse, not after how he'd slammed the door. She could imagine him going down the stairs, anger in every step. The fact was that no one got better after hitting someone; they just hit them again.

After she finished putting her apartment back together,

she took an excessively long shower that made the cut on her cheek sting like a son of a bitch, and worked hard to become as presentable as possible for her afternoon lessons. No matter how artful the application of makeup, she was going to look like she'd lost the battle with someone's fist. Or walked into a door. Or fallen down the stairs. Or lost control of the car she didn't even own. So many potential obfuscations for the sad truth. Not wanting to invite someone in to your shitty situation meant employing lies that made it look like you were protecting your abuser. Which you were.

Allie rehearsed some easy answers to potentially complicated questions and felt as ready as she was going to be by the time she opened the door to Ryan. "Come on in. I hope you're prepared because I'm not letting you off easy today." The best defense was a good offense.

He stood stock-still in the hall, his mouth agape and eyebrows pulled together in a frown. "What happened?"

"Nothing," she said. "Long story, and your mom's paying top dollar for this lesson, so we should get started."

He followed her in, but he said, "Seriously, did you get into a fight or something?"

"Or something. Jazz clubs can get rough." She winked with her good eye, which was an overcorrection.

He put his case on her couch and squinted at her. "What's under that bandage?"

"Ryan, I already have one mother, okay? How about we get to work? You need to warm up and focus on your music. Your concert's getting close, and you aren't ready yet."

That sobered him, maybe more than Allie had meant to. She listened to him play scales and a couple of exercises to warm up, knowing firsthand the vibrations they'd be generating in his head and feeling a corresponding, sympathetic ache in her cheekbone and eye. She'd played just enough before this lesson to know that she wasn't interested in doing more than the bare minimum, not without a truckload of painkillers.

They worked on his piece through the next forty-five minutes, but Ryan kept sneaking looks at her face, each detour making him frown more deeply and puff out his trim but still-adolescent chest. Good Lord. The last thing she needed was another protector. Besides, Cait was clearly better suited to the job, being an Amazon and all.

Allie read him the riot act while he was packing up at the end of the disaster of a lesson. "If you're going to be serious about this, then be serious. Don't waste your time, and don't waste mine. You have potential, but that doesn't mean anything without consistent work and focus."

"But—"

"But nothing. You objectively performed like crap today, and you're better than that. Professional musicians don't get the chance to make an excuse for playing poorly on a bad day; they just get fired."

He crossed his arms over his chest. "I know someone hit you! Who was it?"

Allie mirrored his stance and stared him down, his eyes several inches higher than hers. "Why, what're you planning on doing about it?"

"They shouldn't get away with that."

"How do you know they have? How do you know anything but this kind of 'me Tarzan, you Jane' shit you're falling into like so many other guys? If you all kept your fists to yourselves, there wouldn't be any problems to solve. You get it? Besides, we're here to work on music. My personal life is off-limits."

Red patches of flush colored each cheek, but he nodded and let Allie lead him to the front door, where she stopped him with a hand to his arm. It tensed under her touch, and she pushed down a laugh.

"Everything's fine, Ryan. This is the home stretch for all this practicing, and you're going to do great. Just don't lose focus. Not now."

After a moment, he nodded and gave her a weak smile. "See you next week?"

"Only if you're better prepared," she joked.

His smile went wider. "Yes, ma'am."

She loosened the chain and opened the door to let him out. Nick was sitting on the filthy carpet, his back resting against the stairway's railing. He stood up and stuffed his hands in the pockets of his jeans. She gave him a look daring him to say anything, and he managed to keep quiet until Ryan had descended the stairs and pushed his way outside the front door of the building. Then he said, "Allie, listen."

She took a step back into her doorway and watched her brother's face fall at the motion. "I have another lesson in ten minutes, so you can't be here. If you assure me you'll behave yourself, though, you can come back after five, and we'll talk."

"Yeah, okay. But, Allie, believe me that I get way more sick of myself than you do. You don't know what it's like to live in my head."

She was glad she didn't, and even though it caused the smallest, itchy bump of sympathy, a raised hand cut off anything else he was going to say. "I really don't want to hear it, Nick. I'm not saying you can stay here tonight, but we can talk. Maybe out front, okay?"

He shrugged. "I guess you're calling the shots, so okay."

"Fine, now get out of here so my students don't think you're a perv." She ducked back inside the apartment, locked and chained her door, and gave in to the shakes.

CHAPTER ELEVEN

Cait had been on the phone with Tamara for an hour, and there was no indication that their conversation was going to wrap up anytime soon. Tamara had started by using Cait as a sounding board for her ideas, which was bad enough, but their conversation had then spiraled into an in-depth and seemingly endless discussion about point of view in nonfiction.

"Tamara," Cait said, "I'm far from an expert in this, and writing doesn't have any hard and fast rules, as you know. It wouldn't be much of an art form if it did. I wouldn't deign to tell you what to write and how to write it. The writing is your job."

"Yeah, but now you're my coach, right?"

"No, I'm not your coach. I'm not anyone's coach. I'm an editor, and I'm helping you edit your memoir. Maybe there's some general overlap between editing and coaching when we're talking about larger developmental edits, but I'm more of a surgeon rather than a primary-care physician."

Tamara made a breathy noise. "That's *such* a good metaphor. You should think about writing."

Cait tamped down a sigh. "You couldn't pay me to face a blank page like that, forget about the rejections. Now, we need to wrap this up so I can get to patients who are bleeding out on the table."

"But why don't you?"

She'd let herself get distracted by Pancho licking his nether regions, and it took her a moment to swim back up to the surface. "Why don't I what? Write?"

"No, be a primary-care doctor."

She was still a little lost. "I'm not getting you."

"Why don't you become a writer coach? I mean in addition to your editing? You're so good at giving feedback and instruction that I can actually understand and follow."

"I'm not giving you instructions. I'm making developmental editing suggestions with a lot more context and rationale than usual, and I'm doing that so I don't have to talk you through every little thing." She got up and wandered into the kitchen if only for something to do besides dwell on Tamara's misplaced enthusiasm. "What we're doing is supposed to be editing with a faster turnaround so you can eventually finish revising your book on your own before you're too sick of it to look at it. Finish without me," she said, emphasizing what she previously would have thought was obvious.

"Whatever this is, you're doing a marvelous job, and you should consider doing it more often. I'm sure there's an excellent market out there for it."

"Thanks, but my plate is pretty full. Now to bring it full circle, do you understand the point I'm making about the Ben character?"

A few more back-and-forths finished up their call. Cait leaned against the half wall to her kitchen and turned her phone over and over in her hands, musing again that they were as flipper-like as her feet—long fingers and broad palms that had been advantageous during her swimming career. It meant, though, that even as phones had gotten larger, they still fit neatly in her grasp. Sometimes, she wished that this disruptive device would grow impossibly slippery, swan dive from her fingertips, and shatter against the floor, leaving her blissfully unavailable for a while.

That was not the type of thing a budding writer's coach would think. It was the writing that mattered, not the writer, Cait thought, conveniently ignoring the fact that the writing wouldn't exist without there being a writer first.

Sort of like there wouldn't be music without a musician? She studied the three instrument cases still taking up space in her entryway. She'd crossed a tiny, thin line earlier today and opened the smallest of them without Allie's permission. Inside the hard case, nestled in a bed of perfectly shaped, velvety ridges, was the strangest little trumpet she'd ever seen. It was practically the size of Cait's palm and had a longer, slenderer bell than that of the instrument Allie had been holding when Cait had interrupted her playing. This one was a shiny silver and downright adorable, and she couldn't stop herself from imagining it in Allie's hands, pressed up to her mouth. They seemed like a matched set—in size and likely loudness, just like Cait and Pancho. She wondered how Allie saw it, if she felt complete with just her instrument.

"For Christ's sake," Cait said to herself. As she pushed away from the wall to dispel the image of Allie and the pocket-sized instrument, her phone vibrated unexpectedly with a new email, and she almost got her wish and dropped it. Whatever it was, she decided, she didn't want to know. The day had started out on the worst foot possible with Allie, and it had gone nowhere good since then.

She was still trying to figure out Allie's reaction. Cait had descended into thunderous rages over Allie's playing, but did Allie think she actually hated her at this point? Enough to fear her? She might look like a bruiser, but she shied away from all confrontations, not just the violent kind. In trying to communicate that to Allie, though, she hadn't been able to get any words out, much less the right ones. She snorted. And Tamara thought Cait should be a writer.

It wasn't like she'd helped Allie out so she could feel good about herself either. Allie had needed help, and Cait had been happy to give it. Not just happy but compelled. To be honest, seeing her neighbor in such terrible straits had changed things. When she'd lain in her bed, her door open to Allie in the living room, she'd listened to Allie turning this way and that, muttering to herself with every adjustment. Even after she'd fallen asleep, she'd breathed heavily, like she was trying to play her instrument in her sleep. How could Allie not have someone in her life who would invite her into her bed to be enfolded with physical warmth and affection? Cait barely knew her, but, ridiculously, last night she had wanted to go to her and offer some kind of comfort: a touch, her voice, a fresh ice pack. Whatever animosity she had harbored toward the smaller woman had somehow melted away, transmuted into a kindheartedness—or something more—that Allie couldn't seem to believe she was capable of.

Well, she wasn't the first to think that.

Reminding herself of the email that had come in, she leaned against the back of her couch, which was still host to Allie's bedding, and unlocked her dreaded phone. She uttered a small sound of triumph when she saw Daniel's name in her inbox, bolded and with that lovely little paperclip next to it that indicated an attachment. She practically skipped into her office to open what he'd sent on her big monitor.

This was actually a fun assignment, he wrote. *Even though it was a challenge to keep the original voice in the face of the modifications you wanted…and that it needed. Maybe I've missed a fabulous and exciting career as a ghost writer. Seems like it would be easier than continuing to peddle my own pablum. Oh, and don't worry, I'll think of you next time I need a favor from someone.*

She read the file he'd included, making herself take it slowly and be critical of everything. It was at once familiar and wholly new. An additional section of background laid the groundwork for the rest of the segment, allowing the existing metaphors and imagery to find footing against it before blooming more on their own. The inversion to the structure, going back to a more traditional exposition-then-scene instead of George's in medias res approach of starting literally in the middle of dialog made the piece feel more fresh rather than old-fashioned and gave the reader a much-needed grounding in the story and setting.

One of the best parts of editing was seeing a piece reworked in a way she knew was possible but could never execute herself. This document made her both hopeful and nauseatingly nervous. Would this sway George in the way she needed? She'd told Martha she could get this done, but if this didn't work, she'd shortened the already tight runway needed to make the book at least a critical success, if not commercially notable. Despite the brilliant work Daniel had produced, with its pitch-perfect mimicry, the chip on George's shoulder at this point was vast and impossibly brittle. The smallest breeze—or wrong move— would send it crumbling.

Her fingers hovered over her keyboard as she tried to decide what to do. She thought approaching him through email was the best idea, but she worried that that was because she desperately wanted to avoid another phone conversation with him. She could somehow interrupt Allie and Nick's knock-down, drag-out fight but not dial George's ten digits for a professional conversation—or at least professional on her side of the call. Writers tended to like the printed word, but even so, it would be easy for George to misinterpret what she'd asked Daniel to produce. Her motives would be painfully obvious; he would know that in this case imitation was not the form of flattery it often was.

She sighed. All she could do was hope that he would see enough fawning and effort in the work to leave him open to putting aside animosity and working with her. Even just a little bit, even just on the worst of the issues. She could compromise. She was all about compromise. Look how much she'd gotten on board with tolerating the noise from Allie's apartment.

It took her an hour to write a two-paragraph email to George, trying to achieve the proper balance of blowing smoke up his ass and believability. She wanted him to see something tangible from her editorial suggestions but not feel like she had to get someone else to write it because she didn't think he could. That wasn't true. She thought he was talented enough to turn this book into something spectacular; he just wouldn't get out of his own way.

Once the email was written and she couldn't find any other ways to revise it, it took her another hour to get up the nerve to send it. The instant she did she couldn't stand to be in her apartment, waiting for a response, so she got Pancho's leash and took him out for a walk. It was still officially within the confines of the workday, and Pancho seemed to have an extra bounce in his large step at the novelty of it. Cait could feel it too, a certain illicit freedom. Up to the moment, at least, when she left the building and ran into Allie's brother squatting on the front steps.

Pancho seemed to remember the man; he kept to the edge of the stairway opposite of where he sat. Cait split the difference between them, slowing down just enough to see if there was any evidence of Allie giving as good as she'd gotten before Cait had intervened. He glanced up from his phone and squinted at her.

"The Amazon and her horse-dog."

It sounded like a quote, but it wasn't one Cait was familiar with.

"It's what Allie calls you, you know. The Amazon. I think it's generous, but there never was accounting for Allie's taste."

"You should be in jail."

"You should stay out of our business."

"Gladly." Cait hurried down the sidewalk away from him, Pancho practically glued to her side, almost tripping her up with the pressure of his shoulder and the off-kilter rhythm of his slow trot. What was up with men? She knew it was a gross and unfair generalization to say so, but they had such a need to prove themselves as superior—or at least beyond reproach. And they so often did it by trying to belittle everyone else, women, especially. Domestic abuse, rape, sex trafficking, pornography. Terrible shit happening to women was a damn epidemic, but the fact that it was happening to Allie felt sharply personal.

She pulled her phone from her back pocket and called her momma. As always, she answered right away and sounded bright and shiny in her hello, at least before she sobered and said, "Is everything okay? You usually don't call this early."

"Everything's fine. I was just thinking about Mrs. Lewis a couple streets over."

"Why would you be thinking about her?"

At saying her name out loud, Cait was back in their grocery store, a gangly twelve-year-old unable not to watch Mrs. Lewis reading the label on a box of crackers. Her face was a map of bruises, yellow, purple, and every shade within. Her lip was fat and crusted around a deep split in the upper one. When Mrs. Lewis finally had looked at her, one of her eyes swollen shut, she said, "Get out while you can." Frankly, it had scared the shit out of her.

Cait said, "Whatever happened to her?"

Her mom's quiet was thick and long. "She's in the county institution over in Mulberry. I heard they brought her out of her house one day on a stretcher, and she never came back, wasn't the same. Not that being the same would have been any great shakes for her."

"And Mr. Lewis?"

"Why are you asking about this? What happened to them happened to them and no one else, and it was so long ago now."

Cait persisted. "Did he go to jail at least?"

"Judy never would press charges, no matter how many times the police showed up at her door."

She made a strangled sound that startled someone passing her on the sidewalk. "Why do women do that? They're always giving second chances and making excuses."

"Do you know someone…?"

"No." Cait took another few steps. "Not really. I mean not really on all sorts of levels. Did you know that Mrs. Lewis told me to get out of town?"

"Really?" The word was breathy with surprise. "When was that?"

"It doesn't matter. Forget it. It's just that I think she wanted to leave but couldn't."

"Not everyone is as good at picking up and disappearing as you are."

She squinted up at the bright sky, still afternoon in every way. "Momma, come on. What I did was totally different."

"The end result was the same."

"Please. There was no abuse in our house. If anything, Daddy cultivated a deeply religious indifference." Which, of course, Cait had let him get away with because letting him get away with it was by far the easiest option.

"Who's beating on your friend?"

The bluntness of the words made it hard to swallow for a second. "She's not my friend, and I'm totally uninvolved. But if she were and I were, I'm not sure what I should say to her about what's going on."

"Honey, there's not much you can do in these situations. If they're going to do something or leave, they're going to come to that on their own. They only do it when something in them breaks in the right way. Or the wrong one, for their husbands."

"It's not always a husband."

"No, it isn't, and Judy wasn't the only woman in those circumstances in town. The others hid it better. Or maybe their husbands did." She paused, and Cait stopped when Pancho pulled over to pee against a horribly maligned tree. "Is this why…"

Cait waited, knowing but not believing what her momma was going to say next.

"Is this why you're the way you are? Mrs. Lewis and everything?"

"No, Momma. Like I said, I was born this way, remember? But sometimes I'm relieved that I'm gay and have a much smaller chance of getting knocked around by my spouse." Ditto with being an only child.

"Well, all right." Then, "Does that happen? Between women?"

Cait wanted to tell her that everything that happened in a straight relationship could happen in a gay one, but that was a can of worms she wasn't interested in opening. "Sometimes. Rarely, though. Don't worry, I'm pretty sure I won't end up with an abuser."

"This has been a dark conversation."

"It sure has," Cait said. "Tell me something upbeat, then, while I finish walking Pancho."

"I still don't understand that name. Why does everything you do have to be so different?"

"Pancho Villa was a revolutionary in Mexico. There's something about his face and mustache that looks like my dog. It's not some gay thing if that's what you were wondering."

"I thought we were going to move on to nicer topics."

Cait bit her tongue against reminding her momma that this conversational swerve had been entirely of her own making and instead asked about church and her latest quilting project. It had been years since she'd actually spoken to her father, though sometimes she could hear him doing something in the background of her calls with her momma. He didn't approve of her and wielded a cold shoulder like a blunt weapon, so Cait excelled at staying out of range. Interestingly enough, she couldn't quite tell if her being gay was the biggest of his problems. She had taken Mrs. Lewis's admonishment deeply to heart and worked and schemed and swum her way out of eastern Tennessee and to parts farther north, parts with a mishmash of values, of languages, of colors, of ways of being. Here, she could be herself but still live in the background, slipping in and out of human traffic on the sidewalk and the train. She could avoid standing out without needing to blend in.

It was freedom of a kind unavailable in her hometown, and she didn't miss talking to her father. How her momma navigated her relationship with Cait under his watchful eyes, Cait didn't know, but that wasn't her problem. She had enough problems of her own, so after ending the call with her mother she took Pancho on their longer loop: two miles around the neighborhood with a stop at the dog park. She was a few blocks from home, Pancho's tongue lolling out of his mouth and bouncing with each step he took, when her phone rang. She pulled it from her pocket and hesitated at seeing Martha's name. For a palsied second, she thought about not answering it but called herself ridiculous and picked up.

She said, "You caught me on a walk with Pancho."

"We need to talk. Do you want to call me when you're back at your desk?"

She slowed down, looking for the nearest bench or bus stop so she could sit. "No, this is fine as long as you don't mind traffic noise in the background."

"I just got off the phone with George. Please tell me that it's not true."

Cait sank down on the splintered wood of a nearby bench, motioning for Pancho to sit next to her. "There's the factual truth and then what he might be reading into it."

"Cait!" Her name was a shout that she winced at. "You had someone, what, pretend they were George somehow? I don't remotely understand this. What were you thinking?"

"I—"

"Really, what were you thinking? Now I've got him threatening to pull out of his contract, and this stunt could make us liable for what we've already put into him with zero recourse."

Speaking of breaking, something majorly slipped off the track inside Cait. "I know George is related to that donor, and I know I'm ignorant of what it takes for you to run Grovetree when no one reads anymore, but you wouldn't publish something you didn't believe in. I've tried, I really have, but I've read it four times and still don't see it. Half the experimental bits don't make any statement other than 'look at me,' and his characters, especially his female ones, are practically cardboard cutouts. He can turn a phrase, for sure, but literature isn't just one compelling phrase after another. Martha, I really want to know what excites you because I've never felt more blind than I do with this book."

"Forget about my opinion. You needed to tell me how you felt right away so I could reassign it because it will be published no matter what you think about it. But now you've wasted months and alienated our author. What were you thinking?"

That refrain burrowed deeper inside her every time Martha said it, and now she wondered herself. She gripped the phone until it whitened her fingers and palm.

"I was trying to do my job! I was trying to get him to see how the book could be better. Then, when it was clear he wouldn't listen to me, I tried to tell him in his own voice by having a friend mimic his style and revise a section with some major developmental edits. But he doesn't even want to listen to himself, so I don't know how anyone is going to properly edit the book with him."

"That's my problem, isn't it? And it should have been my problem months ago by now so I could have dealt with it appropriately. You assured me that you had this, and you've spent your time playing at some sort of craft exercise?"

"I get it, okay? You disapprove of my tactics and I kept you too much out of the loop. I wasn't intentionally sabotaging the book or the process. I just erroneously credited George with having the smallest sliver of professionalism. You'd better wonder what else he's going to buck before you actually get to publication. Seriously, what is with him and this book?"

"It's new, Cait, and it's different. It takes chances and is full of sparkling phrases and metaphors."

Cait leaned forward and talked to her knees while Pancho licked her ear. "It's also draggy, showy, and emotionally unsatisfying."

"Be that as it may, I acquired it, and I have a plan for it. A plan that someone else will be participating in as an editor instead of you. I just don't know what I'm going to do with you, Cait. This is a grade-A disaster."

Cait's throat thickened. "I'm sorry. I know I've disappointed you."

"You did worse than that. You lost my trust. Now excuse me while I go try to deal with this."

The line went quiet, but Cait continued to hold the phone to her ear, feeling like it was only that little bit of contact that was keeping her together. This...wasn't good. This was ungood on countless levels, and crying about it on the sidewalk blocks from her apartment would only make it even less good, which she wasn't sure was possible. For once, she wished Pancho actually were a horse and she could ride him back to safety without needing to find her own motive power.

She'd been so stupid, so damn proud, and now Martha was scrambling to get away from her the way Mrs. Lewis should have up and left her husband before it was too late. The stupid analogy made her think of Nick, which got her angry under her hurt and was enough to goad her to her feet and start her walking in the right direction. She wasn't sure what she'd do if he were still sitting on the steps, but it would almost certainly be something foolish and yet deeply satisfying.

When she got within sight of her building, the steps were empty, and she felt a disappointment-tinged relief that deflated her so much she wasn't sure how she would make it up the three flights of stairs to her apartment. She moved through a swirl of emotions: anger, sadness, shame, and a deep, thumping fear. What if Martha pulled all her Grovetree work? How long could she live on half her income before life would catch up to her? Great Danes were not inexpensive dogs to own. How would she keep Pancho in kibbles and treats, given his horse-sized appetite? She'd screwed up so badly, given what was at stake. She'd ended up acting as stubborn as George, but to a much worse end.

She slowed as she neared Allie's door, listening for…what? A lesson or practice session? An argument? The crash of glass breaking? What would she do if she heard that, anyway, given her questionable instincts? Nick was right: it wasn't her business. When she thought about it, given this setback with Martha, very little was her business. So she had better tend to what little she had.

After making sure she was up-to-date on all her current projects and had reached out to a few other publishers she'd worked with in the past, she went to the gym. Wasn't this exactly what weights were for? The push of metal and bodyweight against gravity shoved all extraneous thoughts from her mind. The focus on form and pacing, counting the last couple agonizing reps, all translated to a mental Zen that matched the fatigue of her body. Or at least that was how it was supposed to go.

This session had been dissatisfying in every way but still, somehow, exhausting. She'd resurrected some swim-specific exercises she hadn't done very much since college, and when she finished, her forearms were so exhausted that her hands trembled, making her look like a detoxing drunk. She fumbled with the zipper on her gym bag and ducked, palsied, into the hoodie she'd worn over here. A shower here, while usually compelling, left her flat and just wanting to get home where she could hide with her own misery. She couldn't remember what she had in her refrigerator to make for dinner and didn't care. She'd lost her appetite the instant she'd seen Martha's name on her phone so soon after having sent that email to George, and it didn't seem eager to return anytime soon.

After getting home and taking Pancho out for one last pee, she turned on the shower, ready to let hot water and negative ions work whatever magic they were capable of. She was stripped down to her sports bra and shorts when she heard a sound she couldn't quite place. She told herself to ignore it, but she was apparently as bad at following her own directions as everyone else was. Drifting from the bathroom and to the edge of the living room, she shivered in the cool air of her apartment and told herself she was an idiot. Then she heard it again. A knock. Who? Allie? Did she want one of her instruments at this hour?

She strode to the front door and yanked it open, in no mood to be at all neighborly. Allie was standing in the hall, lips twisted in a small, almost smile.

"Sorry," she said. "I didn't mean…I'm guessing I interrupted something."

"Just a shower. Or almost a shower." She took a moment to look more closely at Allie. The cut on her cheek looked scabby and raw, and the bruising was like the sky before a Nor'easter—ominous and all-encompassing. Her eyes were glassy, and her hair was pinned up in a decidedly haphazard way, one barrette listing off to the side and down as if it were making a break for it. Something in Cait softened despite herself. "Are you okay?" she asked.

CHAPTER TWELVE

Allie tried to keep her gaze leveled at Cait's eyes, but there was just so much of her on display. She wouldn't call her ripped exactly, but strength screamed from every one of her exposed parts, shoulders, core, calves. Even her ankles radiated power. Allie blinked mutely when Cait raised an arm to rake hair back from her face and her bicep bunched with the movement. Thinking was an impossibility, forget about speech. Remembering finally that Cait had asked her if she was okay, she mustered just enough control to answer, albeit incoherently.

"Yeah. No, I mean. But yeah."

Cait's dark eyebrows pulled toward each other in confusion.

"Sorry," Allie said. "I'm being a moron." She took a step toward the stairs to her apartment. "I shouldn't have bothered you."

"Allie." The word was more a demand than anything. "What's going on?"

"Nothing. Or nothing new. I just…never mind. It's stupid."

The deep breath Cait took made her chest rise in a distracting way. "Just tell me."

"Fine. I was wondering if I could stay here tonight. One more night only, I swear. I'm crawling out of my skin downstairs."

"Is Nick there?" Her gaze was so completely on Allie that she felt frozen in place.

"No, but he will be."

"You're letting him stay with you after that?" The surprise in her voice was laced with a disdain Allie felt for herself, too.

"We talked and…You know what? This is between him and me. I didn't ask for judgment, just a place to sleep for one night."

"I'm sorry." Cait pressed the heel of a hand against her forehead. "Come in." She stepped back to let Allie slide into the apartment. This put them closer together than was exactly comfortable, not with all those acres of Cait's skin exposed and the scent of fresh sweat that made Allie want to breathe in more deeply.

She scooted past as quickly as possible and said, "Thanks," when Cait closed and locked the door, drawing the chain for good measure. "I'm not as pathetic as I seem." Mind you, her cheek still throbbed, her left eye looked like it belonged to a drunk version of herself, and she had no idea what she was going to say at her studio session tomorrow, let alone at the jazz gig she had afterward.

Cait turned around, leaning back against the door and folding her arms across her chest. In the background Allie heard the spattering rain sound of the shower running. "I don't think you seem pathetic at all."

"It's complicated."

She laughed. "When is it ever not?" She squeezed past Allie again and walked into the living room. "I haven't put your bedding away from last night, so it's there whenever you're ready. I need to take a shower since I've had my own hellish day, but make yourself at home while I'm cleaning up."

The door to the bathroom closed behind Cait, muffling the shower sounds, which was excellent because Allie didn't need any reminder of what was happening in there. Get a grip, she told herself. This is The Amazon, the woman with a huge bug up her ass all the time.

And the one that had now helped her out twice, she conceded, trying to be honest with herself. She sat on the couch next to the hastily folded bedding from the night before, one small step away from having a panic attack. She jumped up to look for a stereo or a Bluetooth speaker, anything to disturb the just-so quietness of the apartment.

Where was the horse-dog? Was his absence the reason it felt so unnaturally still? She looked around. There was no dog bed out here, though Allie figured that wouldn't stop Pancho from taking up the whole floor if he wanted. She peeked into Cait's office, remembering there'd been a bed in the corner big enough for him to sleep on. It was empty. Had something happened to him? Cait had said she'd had a hellish day. Was Pancho at the vet with a grievous injury? Had he gotten into an altercation with a very bold rottweiler? A triggered pit bull? She should definitely not be here if that were the case. Her keys were in her pocket. She could just slip out, and Cait would get it. She already thought that Allie was very much not in control of her own life. This would just substantiate that.

She was about to turn around and let herself out into the hall when something nudged her lower back. She jumped and barely choked off a scream. Pancho was standing inches from her, his tail making mincemeat out of the air behind him, hitting the wall at the far end of every stroke. What a goofy-looking dog. Then again, size did not always confer dignity. She softened a little at his eagerness and tugged on his ears before scratching behind them. He pushed closer to her, which made her lose her balance and step back before laughing. This dog for sure weighed more than she did.

"Come on," she said, returning to the couch and sitting down. As if this were the most familiar move in the world for him, Pancho stood by her knees and laid his neck and head in her lap, glancing up at her, his eyebrows twitching back and forth as if impatient for what was supposed to happen next. Dogs were pretty simple beings, so what could be next except more petting? She scratched and thumped and stroked all over that heavy head and down to his shoulders, losing herself in

his huffs of breath and the feel of his short fur. He smelled...
lemony? Not any scent she had ever associated with a dog, that
was for sure.

When the bathroom door opened with a click, she put her
hands up like she'd been discovered fondling a weapon instead
of a dog. "He made me do it," she said.

Cait laughed, which made Allie laugh and relax a notch
again. Cait strode closer, still toweling off her hair but at least
fully dressed in a T-shirt and pajama bottoms. The shower had
brought a flush to her cheeks, and the steam that followed her
out of the bathroom smelled remarkably like how Pancho's
head did.

Allie said, "Do you use your own products on your dog?"

Cait's towel stilled against the right side of her head. "If I
did, that would be...weird, right?"

"I would say 'unusual,' but what do I know? The last pet I
had was a hamster in the fourth grade, and that didn't end that
great for anyone."

"Pancho seems to like you well enough."

"I have a feeling Pancho's easy to please." Though he hadn't
liked Nick. Maybe instead of easy to please, it was more like he
had good taste. Allie let herself hold on to that thought for a
moment.

Cait said, "Are you tired or do you want some tea?"

"Hey, just pretend I'm not here. Besides the fact that I'm
holding your dog hostage. I know you had a bad day, and I don't
want to make it worse."

She grasped her towel in both hands in front of her. "I went
to the gym to try to exhaust myself, and I think I ended up even
more wound up. I'm putting on some water for tea. I can make
you a mug if you want it. Or I can try to pretend you're not
here—even though you're for sure holding my dog hostage."

"Tea would be great. Anything but mint."

"Tastes like toothpaste and chewing gum, right?"

"Totally. I don't know how anyone drinks that stuff. You
might as well sip warm mouthwash."

Cait grimaced. "Now that's an image I'd like to forget. I've got some non-minty, calming tea in my cabinet." She swung the towel over one shoulder in a super casual move that was also devastatingly hot and sauntered away. Allie wondered what the hell was wrong with herself. Maybe it was just that Cait was doing her a favor and rescuing her from her own apartment. That was it. Thankfulness was powerful stuff, not to mention whatever endorphins she was getting with this mammoth dog head under her hands. All of which had made her balance precarious.

Behind her, Allie heard Cait rummaging through her kitchen, running the faucet, clinking mugs together, and ripping open a box and the plastic inside it. Because nature, and Allie, abhorred a vacuum, she said, "What do you do at the gym? I ask this from a place of total ignorance since I stay fit by walking to gigs and to get takeout."

"I'll do some cardio to warm up, but I mostly lift." The clicking of the gas range punctuated her obvious answer.

"As in weights?"

"As in weights."

"Oh yeah? What can you bench?" Even as she said it, Allie had no idea what she was asking.

"One seventy."

Allie craned her neck around to try to catch sight of Cait in the kitchen. "Pounds?"

Cait laughed. "It'd be really impressive if it were kilograms." In response to the undoubtedly confused look on Allie's face, she added, "That would be more than twice as much."

"So, you're...strong, then." Allie was a total and complete idiot. Why hadn't she escaped back to her own apartment when she'd had the chance and wasn't pinned down by a horse-dog and the promise of tea, which she suddenly wanted desperately?

"Stronger than average, but I wouldn't win any competitions. I just like the focus of it, the exhaustion I can get from it, and feeling capable, I guess."

"Sounds kind of like playing the trumpet. Once you master it, at least. Even the hard stuff is under your control."

Cait said, "As opposed to all the other hard stuff you have no defense against."

"I have no idea what you're talking about." Allie made sure her words were laced with sarcasm. Still, when the quiet between them grew noticeable, she wondered if she'd misplayed her hand. Finally, she said, "I meant that I understand."

Then Cait was next to the couch again, surprisingly stealthy for her size, just like Pancho. "I can identify sarcasm, Allie. I"— she glanced up at the ceiling—"I don't know how to ask this without you taking it the wrong way."

"I guess there's only one way to find out."

"Why are you here?"

Allie's laugh got caught up in the middle of her throat, coming out more like a gurgle. "Sorry. You're just so blunt."

"Clarity is an asset in my professional life. You don't have to answer." As if to prove that point, she turned toward the bathroom, pulling the towel from her shoulder and disappearing behind the door to hang it up.

It was easier to talk with her out of sight. "I knew this was inevitable with Nick, but for a long time, I convinced myself it would never get physical, that I could just deal with him as a moody bastard, and life would go on. And then I went right to doing what my mom did with my father. Excuses and chances and every ridiculous thing under the sun. I don't want to be afraid of Nick. He was my savior back then. He sacrificed himself for us, and I don't know what to do with that." Besides her therapist, she'd never told anyone that with as much clarity as Cait seemed to like.

The kettle whistled, and Cait walked past her to take care of it. When its shriek choked off, she said, "I don't care what you think you owe him. You can't let him abuse you."

Allie let that hard truth sit in her chest, making it tough to breathe. This woman had seen the direct aftermath of Nick's rage but knew so little of what had come before it. So much could be true simultaneously, but not all of it mattered at some point. "I know that, and I know that it would be foolish to think it'd be possible for him to change now. I wish this could be someone else's problem." She put a hand to her mouth. "God, that sounds so spineless."

Cait set two steaming mugs on the coffee table—using coasters, of course—and moved the folded bedding aside to sit next to Allie. "No. It sounds incredibly difficult, and maybe you don't have to figure it out right this second."

"I don't even really know what my options are. I mean, how does it actually work? My mom could have pressed charges any time the police came to our house, but she never did. I don't want to wait for the next time and hope someone calls the cops. And can it actually work, or will he get a slap on the wrist and still be able to get at me? Not that I think he's a monster who would stalk people in order to hurt them. He just lets something get to him so much that he loses control. It's all so opportunistic it barely seems like a crime." Now that she'd started, Allie couldn't convince herself to shut up, and she was getting more and more wound up. No amount of herbal tea was going to get her calm enough to sleep. She sounded exactly like her mother, and disgust thickened her throat.

"Hey," Cait said and laid her hand on Allie's thigh next to Pancho's neck. It was warm and pressed down firmly but not in a claustrophobic way. "He hit you. That's assault. That should be all you need. You have options."

Allie hadn't noticed that she'd stopped petting Pancho until Cait snapped with her free hand and pointed to the floor at her feet. He lifted himself off Allie's legs and lay down against Cait. Allie said, "You obviously haven't had much experience with domestic abuse."

"No, I haven't, not personally, but I saw enough of it back home to know you need to do what you can. You said he's an opportunist, so remove as many opportunities as possible."

Allie let out a mean laugh. "Your couch is about to get a lot of mileage if you're not careful."

Cait's fingers squeezed Allie's leg and relaxed. "I'll butt out if you want me to, but I'll help, too. It's completely up to you."

Allie groaned. "It's so impossible, and it's fucked me up so hard. I can't think about it anymore." She grabbed her mug from the coffee table and took a scalding sip. "Shit. Hot." She set it back down and fell over onto her side while her feet stayed anchored to the floor. The position was hardly comfortable, but it was somehow necessary. Cait's hand still hadn't moved, and it grounded her in a way Pancho hadn't. She closed her eyes and tried to breathe. "Can we change the subject? Why was your day hellish?"

"Misery loves company?"

"Something like that. Or maybe misery loves distraction."

Cait hummed and sipped her tea. Allie was sure she wasn't going to answer when she said, "I screwed up on a contract in a pretty spectacular way."

"Ouch. What does screwing up look like for you? Because I can't imagine it's the same as for me."

"Have you screwed up before?"

She opened her eyes and gave that some thought. "Only mildly and not recently. If I show up on time and am prepared, I can pretty much guarantee I won't burn any bridges." She thought about turning her head to see Cait, but it seemed safer to keep her gaze on the edge of the coffee table in front of her. Besides, she didn't want to move and give Cait any motivation to remember where her hand was and come up with a reason to remove it. "What happened?"

Cait sighed. "The particulars don't matter. Basically, I let my pride get in the way and made a terrible decision for my career."

"You're a freelancer, right?"

"Until now, yeah, but that might all change."

"That sounds a bit fatalistic, but I get you. Even after ten years doing what I do, I'm sure the gigs are going to dry up one day. Even now, I'm hustling all the time."

Cait's laugh was low and quiet. "Ah, the hustle. Do you ever just want to take a nine-to-five job and have some security for once?"

Allie smiled, which felt weird on her face. "Never. I'd rather play my horn and complain all the time."

After a long dollop of quiet, Cait said, "I listen to you sometimes. You're the good one, right?"

"I'd like to think so. I hope no one tells me if I'm not."

"At least I'm sure that you're not your three o'clock Wednesday lesson. Who is that, Dizzy? Do you share those nicknames with the kids, or are they your own shorthand?"

At that Allie did turn, swiveling her head to look at Cait, who was blowing across her tea in a small billow of steam. "You figured that out?"

"It wasn't that hard. Dizzy and Miles gave it away. Was it supposed to be code or a secret? I didn't mean to pry." She put her mug down and looked at Allie. "I swear, it's not my goal to be difficult for you. I just don't always handle difficult situations well." Her eyes were a warm brown, and the wetness still in her hair made it even darker. Her jaw was strong, but her lips were soft. Allie couldn't seem to look away.

"That's okay. I get it. We all have our shit."

Cait smiled. "I couldn't have said it better myself."

They went on to different subjects, talking easily now, Cait's warm hand a permanent fixture on Allie's thigh, Pancho twitching in his sleep. Allie relaxed into the couch and into the way Cait's smile quirked one side of her mouth up higher than the other. This was nothing like how she'd imagined the evening going, but now that she was here, she wouldn't have it any other way.

The sun was streaming through the window in full-blown morning when Allie woke to the strangest noise. It wasn't an alarm but was rhythmic in a droning sort of way. Eyes closed, she tried to puzzle it out, along with other things like the slight smell of lemons and the unfamiliar weave of the fabric under her cheek. The noise returned, a strangling, stuttering sound like a flugelhorn in real distress. She opened her eyes. Cait sat at the end of the couch, her head thrown back against the cushions, snoring like a freight train. Allie wanted to laugh but stopped when she continued to take stock of the situation. Her legs were draped over Cait's lap, and one of Cait's hands was warm on her shin under her hiked-up pants, the other drifting closer to her knee. Their tea mugs reposed next to each other on the coffee table. Pancho raised his head at Allie's movement, making his tags jingle once. Cait snored again.

They had talked so much and so easily. Cait had been nothing like Allie had thought she was. Quiet, yes, but also both warm and fierce. She was sometimes funny but always genuine. She'd placed her hands on Allie in a way that spoke of comfort more than anything else but was still insistent and full of intention. Cait snored again.

What did any of this mean, though? Was Cait even clear what she'd done in comforting Allie this way? Was Allie even interested in anything with Cait beyond the salvation of the night before? She examined Cait's profile, her mouth open in apparently deep sleep. Cait had become familiar literally overnight, and Allie liked looking at her, watching her mouth form words. Allie liked her rippling forearms and this feeling of intense competence that radiated from her like the lemony smell of her soap. Allie liked Cait. The thought made her panic a little. Everything was jumbled now, Cait changing right in front of her eyes, Nick sleeping downstairs while she was up here, her face impossible to hide. She wanted to stay like this the rest of the morning, a desire so out of left field that she gingerly moved her legs from Cait's lap and shook the woman's shoulder in a firm, businesslike way.

"Hey, wake up."

Cait made a noise that felt like a squint and lifted her head, hissing in breath and pressing her hand to the back of her neck. "Oh my God. Ugh." She closed her mouth and audibly swallowed. "What happened?"

"You fell asleep. We both fell asleep. You were snoring."

Now the squint was in Cait's eyes. "My neck feels like someone stepped on it. Why'd you let us do that?"

"Uh, I think I lost control of the situation when I went comatose. Did you think I would carry you to bed? Or could?"

Cait's fingertips were white where they squeezed her neck. "You know what I mean. I was snoring? Jesus, why not? Of course. And now I need to go to the damn chiropractor."

"Wow, okay. I'm sorry I woke you up." Allie scrambled off the couch. "I'll let myself out, then."

She was at the door before Cait said anything. "I didn't mean that. My neck is killing me, and you—"

"I, what?"

"Were here."

"Not for long," Allie said and let herself out into the hall, working hard not to slam the door behind her. She hurried down the stairs to her floor and had her key in the lock before she remembered why she hadn't been in her apartment in the first place. She and Nick had talked yesterday, and he'd apologized. Allie had known it was genuine, but that didn't mean she'd believed it. Or, rather, she believed it but didn't believe it actually meant anything. But because she believed it and was an idiot, she hadn't taken Nick's key away from him and now didn't know what would greet her when she opened her door.

She stupidly hoped that Cait would come after her, apologizing in her own way and enticing Allie back to her apartment, that apartment that was warmer than it looked and full of a comfort she'd never thought to imagine before. But the stairway was quiet, so she turned her key and went in.

Nick was asleep on her couch in his boxers, his flabby belly pushing against its elastic waistband, his cheeks shaded with pale-brown stubble. If only she didn't love him. If only she hadn't just spent the night on a different couch, one where she'd felt understood and safe. At least for a while. But she was here now. She'd made choices. Now all that was left to do was live with them.

CHAPTER THIRTEEN

Cait couldn't get over how thoroughly Allie had made her forget the trouble she'd gotten herself into. In fact, she couldn't get over a lot of things: how easy it had been for them to talk, how her hand had been drawn to Allie's thigh, how quick Allie had been to smile once they'd both relaxed, how soft the skin had been on her leg. And, of course, how ridiculously wrong it had gone at the end. Literally anything would've been better than first snoring—and drooling too, no doubt—and then basically driving Allie out of her apartment with her short-tempered remark. Well, who could blame her? She'd just woken up, she was in pain, and she was mortally embarrassed.

But, really, what had she thought she was doing in the first place?

When Allie had arrived last night, her effort to sound matter-of-fact had been clear, but her upset had felt visceral to Cait. It had been impossible not to try to comfort her, even if it were just by providing a steadying touch that went on far longer than Cait had anticipated. Her hand had fit perfectly there, blanketing Allie's thigh. She had felt useful in her largeness for a change, able to ground Allie in a meaningful way. It had worked, too; Allie's frenetic musings had slowed down, shifting things into a calmer gear.

And then their conversation had been effortless. Comrades-in-self-employed arms, living in reach of or truly within the arts, coexisting in this same building, on the same street, in the same neighborhood, in the same city. They had more in common than Cait could have imagined, and they'd passed time and a couple of mugs of tea, getting more and more comfortable until...what? Cait couldn't exactly remember beyond getting relaxed and overpoweringly sleepy.

She rubbed a hand over her face and groaned, which made Pancho clatter to his feet, flap his ears in a shake, and bump his snout against her neck. The day was going to have to start, no matter if she wanted it to or not, no matter if it was going to be one unsavory thing after the other, just like the day before. The thought of running into Allie on the stairs was so untenable she didn't even change out of her pajamas before grabbing Pancho's leash from the hook by the front door, stuffing her feet into her gym shoes, and heading out. Pancho trotted next to her down the hall and around the stairs until they were outside and making tracks away from the apartment building.

Running away like this was ridiculous. She and Allie had made a connection—exactly what kind she wasn't sure—a connection that she was now going to ignore and continue to sequester herself in her apartment like a frightened child. Lauren had been right. She was defective. She hid behind judgment and fear and excuses and lived her life exclusively on the page, immersing herself in her work, in other people's stories, in order to forget that she didn't have a life of her own.

Not that Allie even wanted to be part of Cait's story. Cait had offered her a convenient place to crash, but she was otherwise an unremitting annoyance, critical of every noisy aspect of Allie's life. Much as Allie was critical of Cait's own relentlessly quiet, well-ordered, sterile life.

Somehow, though, what had seemed nothing other than a major imposition and a distraction had turned into something unexpectedly different. If Cait were a writer, she might have the words for it, but as an editor, all she could do was decide to cut, add, or rearrange the words of others. Doing more than that required developing intentions she hadn't yet honed for herself.

Her phone rang, and she wished she'd left it back in the apartment instead of habitually stuffing it in a pocket. She looked at the caller ID, and her stomach clenched. Martha. It was both early for Martha and late for Cait, since she'd slept away half the morning in a ludicrous position that still made it painful for her to turn her head. Nothing good would come from either answering or not answering the call, so she defaulted to at least being a professional, despite walking down the street in her pajamas.

"Good morning, Martha."

"Cait."

"Are you calling to fire me?" She blamed her stiff neck for her award-winning frankness, though she was starting to wonder if it were more of a chronic condition.

"At least I can always be straight with you. So many people of your generation are delicate flowers wilting in the slightest criticism."

Yeah, like George, though he didn't so much wilt as completely reject what he didn't like without the most basic acknowledgment. "So, that's a yes?"

"I thought we might discuss things first."

Cait stopped at a fire hydrant. Dogs and hydrants. There should be a scientific study about it. "I'm sorry. I screwed up and made the wrong call. I was overconfident in me but also in George, to be honest, and I'm not interested in falling on my sword any more than that." That last bit of sass wasn't called for, but this was Martha. They knew each other; this was how they rolled, at least usually.

"Do you know how much this pains me?"

"If by this you mean firing me, then I think it might pain me a little more." The breeze cut through her thin T-shirt, making her shiver.

"I'm not firing you, Cait. But you need to earn my trust again. We have another title by an author you've worked with in the past coming in the next couple months, but you won't be on Michelle's next book or anything other than that one for the time being. To have you hang me and the press out to dry like that was a personal betrayal. It's going to take some time to come back from that."

That Martha was being as hard on Cait as she was on herself was both warranted and not. This was a pretty spectacular failure, especially considering how important this book was to Martha, but it faded to near insignificance in the face of all the many, many projects she'd gotten right over the years. Cait couldn't keep herself from asking, "Who did you assign George's book to?"

"Frankly, that's none of your business."

Cait squeezed the back of her neck with the hand holding Pancho's leash, making him move several shuffling steps closer to her. "Fair enough. I appreciate this chance and am sorry, again, for letting you down."

"I'll be in touch when the next book is ready for you."

"Thanks, Martha." Before she could say goodbye, the line went quiet, and Cait dropped her head back, beseeching the unclouded sky and triggering a spasm of pain in the base of her skull. "Fuck," she said, but the word came out quiet and defeated. "Come." Pancho fell into step with her in a tight heel. What did Nick say that Allie had called the two of them? Oh yeah, "The Amazon and the horse-dog." For years, that had just been the way it was, the Amazon part at least, but now the description chafed like sand in a bathing suit. All of it rubbed her the wrong way, and she wasn't sure she'd be able to make rent next month without her regular Grovetree work. She still had pending invoices in to the press, but she'd put so many of her eggs in that basket that things were going to get uncomfortably tight more quickly than she wanted to admit. Could she be bold enough to bill for all the time she'd spent on *Put Title Here*? Maybe Allie could be that brazen but not her.

Back in her building, she slowed in front of Allie's door despite herself and listened. All was quiet on the third-floor front. Cait supposed that was good, but it didn't feel it, just like the frayed remnant of rope Martha was dangling for Cait to hang on to and maybe climb. Despite her size, she had always liked the rope climb, especially the view from the top. This rope, though, didn't seem capable of holding her weight, let alone taking her where she wanted to go. Not that she knew exactly where that was right now. She reluctantly pulled herself away from Allie's door. Allie might not even be in there. Besides, the last thing she wanted was to be caught in such an unaccountable position. She had enough wrongs dogging her as it was.

The next week was more of the unnerving same. Working with Tamara took ten to fifteen hours each Monday to Friday, depending on how much work her packet required, and she had another book and several technical articles to get to, but Grovetree pulling the rest of her projects was going to hurt. Anticipating her diminishing queue of work, she'd been emailing the writers and editors in her network, looking for referrals, but she wasn't having much luck. Didn't everyone think they had a book in them? A family history, if not the next *Lord of the Rings*? They wouldn't be fun, but a good portion of those desperately needed editing, and they would make for a steady pipeline of work.

In her weaker moments, she perused the ads for editors on job boards and actually updated her résumé. What she liked about freelancing, though, was the variety. The thought of giving that up, not just in terms of subject matter and form but in the range of writers she worked with made her cringe.

She continued to sequester herself, avoiding going in and out of the building—except to take Pancho out and hitting the gym, which helped her nerves but made her wonder if she'd have to drop her membership in service of belt-tightening. Whenever she did leave, she waited until the hallways were stone quiet when she opened her door or when she heard Allie or one of her students playing in the apartment downstairs. She became a ninja when traversing thin carpet and creaky stairs, even holding Pancho's collar and tags in her hand for the trip to keep them from jangling. She admitted that avoiding Allie was the biggest aim; Cait's feelings on that matter were as fraught as her financials. This hiding was a kind of subterfuge she'd engaged in before, but for the first time it felt distasteful. Cowardly.

Finally, she really had to escape her apartment, not only because it was a full day of lessons and practice sessions but because she needed to grocery shop or go hungry. She left Pancho with his favorite chew toy and made a day of it, heading first to Diesel, the coffee shop that had become a comfortable refuge over the last couple of months—at least when she wasn't shoehorned into the bar seating. The hiss of the steam wand, the frothing of foam, and the grinding of beans were low-level background noise that was also predictable enough to ignore. Besides, sitting there made it nearly impossible for her to talk to anyone on her phone, something she'd been avoiding exactly as earnestly as she'd been dodging Allie.

She had a table to herself today, but it was too close to the front, where customers coming and going and passersby on the sidewalk seduced her with ample distraction from what she was trying to do on her laptop. Still, she'd take it and not complain—or at least not very much. Tamara's weekly email dropped when she was an hour into trying to work and on her second cup of coffee. Cait steeled herself for the torrent of pointless words that usually accompanied her weekly attachment but stopped short when she saw just one: BREAKTHROUGH.

The arrangement they had developed depended almost entirely on Tamara's energy and belief. Cait didn't skimp on her critique of the pages Tamara sent and worked hard to give oft-repeated feedback in new and inventive ways—if only to keep boredom at bay. Her heart hadn't much been in it, though, especially since weeks of back-and-forth hadn't seemed to make much of an impact. She was intrigued now despite herself.

She opened the attachment and started to read, making it to the second page before stopping and laughing. Not in a *haha funny* way but in a *huh, this is different* way. She leaned forward and worked through the fifteen pages she'd been sent, not at all distracted and definitely smiling. Tamara had done it—or at least some of it. She'd finally figured out how to work with exposition and scene. The dance between the two had been tripping Tamara up this whole time. The approach was somewhat counterintuitive, but sometimes, in order to give scenes the motion they needed, writers had to slow everything down first with some exposition. That enabled them to ground characters with their essential traits before the reader watched them play out in the real time of the story. Yes, Cait thought while she read. Exactly right. Well done, Tamara!

When she sat back and pulled her gaze from her laptop screen, she discovered Allie was in line—and looking at her. The bruising on her face had been reduced by now to a little yellowing at her hairline and by her ear, though makeup might have also contributed to producing that effect. The swelling in her cheek had gone down, and the cut was much less angry looking, though it was still scabbed and red. Cait had a nearly uncontrollable urge to touch her again. To kiss her until they were both breathless. What the...? Before she could stop herself, she said, "Hi. How are you?"

The people at the table between them glanced over at her, but she ignored them, keeping herself focused on Allie. Allie's lips pressed together, which Cait realized was easy to see at this distance because they were such a rosy red next to Allie's creamy skin and golden hair.

Cait rose halfway from her chair, which only made Allie's lips clamp more tightly. She sat back down and raised her hands as if trying to calm a wild animal. "I—" she started, but Allie shook her head.

"I'm fine," she said and turned forward in line, pointing her gaze decidedly away from Cait.

Cait's stomach churned against the coffee she'd already consumed, and she felt a lurching combination of competent from Tamara's email and inept from Allie's reaction to her. She had meant to figure out a way to talk to Allie over the last week, but she'd known she'd get exactly this reaction, which while totally reasonable, wasn't something anyone relished. She watched Allie progress in the line, finally moving to the area where she'd pick up her drink. Staring too blatantly at her could incite Allie's anger—or her fear—but Cait couldn't stop, not when she realized she had no idea what Allie really was thinking.

She could do this. She could communicate, she could make herself heard, and she really wanted to do both with Allie. After all, she had somehow made herself understood to Tamara of all people, causing a breakthrough in a situation she hadn't felt remotely in control of. Ignoring her laptop, she watched Allie as she waited for her drink, doctored it with honey, and sipped it to test its flavor. When, with a small nod, she made her way back up to the door, Cait moved to intercept her.

"I screwed up, okay?" she said, her new refrain. She stood in front of Allie. "I do that a lot. I mean, not with grammar but with stuff like this." Her hand waved back and forth between them. Her voice was a bit too loud, though, and too many people had turned away from the work they were supposed to be doing and into the distraction she was providing. She lowered her voice. "Do you have a minute?" She indicated her table with a nod.

"I have a lesson," Allie said.

Cait checked her watch. "Not for a half hour, right? That gives you at least five minutes before you need to leave, and you could still have a leisurely walk."

Allie shifted over to let someone exit past them but made no further moves toward Cait's table. "What do you want, Cait?"

"To tell you what I was too stupid to tell you that morning." To kiss you senseless, her libido unhelpfully added.

"I don't have time for this."

"Please." Cait pressed three fingertips to Allie's forearm as lightly as she could manage. She couldn't help herself. She didn't want to help herself, and Allie didn't pull away.

"Seriously, I don't have time, not with the line I just stood in."

"Tonight?"

"I have a gig."

"Where?"

Allie rolled her eyes. "Like you want to go to a jazz club after your bedtime."

"Where is it?"

Allie told her and pulled her arm gently away from Cait's hand. "I have to go." For a moment, she looked like she was going to say something else, but she just turned away and pushed out the door. Cait watched her walk down the sidewalk before slumping back behind the shield of her laptop. That could have gone worse, not that she wanted to imagine the alternative to what had just happened. She looked up the club Allie had mentioned and mapped a route from the apartment building to it. She checked its website to see when Allie's group was playing, then ordered another coffee, hoping to be able to stay awake that late.

Cait was significantly more confident than she should have been while riding the T past Harvard and Central Squares and over the Charles River into downtown before changing to the Green Line and heading out of town again. She was wearing her newest and darkest pair of 501s, her crispest button-up shirt, and a light cardigan, and the high she'd gotten from Tamara's progress plus Allie's backhanded kind of invitation was making her feel like she was on the right path for the first time in months. She wondered where it might take her. She was pretty sure she didn't like jazz, but she wasn't going to let that stop her from being on time getting to Wally's Club, which sat between Back Bay and the South End. She was going there to see Allie, not really to listen to her play, though she guessed Allie's trumpet was like a vital organ to her.

She had her phone, of course, as well as a pair of earplugs in one pocket in case things were out-of-control loud and enough cash in her other pocket for a drink if she needed to become desensitized in order to make it through the night. It felt like she was heading into the wilderness, hoping to survive with just what she could carry in her own two hands.

Was this why Lauren had left her? Because Cait been unwilling to go on these kinds of adventures? She always had had work to do, which was simultaneously true and not true. Cait hadn't had any problem staying up until all hours talking to Allie that night. She hadn't thought about work a single time—aside from commiserating with Allie about the trials of freelancing. She'd dedicated herself completely to the pursuit of making Allie feel better and staying in close proximity for as long as possible.

She could have gone to her bed at any point when she'd started to feel tired, but she hadn't. She'd urged Allie to stretch out. She'd stayed sitting under the weight of Allie's legs, relinquishing even the amount of control required to avoid a sore neck in the morning. She'd gone from hating Allie in the beginning to liking her quite a lot, and she had to see if the same was true for Allie. Because, until her massive brain fart that morning that had derailed everything, it had seemed like maybe it was.

The club was small, tucked in at the ground level of a brownstone like any other in this area of the city. She opened the door to loud music, showed her ID, paid the cover, and edged along the side of the room to reconnoiter and see if she could spot Allie, who wasn't on stage. No one was, actually, and the music that was being played too loud was of the prerecorded type. She moved along to the bar on her left, perching half on a stool as if she would take off at the slightest provocation. It wasn't terribly busy yet, and the woman behind the bar asked for her order just moments after she pulled her gaze from the empty stage and glanced at the bottles lined up in front of her. If only for something to do with her hands, she chose a Goose Island lager and took a single fortifying swig from the brown bottle, the glass frosty against her fingers.

She was massively out of her element and wished she hadn't been so prompt, but she'd left on time and had caught the two trains quickly. Now she wished she'd taken some time to walk around the block and maybe get mugged. But she hadn't, so she was there in time to see a bass player step on stage and lift his instrument from where it lay on its side. A man settled in behind the drums, a woman sat at the upright piano, and Allie hovered between them, her trumpet glinting dully in the bright lights. Cait didn't want to stop watching her exactly as much as she wanted to run away, so she stayed rooted to her stool, peeling the label on her warming beer.

Allie had invited her, right? She wouldn't have told her where the gig was if she hadn't wanted Cait to come, but that didn't make her feel confident at all. She was glad for the spotlights that seemed to be shining right in Allie's eyes because that might make the rest of the club invisible to her, leaving Cait an opportunity to escape.

The drummer counted in the beat, and Allie's now-familiar sound announced her entrance. Instead of slinking out of the club, Cait found herself smiling as Allie swayed to the beat, accenting certain parts with small sideways hip thrusts. She wore a blue dress that matched her eyes. It had a flare at the bottom that swung just above her knees, and her heels did something magical to her legs. The light caught her hair and did, in fact, make her look like an angel, but the way she could make her instrument speak was far more earthy.

As for the music itself, Cait decided she didn't hate it. She realized, in turn, that there were different variations of jazz, just as mysteries had a practically infinite number of subcategories. Cait had no idea how to describe what this was, but it definitely wasn't the screechy and self-indulgent stuff about which she'd formed her first impression of the genre.

Cait couldn't unstick her gaze from Allie, who seemed totally in control, who was making what she did look—and sound—effortless. This was mastery, and Cait was caught up in it. So much so that she didn't stir when the small group took a break after their first set and Allie marched in front of her, arms crossed over her chest and eyebrows raised. Her lips were even redder than they had been at the coffee shop and were marked with a bullseye-looking circle of anger from her mouthpiece.

Cait smiled. "Hi. Want a drink?"

Allie's eyebrows pulled down into a frown. "Why are you here?"

"To talk to you."

"I'm at work."

"Right, I know. You're doing a great job." Cait sounded like she'd drunk this beer and two others, though she'd barely made a dent.

Allie rolled her eyes. "As if you'd know."

"I don't hate it, so that's really something."

"High praise, thanks." She leaned closer to the bartender. "Fizzy water, please."

"With lots of ice?" the bartender asked with a smile that felt flirty to Cait even though it was basically a normal I-want-a-tip grin.

Allie nodded. "You got it."

"Coming right up," the woman said, and Cait felt irrationally jealous that they knew each other—further, that the bartender was familiar with what Allie drank.

"I know you're busy now," she said. "Or, you know, occupied. But what about after?"

"What about after? What are you getting at?"

"What do you do after this?"

Allie squinted. "What do you think I do? Go home and go to bed."

"Can I walk you? It's not as far as you'd think if you cut through some places."

"Contrary to what you might believe, I don't have a death wish. I take a ride share."

"Come on, once you're off this particular street, it's fairly safe, I think. We could walk all the way to the Charles, at least."

"Maybe if you're six feet tall and a wall of muscle." The bartender took that moment to slide Allie's water over to her. Allie nodded her thanks and took several long swallows before gripping her forehead in her fingers. "Ah, cold headache."

Cait said, "Press your tongue against the back of the roof of your mouth. It'll go away."

Allie gave her a look of disbelief that was crookedly adorable, but after a moment, one of her eyebrows shot up. "Huh. How'd you know that?"

"I read a lot. I also know that incarnations of the trumpet have been around for three thousand five hundred years."

"Yeah, in King Tut's tomb and other places, though my valved version didn't become the standard until closer to 1900." She took another swallow. "You're trying to butter me up."

"Is it working?"

"I'll tell you after the next set." She downed the rest of her water and waited for a refill from the bartender before turning around and, without another word, heading toward the sign for the restrooms.

Another set? Cait checked her watch and gave an inward groan. Was it always going to be late nights with Allie? Whoa, she told herself. There was nothing "with" Allie right now, much less anything like an always, so she would have to take whatever she could get. She swigged her warm beer and grimaced. It was probably for the best that she'd made this drink undrinkable. The cards may have been stacked against folks back home in Appalachia, but they didn't do themselves any favors with their drinking habits, either. Way too many people imbibed way too much, even her holier-than-thou father, who made a habit of drinking himself to slumber most Friday and Saturday nights.

Tonight, though, she wanted to feel a little loose and daring, and that wasn't going to happen without some assistance. So she bought a new beer and went to work on it, making a mental list of what she hoped to accomplish. She wanted Allie to absolve her for being such a fright the morning after their lovely evening together. She wanted to be likeable, the kind of person that others trusted to edit their books. Or to be their friend. Or, you know, to kiss them. 'Cause, yeah, that's what Cait wanted. The red bullseye that Allie's instrument left on her mouth was a target that she was particularly interested in.

Most of the beer was gone before the band's break was over. As they prepared to take the stage again, she turned her head toward it, and the room grew fuzzy around its edges. Right. She was a freaking six-foot-tall "wall of muscle," but she couldn't hold her liquor worth a damn. The room snapped back into focus as the group started up again. The woman at the piano and the man on drums sang a couple of old standards but gave them a fresh take. The room, now teeming with bodies all radiating at 98ish degrees grew warm, and she slipped off her cardigan, draped it over a leg, and rolled her shirt sleeves up to her elbows.

Resting her bare forearms on her thighs, she listened intently. Music had never been her thing, especially jazz. When she'd been at college, she'd found those who liked it to be affected and generally intolerable. While she didn't have much use for any kind of music—it just distracted her from what she was actually interested in—tonight she felt open to it in an atypical way. Obviously, part of that could be attributed to her newfound affection for Allie, but as the beat, swingy and bluesy, invaded her cells and asked them to come along for the ride, she could almost fathom the appeal. Watching the joy with which Allie performed helped her understand Allie's devotion to her craft and her desire to stay up late and play for an audience.

As an editor, Cait lurked behind the scenes of the art she was associated with, bringing out the best in the artists she worked with, rarely acknowledged but basking in their reflected glory. Her goal, actually, was to erase her and the author from the work completely, enabling the reader to be subsumed directly into the story and not to surface until it ended—or they had to pee. Hadn't that been one of her problems with George's manuscript? The author's hand had been far too evident. It was the same with Tamara's work. It had been forced and awkward, not to mention disorganized. But she had helped her fix that, hadn't she? She'd led Tamara to a breakthrough, which, she had to admit, was even more rewarding than editing a more established writer. If she were honest with herself, she wanted more of the coaching…and she might have room for it now that she was on such severe probation with Martha.

She spent the rest of the second set half listening to music and half scheming how to find more coaching customers. When it was over and she joined the crowd's standing ovation, she was still a bit buzzed. Her joints were relaxed, and her head was bleary around every edge. She stayed at her stool while Allie walked off with her instrument and, again, passed under the restroom sign, headed toward a green room of some sort, no doubt. The place started to empty out like a fog burning off in the morning. She was halfway through tugging the label off her beer bottle when Allie reemerged, a black bag slung over her shoulder, walking between the piano woman and the drummer man. The three of them stopped in front of Cait.

"Cait, this is Jennifer and Mike Collins," Allie said. "They're the married beating heart of our group. Guys, this is Cait, my upstairs neighbor."

The couple exhaled in simultaneous ahs, and Cait could only imagine what Allie had been saying about her for the last months. Cait said, "I'm not a music person, but—"

Jennifer interrupted her. "Yeah, we got that impression."

"In my defense, the trumpet is quite…" Cait cast around for the right word.

"What about 'bracing'?" Allie suggested wryly.

"Excellent. Yes, bracing. All of you were really good together, though. It's nice to hear Allie play with a group instead of only practicing."

Mike said, "We're just having fun. You should hear us when we have a sax player again."

"What happened to your last one?"

Allie said, "Long story. Don't you two have to get home now that you've been introduced?"

Jennifer said, "Allie never has people coming to watch us."

"We always play on school nights."

"Excuses excuses." She slipped an arm through Mike's. "Good to meet you, Cait. Get home safely." Then they were gone along with most of the rest of the patrons, and Allie was standing alone in front of Cait, her thumb rubbing back and forth across the red marks on her lips.

Allie said, "What now?" She glanced at the bottle in Cait's hands. "Please tell me that you didn't drink to excess. I can't deal with dealing with you like that."

"No, of course not." Cait set the bottle on the bar and slipped from her stool. "I was still wondering if you'd let me walk you home."

Allie laughed. "That again? Are you serious? In the middle of the night? That's just asking for trouble. I haven't done that since I was a stupid college kid."

"Oh. Are you worried about being messed with?"

"Isn't everyone?"

Cait stayed very quiet.

"Seriously? You've never fallen into trouble just walking down the street?"

"I feel like I should apologize, but I can't help the way I look."

"I can't believe you can just go wherever you want whenever you want to. Sometimes I can't even make it through Davis Square without some guy trying to take advantage."

Cait said, "If you walk with me, you'll inherit my luck. Seriously, I don't know, but I've never, ever been messed with walking around the city, and I know I went into some neighborhoods I probably shouldn't have when I was young and stupid."

"Are you telling me you want to take me out to Roxbury or down to Dorchester?" Allie's tone didn't sound as harsh as her words.

Cait succumbed to nervousness and slipped her hands in her pockets. "No. I'm asking if you'll let me walk you to Harvard, and we'll take it from there."

"You know that's at least three miles, right?"

Cait nodded her head toward Allie's shoulder. "What if I carry your bag?" She held her breath.

Allie shook her head a little but said, "I reserve the right to hop in the nearest Uber at any moment. You're lucky I'm wearing comfortable shoes."

"I only have comfortable shoes."

"Good for you. Are we going? Because I'd like to make it home before it gets light out." Allie held her bag out to Cait, who shouldered it.

It wasn't heavy, and Cait asked, "How valuable is what I'm carrying?"

"To me or on the open market?"

"Either. Both."

"Irreplaceable and not terribly expensive at the same time. Lead the way."

CHAPTER FOURTEEN

Allie wasn't sure what she was doing. Somehow, after months of saying nothing but no to Cait and still offended by what she'd said that fateful morning, she couldn't seem to summon the animosity required to take a stand. Though she wished it didn't, that surely had something to do with the way Cait's jeans hung from her hips and the deeply open collar of her crisp, white shirt. And, of course, her quiet kindness the other night. Both nights. It had been such a departure from their previous acrimonious interactions that Allie was still trying to wrap her mind around it, though Cait seemed to have had no problem doing so. They walked over to Mass Ave and turned toward the river. Allie told herself she could grab the T when they crossed it, but she had a sinking suspicion she wasn't going to want to.

Allie nodded as they passed a homeless person huddled amidst blankets in a dark storefront. "You really never get messed with?"

"It's the size, I think. Even if they don't think I'm a man, which is common enough, I'm not the easiest target."

"You don't look like a man."

"Put a hat and peacoat on me, and no one thinks I'm a woman." Cait shrugged. "I don't blame them. We all live by snap judgments."

"Well, I've looked everywhere, but I can't find the 'Go ahead and screw with me' sign I must have on me somewhere. It's been open season on Allie recently."

Cait stopped. "Do you think it's your fault that Nick went after you?"

"No," Allie said. "No. I mean, no, right?"

"Absolutely not. Not in a million years."

Allie tugged on her hand. "Come on. If we stop walking, I'll get cold. I don't know how you're not freezing in just that shirt."

"I run hot, so you can have my cardigan if you need it. My last girlfriend sometimes put a pillow between us to deflect my body heat."

Allie laughed. "She was a fool. Sometimes I wear two pairs of socks and a hoodie to bed to make it through the night." They walked a half block in easy quiet. "I know it's not my fault with Nick. We've just been through so much together, and he didn't have to turn out like this. Maybe if a couple of things had gone differently…But they didn't."

"You can't—"

Allie interrupted. "I know, and I don't want to talk about it. Not now, at least." The Boston night was too bright to see stars, and a siren wailed in the distance. "I don't understand this. I thought you hated me. I thought you hated everyone." She glanced over in time to see Cait smile.

"I like to consider myself an aggressive introvert."

"Emphasis on aggressive?"

Cait shrugged. "You could say that. I think it's one of those, 'It's not you, it's me,' things."

"I get it. You don't like the inane daily interactions that grease the wheels, so to speak."

Cait grimaced, her eyes narrowing with it. She looked like she had when Allie had woken her: pained. "It's not that. Well, it's partly that." She laughed. "But only partly. I don't like to have to manage how people react to me. The height, the shoulders, the dog. It's a lot for other people to deal with, so I mostly try to avoid it entirely."

"How young were you when you got this tall?"

"Twelve. It was a constant bewilderment to me and everyone around me. Then I put on muscle. Then I came out. Inside I'm this quiet, contained person, but outside I'm…"

"The Hulk, but in a good way?"

She huffed a laugh. "She-Hulk, please. I've gotten over trying to make myself small to fly under the radar, but I'd still much rather not draw the kind of attention I do. And my work needs quiet and focus. I won't say my behavior was exactly justified when you started working at home, but you're really, really loud."

Allie nodded and went out on a limb she hoped would hold her. "This sounds a lot like an opposites attract scenario."

Cait cast her gaze up to the sky. "It's not just me?"

Allie captured Cait's hand in hers. "You've been unbelievably kind to me after first being an unbelievable asshole. Good thing I don't hold a grudge."

"What if I promise to make it up to you?"

"Don't let me stop you from trying."

They walked slowly along the river, downtown fading behind them and the water of the Charles dark and rippling to their left. Allie felt stupidly safe walking next to Cait. It wasn't just her size but this calm quiet that radiated from her. And the thoughtfulness. Cait was obviously shortening her lengthier strides to match up better with Allie's, and this charmed her more than anything had in a long time. The tempo of their steps was great, too, not largo or allegro but the perfect in between: a steady forward motion without hurry or languor. The city was beautiful without a bunch of people around, and Allie could kind of get Cait's "aggressive introversion." It was downright amazing to be out at night without having to have all her antennae extended for hints of danger in the shadows—or even right in front of her.

After a while, she asked the question she'd been wondering about for days. "What was bad about your day that night? I know you said you'd screwed up on a contract, but what does that mean for you?" Somehow she knew that, whatever happened next between them, that night would always be *that night*.

"Nothing worth going into."

"Does that mean you don't want me to ask or that you don't want to tell?"

Cait smiled and squeezed her hand but let it fall from her grip. "Neither."

Allie waited for her to expound, but Cait just slid her fingers in her pockets and kept walking. A flare of annoyance shot through her. What was she doing? Looking to let one pleasant night erase weeks of fairly inexcusable behavior? It felt a lot like what her mom had done with her father over and over again. She had already been hit by her brother. Was she destined now to become someone else's doormat? Was she actually attracted to that? The thought made her shiver.

She stopped walking and pulled out her phone. "I'm going to get a ride back home. You should keep walking. But, oh, give me my trumpet." She reached out her hand to where Cait had turned around after taking a couple of steps beyond her. "Please," Allie added.

"I did something."

"No. I just want to get home." She was such a wuss. How was she ever going to stand up to Nick when she couldn't lay some honesty on this perfectly innocuous woman in front of her?

"Okay. I'll ride with you, then."

"I know you'd rather walk."

In the light of the nearest streetlamp, Allie saw Cait's eyebrows draw together. "Only because I had company. Only because I thought you'd like it." She stared at Allie as if waiting for an explanation that Allie had promised, but her mouth was gummed up. Finally, Cait sighed, the sound almost lost under the sparse traffic on Memorial Drive. "All right. I get it. I got ahead of myself again, or sideways, or something." She laughed in a choked way. "Things are so much easier in books. I'm sorry if I made you uncomfortable." She handed over the case, but Allie didn't take it. "Here, your instrument."

"You know what? You always assume everything is about you."

"Oh, believe me, I know that almost nothing is about me, even when I wish it were."

"Fine, then let's get a couple of things straight," Allie said with some edge to her tone. "First, unless it's a yes or no question, any one-word—or one-word adjacent—answer is conversationally unacceptable. Second, it's not my job to work at you until you talk, like some black-hooded torturer. I would hope you'd want to talk to me of your own accord. Third, I'm not interested in men, and thankfully you're not one, so don't make me treat you like some goddamn neanderthal."

With each point, Cait's mouth had opened a little wider and her eyebrows had crept up closer to her hairline. "Uh, okay? You have rules. I get that."

"I don't have rules, Cait. Or not ones beyond behaving with basic human decency. I'm not going to be the kind of person who excuses you for your behavior, who overlooks unsavory things you should take responsibility for yourself."

The hand holding the gig bag dropped down to her side, the case swinging a few inches above the asphalt of the path. "You think I'm unsavory?"

"No! You are kind of maddening, though."

"I'm guessing not in a good way?"

Allie laughed despite herself. "Jesus, Cait. When I ask about your life it's because I want to know. When I want you to take responsibility for yourself it's because no one in my life ever did, and it's like a black hole of suckiness that I'm constantly this close to falling into. We all have our own shit, dirty laundry we're not eager to air, but if you want something here"—she flicked an index finger back and forth between herself and Cait—"that's the price of admission."

They looked at each other for a while. Allie shivered under Cait's cardigan, and Cait tightened her grip on the trumpet case's strap, her whitened knuckles standing out in the path's lighting. "Do I have to tell you my life story right this second or can it be parceled out over a few days? I mean, it's not that interesting, but it's enough that I don't want to get into it this late at night."

"No. Just tell me why you had a bad day."

Cait stared up at the streetlight. "I got fired." Allie was pretty sure that was going to be the end of it and that she'd now have to navigate even more awkwardness between them until either she or Cait moved out of their building. But Cait dropped her gaze to Allie and said, "I screwed up. I was overconfident and a little unprofessional. I lost the trust of the woman who has been singlehandedly responsible for half of my work and income." She grimaced. "I really, really want to blame the egotistical writer I couldn't connect with, but I know that's a cop-out. And now I have to figure out how to make my rent next month and maybe go into this other direction where I have less than zero confidence I can find enough clients, much less be effective to the degree that I'd have to be in order to live with myself." She took a deep, shaky breath that raised her shoulders and released them on her exhale.

"Thank you."

"Yeah, right. More evidence of what great girlfriend material I am. You'd better call for your ride; it might take a while this time of night."

"You really are impossible." Allie stepped closer to Cait. Her height was dizzying at this angle but kind of nice, and she could feel Cait's body heat even without actually touching her. "Are you going to kiss me or what?"

"I'm pretty sure I'm not the only impossible one here," she said before she put an arm around Allie's back and leaned down.

Cait's lips were warm, firm, and undemanding, and they tasted like the best parts of beer, hoppy and alcoholic. Relaxing into both the kiss and the embrace, Allie tested the shape of Cait's lips, the curve and plumpness of the bottom one and the sharp dip around the dimple above the upper. She stood on her tiptoes, erasing some of the distance between them and prompting Cait to tighten her arms around her to hold her in place. She felt warm and safe kissing Cait, but she wanted more. Once again, it fell to her to take the initiative to move things a notch deeper. Luckily, it took little more than a quick brush of her tongue on Cait's bottom lip for Cait to get the hint.

Allie fell into their kiss, the warmth and wetness of Cait's mouth, the firm press of Cait's arm around her back, and the movements of their tongues, which mirrored their previous walking pace—perfectly timed and able to be maintained for hours. Allie's hands found the soft skin at the nape of Cait's neck just under the collar of her shirt, fingers drifting up into her dark hair and tugging her closer. Allie opened her mouth wider to Cait until she felt one particular swipe of Cait's tongue so acutely that it resonated down into her knees. She pulled back so they wouldn't be arrested for public indecency and rested her head just below Cait's chin, her ear receiving and deciphering the Morse code messages from Cait's heart through the open vee in her shirt.

Allie said, "That was…"

"Yeah, exactly."

"We should go home."

"Finally, we agree on something."

During the ride back to North Cambridge, they sat quietly but close, the length of Cait's thigh burning against Allie's, her gig bag on her lap the only thing grounding her—well, that and the overpowering vanilla scent of the clutch of air fresheners hanging from the rearview mirror of the ride share she'd called. Even though there was little traffic, the ride seemed to take forever, which gave Allie the opportunity to wonder what exactly was going to happen when they got to their building. More kissing, definitely, and she couldn't help fantasizing about unbuttoning that starched shirt of Cait's and exploring underneath it.

It wasn't until they pulled over in front of their building that she thought about Nick, who likely was sacked out on her couch. Oh, he'd have a field day with this turn of events. It would be pure psychological warfare, focused not only on her, but also on Cait. And Pancho, another victim of an assault by her brother—who was damned lucky Pancho was the best-behaved dog she'd ever met.

This was going to be a disaster. She shouldn't have thought about starting anything with Cait until she'd dealt with Nick, whatever that ended up looking like. Not that she'd thought through any of this. Hating herself for being such a weakling, she wished he would simply suddenly decide to move along of his own accord.

They were at her landing, holding hands, when she stopped. "I can't go home with you."

"I…hadn't asked?"

She squeezed Cait's hand. "But you were thinking it."

Cait smiled. She had a beautiful smile when she let it light up her dark eyes. "I think a lot of things."

"To be fair, I was thinking it, too."

"But you can't."

Allie shook her head. "It's stupid, but—"

Cait kissed her quickly, interrupting her. "If you feel it, it's not stupid. Is it Nick?" Her voice dropped to a velvet whisper.

Allie nodded.

"Can I help?"

She shook her head. "You can kiss me again, though."

They lost several minutes making out in the hallway, pressed into a corner next to the fire extinguisher. Now that they'd gotten the lay of each other's land, they dove right into the good stuff. Cait's tongue was soft but not indecisive, and Allie thrilled at how Cait used it to explore her mouth, her tongue, her teeth, even flicking at the roof of her mouth. Cait's hands strayed south to Allie's ass, cupping her flesh through her dress and lifting her up to her toes. Allie got dizzy like she'd just played an impossibly long run on her trumpet, and when she finally stepped back, her face was so hot with a flush she thought it must be glowing in the dimly lit corridor.

Cait's voice was low when she said, "Your lips are amazing."

"You're not too shabby yourself."

"No, really. They're mind blowing. I think I need to put mine on some sort of training regimen to keep up with yours." She dipped her head to kiss Allie again. "I'll see you soon, right?" The weight of a real question made her words rough.

"I'm about to change my mind and go upstairs with you."

"But you can't."

"No, I can't."

"Okay." She leaned in for one last, soft kiss. "I'll see you soon," she said with the firmness of fact.

"Definitely."

Allie listened to Cait climb the steps to her floor, unlock her door, and open it, sounds that were followed by a flurry of excited dog noises and loud whispers from Cait. Then the snick of a lock in the hall's quiet. Before going in her own apartment, Allie pressed her forehead against the jamb and took a few breaths. She was a fool for not following Cait upstairs, but she had to grow up and solve her problems at some point, and Nick was officially a problem.

She entered her apartment, dropped her gig bag at the door, and watched her brother sleep, peacefully dead to the world. If only he would stay that way. If only he'd managed to escape the cycle their father had started. But he hadn't, and if Allie wanted anything different, if she wanted to be the person she hoped she could be, she had to find her own way out.

Nick was at her breakfast bar, slurping his way through a bowl of cereal. His stubble had grown stubble, leaving him well on the way to an unattractively scruffy beard. "How was the gig last night?" he asked around a crunchy mouthful.

Allie raised an eyebrow at his interest but said, "Good. Fine. We're really missing Patrick on sax."

"So get him to come back."

"No one wants him. We just want his sound."

"Talk about splitting hairs."

"Yeah, well, interpersonal shit is important in a small group, and what he did was just wrong."

He chewed for a contemplative minute. "Sounds like cancel culture to me. Did the ladies vote him out?"

"It was unanimous, you asshole."

"Speaking of, you're out of Frosted Mini Wheats. Oh, and milk."

"I'm shocked. I wonder how that happened." She grabbed her phone from the end of the counter where she'd left it the night before. "I need to step out for a minute."

She was at the door when Nick said, "Visiting your beastly girlfriend upstairs?"

"Funny," she said around a tightness in her throat.

"I know you want to get all down and dirty with her. Scale that tall drink of water. At least if she wasn't such a tight-ass."

She turned back around to look at him. "You need to shave. Like yesterday. No one's ever going to want to scale you looking like that."

"Haha. You'd be surprised."

He went back to flipping through the *Rolling Stone* at his elbow, and she slipped out into the hall. She did have an urge to zip up the flight of stairs to Cait's apartment and, yes, scale that tall drink of water, but she just sat on the stairs below her landing and called Maggie. Her friend answered, still clearing sleep from her throat.

Allie said, "Too early?"

"Everything is too early when you're pregnant. This thing is sucking away my life force, and I'm still only in my second trimester."

"I'd say I'm sorry, but I don't think you are, so tough luck."

"Yet again I'm blown away by your talent for comforting me."

"Are you in the studio with me tomorrow?"

"Yeah. Berklee again, right?"

"Okay, cool."

After a pause, Maggie asked, "What's going on? You're being weird, and you sound like you're in a stairwell or something."

"That might be because I'm in a stairwell." She picked at a loose fleck of white paint on a curved balustrade. "Nick's in my kitchen working his way through my cereal collection, so I'm getting a bit of privacy."

Now she hummed. "What do you need privacy for?"

"To tell you I kissed her. Or she and I kissed. Equally and at incredible length."

"Yes!" The shout made her take the phone from her ear.

"You're happy? And you know who she is?"

"I just won twenty bucks off Ron. I totally knew you two would get it on. How did you get over hating each other?"

Allie leaned back uncomfortably against the stairs and gazed up to where Cait's door stood, out of sight. Had she already been out with Pancho this morning? Was she still freaking out about her job situation or was she reliving their time together like Allie had done before she'd rolled out of bed?

"Earth to Allie."

She laughed. "Sorry. She's…she really helped me out twice and is actually incredibly sweet if you wash away the crusty bits."

"Good?"

"Yeah. I mean, we'll see. She might turn into a monster today and ruin it all." Allie straightened up to save her back, thinking of Cait's misery. The first time they'd touched, Allie realized.

"What's going on?"

"Nothing. It's just really early on." There, on the stair between her feet was something that looked like a melted cough drop. This carpet was so foul, but Allie made no move to rise.

"Yeah, but I bet the sexual tension is through the roof."

Allie smiled. "Did I tell you she lifts weights? Her forearms are swoon-worthy. I almost went home with her last night."

"But?"

"We both have some things to sort out."

"When are you going to kick that brother of yours out of the house? I can't believe he closed that door right in front of your face and claimed he hadn't seen you."

The lie she'd told Maggie about how she got the cut and bruises on her face made her feel sick now. Still, she didn't correct the record. "I think he's nearly as sick of me as I am of him. You know siblings."

"You can't get my sister and me in a room for more than an hour without a catfight breaking out. I just hang on to the fact that my husband is objectively hotter than hers."

"You're a professional musician. How does anyone beat that?"

"Yeah, but I play the nerdiest instrument short of the bassoon, so that only gets me so far. Now, if I played the trumpet..."

"Oh no you don't. If you picked up the trumpet, you'd put me out of business. You're not going to give it up when you move to the 'burbs and pop out that kid, right?" The question came out in a blurt, fully formed and urgent, before Allie even knew she was going to ask it.

"Uh, where did that come from?"

"Painful history?"

Maggie's breath hissed through the phone. Allie didn't know whether to be pleased that she seemed to be giving the question serious thought or even more scared. Finally, Maggie said, "Honestly, I can't tell you. That's not my plan now. I can't imagine not playing professionally and having that life. But I also can't really imagine what it's going to be like to be a mom. You know?"

"Sure, of course. I'm really happy for you guys."

"I'm not going to abandon you, Allie. We'll always be friends."

With some more inanities and lewd comments, they hung up with a promise to grab coffee before their studio session. Allie didn't move from her perch on the stairs. She'd heard that assertion before, multiple times, and it had never once come true. They meant it at the time, but people invariably moved on without Allie. It wasn't even Maggie's loyalty she was questioning. Maybe they'd stay friends, maybe they wouldn't, but things changed, and the bonds of blood won out in general, shared chromosomes cinching those kinds of families tight together into an indivisible unit, one hopefully filled with love and devotion. The blood bonds in Allie's life, frankly, sickened her. Which is not to say those unfortunate relationships didn't still pull strongly at her.

She knew she was poking this bear with Maggie because of the impossible position she was in with Nick. She'd seen how people went from chosen families to blood, but how was she going to manage doing the opposite? Things had changed now, and it was up to her to change along with it.

CHAPTER FIFTEEN

The week after the jazz show, Cait saw Allie every day, getting together with her even just for a quick chat between Allie's lessons, both of them standing in Cait's doorway, whispering and kissing and trying to keep the dog from weaseling his way between them. Over time, they progressed further into the apartment, finally making it as far as the couch, where they tangled together in a slow, delicious make-out session. One Cait would be happy to repeat ad nauseum until they closed the gap between living room and bedroom.

Grovetree had already taken away a lot of work that wasn't related to the George debacle, so she had empty hours to fill. She whiled many of them away thinking about Allie or listening to her play downstairs. The rest of the time, even when she was at the gym, she worried. No topic was exempt. She worried about Nick lurking in such close proximity to Allie. She worried that she was temperamentally unsuited to be a writer's coach even though she might be able to make a decent living doing that and start right away, given the interest she'd seen from just Tamara's network. Ridiculously, she worried about what she was going to do when she would have to put Pancho down in a heavy handful of years. How could she ever bear having another dog? And she worried about failing Allie before they'd even really gotten started.

Allie wasn't going to excuse her, treat her with kid gloves, or police her. Allie expected her to take responsibility for herself in whatever relationship they might have. That sounded totally reasonable on its surface, but it was going to require a kind of volunteered openness Cait had never been very good at giving. Aside from the resulting loneliness, everything was easier when she kept other people at a distance—a tactic that manifested in a hundred different ways, all of which Allie apparently saw right through. Maybe other people had, too, but they hadn't challenged her behavior the way Allie had while standing on the river path. "Unsavory."

Why was she agreeing to move even one single step away from being considered unsavory when this approach had worked so well for her?

Maybe it was because Allie seemed to want them both to do better. Wasn't that the best kind of partnership? The kind where each person helped lift the other up instead of beating them down? Where there was understanding of both strengths and weaknesses, where one wasn't faulted for needing to do better but challenged to rise up? It sounded like the stuff of fiction, but Allie seemed to want to make it real. It went beyond what she'd said by the river. Between stolen kisses (Cait wasn't sure exactly why they should be considered stolen), she had talked about knowing she needed to take steps with her family and her disappointment in herself for not having managed to do so yet.

"Soon," Allie had said, "I promise you. Very soon."

Cait believed her and felt a surge of her own can-do mentality in response. But then they inevitably left off talking and began to kiss again (Cait's couch had seen more action in the last few days than in the three years before that), and Cait was lost.

As far as she was concerned, Allie's lips were one of the wonders of the world. They were conditioned by years of playing, and she had a kind of control over them Cait hadn't even thought possible. They reduced her insides to a molten puddle of need, made it hard to see straight when the two of them pulled apart, which they always did. Cait knew the taste of Allie's neck and the softness of her belly. She knew the weight of Allie's breasts in her hands and the heat of Allie's breath on her cheek. Unfortunately, she also knew too well what it was like for Allie to pull back and slide to the end of the couch, running her hands through her hair to tame it. She knew Allie wanted more—she could see it in the rapid rise and fall of Allie's chest and the flush in her cheeks—but her hesitation was a physical thing, and Cait was mostly okay with it.

There was still an element of whiplash involved in their being together in any way, after all, let alone this one. It had been only a couple of months since Cait was yelling at Allie and Allie was telling her to use earplugs and get over it. They'd turned into caricatures of themselves in their little feud and maybe wouldn't have moved on if it weren't for Nick. The dog slapper. The family problem Cait had gotten in the middle of, not that she was sorry about that one bit. Helping Allie had made her feel better than she had in ages.

Not that her own family was easy, as Allie was about to see. She was in the middle of her weekly call with her momma when Allie knocked on her door. She let her in, holding up a finger and sweeping her hand toward the couch, hoping that Allie would take the hint and get comfortable while she finished on the phone.

"Nothing's going on with my friend, Momma. Everything's fine. Or as fine as it can be," Cait said.

"I was thinking the police aren't good at that sort of thing."

"That's abundantly clear." And such an abundantly common conception that it had to be at least a little bit true.

"I mean that other organizations are around to help. Shelters. Churches."

"I know what you meant. I don't disagree. But I also think involving the police might be necessary at some point."

"Well, of course. Look at Judy. Anyway, did I send you a picture of my latest quilt pattern?"

"You sure did, Momma. It looks very pretty. I like the geometry in it."

"When are you going to let me make you one?"

It took everything in Cait's power not to tell her that she'd want one for a wedding present, whenever she got married. "Maybe when I stop renting and can paint my bedroom however I want to."

Cait settled on one of the bar stools at her kitchen counter and watched Allie curled up on the couch, flipping through a magazine. She hadn't even kissed her hello and was about to get up and do just that when her momma said, "I don't think your father would like me making one for your bedroom."

Cait stood but couldn't find words through her outrage. She sat back down, noting that Allie was now watching her. "I guess I'm not surprised, but you don't have to do everything he says."

"I don't. Of course I don't. But there are boundaries, and respecting them is part of respecting our marriage."

"Even if they're wrong?"

"Cait."

"Even if they're hurtful?"

"You know it doesn't go well when we talk like this."

Cait laughed. "Gee, I wonder why. If you want to make me a quilt for my depraved bed, then you should go ahead and do it. I'll—" She was going to say send you pictures of me and my girlfriend under it but stopped herself just in time. She breathed a deep breath in and out. "I'm sorry for that. I have to get going. I'll call you again, okay?" She didn't wait for an answer before hanging up.

Allie was still watching her. "That escalated quickly," she said.

Cait nodded.

"Your mother."

She nodded again. "I broke a bunch of implicit rules there."

"You also have an accent when you talk to her." Allie smiled, wide and toothy.

"It's hardwired, especially when she gets under my skin."

"Are you going to come over here or what?"

Cait slinked over to the couch and sat next to Allie, who took her hand and kissed each fingertip. "I don't talk to my father, as you may have gathered. They're religious, to say the least. And rural. And ignorant. But my momma overlooks my deviance. Mostly."

"Ouch. Does it help at all that I really dig your deviance?"

"It does, actually. It helps a lot." Being able to smile this close to that phone conversation felt weird but good.

"Do you want to talk about it?"

Cait wasn't sure what the right answer was, but she suspected she was going to get it wrong either way.

"Hey." Allie touched her cheek. "It's not a trick question. You don't see me waxing poetic about my father or brother, do you? Or getting into why you were talking about my situation with your mom. Everything's fine."

Cait reviewed her side of the phone call. Her smile muscled through trepidation. "I talked about you because you're part of my life, have been for a while now. Forget about that, though. What would poetic waxing look like about Nick?"

Allie laughed. "Probably a dirty limerick."

"God, now we totally have to make one up."

They came up with bawdy rhymes for a while, Cait well aware that she'd sidestepped any further conversation about her own family. Then they devolved into making out again. Cait had Allie flat on the couch and was settled between her legs, holding her weight off Allie on arms bent deeply at their elbows. While they kissed, which was about all Cait could manage to focus on, Allie's hands roved across her back to her shoulders and down over her upper arms, her button-down lying crumpled at their feet. Allie completed this grand prix route several times before she groaned and pulled her mouth away from Cait's.

"I swear, I'd think I was straight if you weren't so incredibly soft."

Cait settled on her elbows to give her arms a rest. "Um, you know I'm not a man, right? The peacoat and hat were just an example."

"That's not what I meant. I just never saw the appeal of muscle until now. Yours is smooth but solid, and your skin is like velvet—what lotion do you use?—and the combination is blowing my mind."

"But I'm a woman. I like being a woman. I'm all in on both sides of the lesbian thing."

Allie snuck a hand between them and cupped Cait's breast, thumbing her nipple through her bra. Cait had to close her eyes for a minute at the resulting sharp pang of want between her legs. Allie whispered, "I know all about it. Well, maybe not all yet, but I have a pretty good idea. You know that thing about there being more of you to love? You're like a Michelin-starred all-you-can-eat buffet." She lifted her head to kiss Cait's neck.

Because she was a total idiot, Cait said, "I know you used to call me 'The Amazon.' Nick told me."

Allie shifted back, and her hand stilled on Cait's chest. "I didn't know you then."

"You definitely weren't attracted to me, though."

"I wouldn't say that, but you were all business all the time, and you had Pancho…it made a certain impression."

"What changed, then?"

"What are you getting at?" Allie asked and relinquished Cait's breast to tuck a lock of hair behind her ear.

"Nothing, forget it."

Allie pushed at Cait's chest to get out from under her. She sat up, running her hands through her light hair. "I thought we agreed not to do that."

"Seriously, it's nothing." Cait sat up as well and leaned away from Allie, cursing herself while feeling around behind her for her shirt.

"Did I not make it clear just now that I want to devour you?"

Cait could feel that her smile was weak. "You may have compared me to a buffet."

Allie took Cait's shirt away from her and climbed onto her lap. "I don't know, babe. You were imposing before and never hung around long enough to ogle, if you know what I mean."

"Sure, I get it. How I am with people isn't an accident."

"We all have a public face." She put her hands on Cait's neck, thumbs brushing her jaw in emphasis. "I just find having a different one useful."

"That's because you're universally attractive."

Allie laughed. "First, if you only knew how many women have turned me down, you'd know that's verifiably false, and second, you hated me just a few weeks ago, too."

Cait felt her widened smile in the push of her cheeks up toward her eyes. "Hate's such a strong word. Finding you annoying didn't mean I couldn't think you were hot at the same time."

"Ah, the truth comes out."

"You asked for honesty."

"Fine," Allie said. "If we're being honest, I liked your eyes and your cheekbones, and I've always had a thing for tall women. I don't know why, but you all make me go weak in the knees."

"But you think I'm kind of like a man." Cait hated that this particular insecurity of hers wouldn't stay submerged under her usually thick skin right now, but having Allie so close made her want to make sure they weren't separated by artifice.

"Cait, no. Absolutely not." Allie's fingers gripped at the back of Cait's neck. "I'm serious. I would never have allowed you to help me if you weren't a woman. You were so gentle and caring. Your insecurities blow me away—in a good way but also because they're incomprehensible to me. I am in awe of how you take care of yourself, your discipline, the mouthwatering results, and how incredibly safe you make me feel." She gazed into each one of Cait's eyes in turn. "Or maybe that last one is Pancho. It's hard to tell."

Cait snorted. "I totally forgot to train him as a guard dog."

"All he has to do is lean on intruders."

"Lick them into submission."

Allie said, "Now that I've been downwind of a fart or two, I think he should just gas them."

"God, he really knows how to clear a room, doesn't he?" Cait glanced over at the beast in question, who was lying sprawled out on the other side of the coffee table. He blew out a huff without raising his head. "One time I actually had to vacate the apartment—even after opening the windows. I was almost overcome."

Allie's hands slipped down to the tops of Cait's shoulders and massaged the muscles there. "Are we going to keep talking about dog farts or are you going to give me a chance to show you how beautiful I think you are?"

"When you put it that way..."

"Farts it is, right?"

"Farts all the way."

On that note, they started kissing again, seriousness sweeping everything out of their path but lips and tongues, fingers and skin. Having Allie on her lap, warm and close, brought Cait completely into the here and now, offering an escape from any worries or thoughts that weren't related to how good she felt and what Allie might do next to make her feel even better. Allie was vocal in her appreciation of Cait's body and what she was doing, too. Thanks to another burp of self-consciousness on Cait's part, that initially felt forced. But only momentarily. In a nanosecond, the sounds Allie was making were adding fuel to the fire of Cait's arousal.

Allie kissed the flat plane of her pec at the top of the rise of her breast, sucking on the skin. "Jesus, Cait. You're fucking magnificent." Her hands found the button fly of Cait's jeans and opened it with one sharp tug. They both groaned at the move.

Cait moved her hands under Allie's ass, tightened her grip, shifted her feet, leaned far into Allie, then carefully and slowly stood up from the couch, taking her with her. Allie curled her arms around Cait's neck and locked her legs around Cait's hips, and they swayed for a minute, kissing deeply. Cait took several steps toward the bedroom, then stopped.

Into Cait's neck, Allie said, "Are you showing off now? Because it's totally working."

"I want to take you to bed, but I don't remember if you have something later or not."

"Are you kidding me? I wouldn't care even if I did."

"Yes, you would."

"Fine. Since you've wiped everything from my mind but yourself, take me over to the counter where my schedule is. I don't think I have anything, but I never trust myself to remember."

Cait walked them to the kitchen, feeling a pleasant strain in her shoulders and forearms. "Practice," they both said in unison. Cait said, "And that means?"

"Take me to bed right now."

"I like that answer." Cait headed in the right direction, stopping inside the bedroom to kick the door closed behind them, knowing it would be a tactical error to let Pancho in while she and Allie got more closely acquainted.

"I can't believe how easily you're carrying me and how turned on it makes me. And it's because you're a woman, in case you wondered. Your strength moves me, okay?"

"I think we should stop talking." Cait deposited Allie on the end of the bed.

"Take off the rest of your clothes. I want to see you."

"I guess that kind of talking is okay." Cait smiled and let her jeans slip all the way off her hips, which was easy given how much they'd slid down since Allie had undone them—and Cait's mind—back on the couch. She kicked them out of the way and glanced at Allie, who was staring at her.

"All of it," Allie said, her voice low and her hands gripping the edge of the bed.

Cait unhooked her bra and used two thumbs to push her underwear down, letting them fall around her ankles. She kept her gaze trained on Allie the whole time. For her part, Allie scanned the full length of Cait's body, her mouth opening as she did.

"Come here," she said.

Cait did as she was told, not sure how Allie had become the one in charge but not minding it one bit. She cupped Allie's head in her hands and moved it to the perfect angle to kiss her. The combination of their kiss and the soft trailing of Allie's fingertips over her back and down her ass fried the synapses of her brain. Her knees trembled as Allie's hands continued to wander, cupping the backs of her thighs, thumbing the indented path next to the flare of her quad. Her movements felt both sensual and tender, and the combination urged Cait to lose track of time and space.

"Your turn," she said roughly.

Allie wasted no time unhooking her bra and unzipping her skirt, shimmying out of them and her panties, a black, lacy pair Cait wanted to take her own time examining on her later. Then finally they were in bed, covers kicked to the side and early evening sunlight slanting through the window blinds and across their skin. The feel of them pressed fully together made Cait's breath catch; she released it in a groan that Allie echoed. All their talking was over now, and they communicated with breath and touch.

Allie pressed Cait into the bed and ranged across her chest, mapping it with her lips and tongue until she settled on a breast, taking its nipple into her mouth. Cait's back arched with no conscious volition, and her arms encircled Allie and held her close, tracing patterns on the soft skin of her back with her fingertips. With Allie's mouth came a sweet ache of desire. Cait wanted to give as much as she possibly could to Allie. She didn't care what was going to happen next as long as it was more.

Allie's mouth kept coming back to hers, kissing it so deeply and thoroughly that Cait could barely breathe. Between kisses, Allie found the pulse point in her neck, sucking on it lightly. Cait whispered, "I want—"

"I know. Me, too."

"No, I want to—" This time Cait was interrupted by Allie's hand sliding down her belly to mere inches away from where she could feel her own heartbeat pounding between her legs. Her breath caught and released in a low moan. "Okay, I want you. Please, Allie."

Allie took her time getting there, stroking the inside of Cait's thighs and her belly, cupping her ass, which Cait lifted off the bed in her need. Allie's palm pressed against her, applying pressure to where she was throbbing with arousal but stopping short of anything that might satisfy her. This went on for so long Cait was practically hyperventilating.

"Please," she whispered, and Allie complied, sliding her fingers through Cait's wetness then back up to her clit, where she set up the most delicious tempo of touches, circles as regular as the scales she practiced. Cait gripped Allie's shoulders and breathed at the ceiling, watching colors rise and fall behind her eyelids, in a place past language and worry, a realm of pure sensation. Not just that but the intimate knowledge that it was Allie touching her, whispering something she couldn't hear, pushing her to let go, surrender, fall into the abyss. An orgasm roared out of nowhere and ripped a low cry out of her while her muscles tensed and shook before finally falling still.

When at last she regained the feeling in her limbs, Allie was draped half across her, arm and leg heavy across Cait's torso, her head on the junction of her shoulder and chest. They breathed for a while before Allie said, "Your heart's going crazy."

"Gee, I wonder why."

"It was okay?"

"It was so okay I forgot how to think."

Cait could feel Allie's smile that ended in a soft kiss. "Good."

"As soon as I can move, you're next."

"Don't rush. I'm incredibly comfortable."

The sound of Pancho shaking his head, flapping his ears and jangling his tags, filtered through the closed bedroom door. Cait listened, waiting to hear the huff he always made when he lay down and settled in.

Allie said, "He'd have a bird's eye view if he were in here, huh?"

"Oh yeah. I have some strict boundaries. He is a dog, after all."

"Your boundaries go beyond animals, I think."

"I thought we were having sex, not psychotherapy."

Allie snorted. "That's way too many syllables for pillow talk."

"Fine." Cait turned the tables, covering Allie with her body. "Sex it is." She kissed Allie deeply and thrilled when she dug her hands into Cait's hair and tightened her grip, opening her mouth wide for Cait's tongue. Holding herself up on one elbow, Cait freed the other hand to trace down Allie's torso from her neck to her hips, coming back to caress a breast until its nipple was a hard press against Cait's palm.

Cait kissed below Allie's ear and whispered, "What do you want?"

"Just you. All of you. I want your weight, your mouth, your hands. I want you inside me. Everything."

She let herself cover Allie and press her into the bed, closing her eyes with sensation when Allie's legs wrapped around her like they had when she had carried her in here. Her hips lifted against Cait, and her short nails pressed into Cait's shoulder blades. They rocked together, breathing into each other's hair and neck, creating the most tantalizing friction and ratcheting Cait's arousal back up from its previous satiation.

Cait slid a hand between them and, finding a hot pool of wetness right where she wanted to be, abandoned herself to her desire and pushed inside Allie. She breathed out a low moan that was matched and surpassed by Allie's own vocalization. "More," Allie said, and Cait complied, pulling out enough to insert a second finger and finding her own rhythm and a sensation that made her previous arousal seem like nothing. She pressed her thigh against her hand, pushing as deeply into Allie as she could, over and over, the base of her thumb pressing into Allie's clit with each stroke. After a long, delirious time, she felt a tightness in her own body that echoed the one she was feeling in Allie. She ground herself against Allie's thigh and rocked along with the motions of her hand, creating the pressure that made another orgasm build inside her, rising up through her belly and chest. When Allie keened hoarsely and with abandon, tightening around her hand, Cait came again, fast and strong.

She fell back on the bed next to Allie. Breathing as hard as Cait was, Allie searched around her until she found Cait's fingers and held them tight.

"Okay?" Cait asked.

"I'll tell you when I can feel my face again, which might take a while." Allie brought their hands to her lips and kissed Cait's knuckles before settling their clasped fingers on the middle of her chest.

"You feel really good. I think that may have broken me a little."

Allie's laugh was quiet. "Are you as out of sex shape as I am? At least you've been to the gym. If we keep this up any longer, I'm going to be sore tomorrow."

"I need a minute to recover."

"Lightweight."

"Literally no one has ever called me that."

Allie shifted to her side and looked at Cait, her arm tucked under her head, her hair drifting across her bare shoulder. "You're delicious. All of you. You know that, right?"

Cait's grin was weak. "Maybe if you tell me a few more times."

Allie cupped Cait's jaw. "Good God, woman. I—" She stopped. "I think you're wonderful. Period."

CHAPTER SIXTEEN

Cait's skin was velvet, her lips just the right plumpness, her fingers long and sure. They'd been in bed for hours, and Cait was making noises about taking Pancho out, but Allie kept getting in her way, finding new parts of her body to marvel at. It was almost like she'd never slept with a woman before, which was untrue, of course. But she'd never slept with one quite like this. When Cait lay back, spent after an orgasm, which Allie couldn't tire of giving her, her whole body relaxed and melted into the bed, muscles slack. She was the best full-body pillow, ever. But when she turned the tables and took charge, she was strength and power. Allie didn't know which she liked better and was happy she didn't have to choose. She was focused at the moment on Cait's abs, which manifested as a soft, smooth belly that hid slabs of muscle on each side, stretching from her hips to the bottom of her rib cage. Allie traced them up and down, making Cait clench. Which made them harden and stand out from the rest of her body. Which made them even more irresistible to touch.

"That tickles." Cait tried to shoo Allie's hand away.

"I know. Isn't it delightful?"

"We have different definitions of the word."

"What did you say? Opposites attract?" They surely did, if the time they'd spent in Cait's bed was any indication. Sex with Cait was a slowly unfolding marvel. So many dichotomies: soft and hard, surrender and command, attentive and abandoned. Her kisses were single-minded, and her fingers... Allie gave an internal shiver. When Cait was inside her, she could feel it everywhere. Right now, she was so spent that she didn't think it was physically possible to get out of bed. Not that she wanted to. Under these sheets and comforter, beside this incredible woman, it was warm and safe and the perfect kind of quiet.

Her stomach growled, embarrassingly loud.

A smile curled the corners of Cait's mouth. "I was kind of thinking the same thing. Pancho probably is, too. I'm surprised he isn't complaining yet."

"Imagine if he were a kid."

"That would be...different." She turned her head toward Allie, brushing some dark hair from her face.

"I'm not saying I want one, in case you're wondering. At least not right now. I just keep losing friends and colleagues to them."

"I'm happily in the dog zone right now."

"It's just that when you really have only a chosen family, it's hard when the people you choose end up choosing their 'real' family instead."

Cait reached over and traced Allie's eyebrow with her thumb. "Does it help that I'm choosing you now?"

Her stomach growled again. "Definitely. It would help more if you could rustle up some cheese and crackers or some other kind of snack. If you can believe it, I want food even more than another orgasm. For the moment, at least."

Cait kissed her. "That really is hard to believe, but your wish is my command." She got out of bed with a groan, looked around the floor for something she couldn't seem to find before pulling her jeans on commando and putting her hand on the door. "Ready for me to let loose the hound?"

"Oh, God. What if I say no?"

"It'll probably happen anyway. Brace yourself."

She opened the door to Pancho standing there, wagging his tail so hard his butt was moving with it. He snuffled and squirmed when Cait petted him, thumping his side and scratching behind his ear. Then he noticed Allie lying in bed, the sheet clutched to her chest. He hurried to press himself against the side of the mattress, using his tongue to bridge the last of the gap between him and Allie's face.

Allie laughed. "I know. We were ignoring you and making all sorts of strange noises. Hello. Hello." She called out to Cait, "Should I get dressed and take him out?"

"I'm pretty sure you should never get dressed again. Don't worry, I'll take care of him. Pancho, come." She snapped, and the dog peeled away from his love assault on Allie to trot out of the bedroom.

Allie said, "Don't forget. Your shirt's over by the couch. I don't want to share that magnificence with—" She was interrupted by a loud knock on Cait's door.

Cait said, "Just a sec," but before she even had a chance to retrieve her shirt, the knocking came again, a hard thumping this time. Allie's chest tightened, but she told herself she was being paranoid.

"What in the world?" Cait mumbled. "I'm coming." There was more pounding, and after a moment Cait appeared in the bedroom doorway, buttoning the last button on her shirt. Her voice was low and tight when she said, "It's your brother."

As if to prove the point, Nick shouted, "I know you're in there, Allie. What? Are you doing the nasty with that big dyke?"

Cait's mouth pressed into a firm line. Allie said, "Ignore him. Don't engage. He'll go away."

"Allie, get the fuck out here. I know what you're up to, you carpet muncher." *Pound pound pound.* "You can't hide from me. Don't even try it since I've got your fucking trumpet here with me."

Allie sat up at that. "He wouldn't. Cait, he wouldn't, right?"

"I didn't see it through the peephole, but let's not take any chances." Cait turned and strode away. Before Allie could say anything to stop her, she heard the snick of the lock, the jerk of the door opening, and Cait saying, "What?" The word was sharp and loud, kind of like the blat of a trumpet.

Fuck. Allie was out of bed in a shot, casting about for clothes that might cover her. In the other room, she heard Nick laugh a scary laugh.

"I think you should go before this turns into anything serious." Cait's tone was low and firm.

Allie pulled up her skirt and ducked into Cait's pajama top, backward and inside out, doing anything not to be in here naked.

"You don't know what you're talking about. Allie! Come on, you little pussy licker."

"Knock it off." Cait's voice was louder now and shaky.

Allie hustled out of the bedroom and toward the door. "What the hell, Nick?"

He laughed again when he saw her in clothes four sizes too big. "You and The Amazon?" He'd been bluffing about the trumpet; his hands were empty, which enraged Allie.

"You need to get out of here right now," Cait said.

"Or what?" He got right into her face. Pancho started to bark, standing next to Allie with his hackles raised.

Without looking away from Nick, Cait said, "Allie, call the police."

Nick laughed. "I'm really fucking scared. Do you see me shaking?"

Allie tugged at Cait's arm. "Don't." Pancho was still barking, and she willed everything to go back to the way it had been, quiet and calm.

"I said, call the police."

"Did you find another daddy now, Sissy?"

Cait's hands balled into fists, the hands that had just touched her so tenderly.

"No!" Allie yelled. "Just stop. Both of you."

Nick shoved Cait, sending her reeling into the wall behind her, her head whacking the plaster with a flat thud. Before she could recover, he had his forearm across her neck and was leaning right into her face. "I don't know what you're doing to my sister, but she doesn't need any of it."

What did Nick think he was doing? Allie pulled hard on his arm, and Pancho barked even louder. "Stop it. Let her go. Please, Nick, don't do this." She hated the pleading in her voice.

"You're such a fucking hypocrite, thinking Mom and me are such sad fucking sacks, thinking you're so much better than I am, and then you go and fuck someone you hate. It's disgusting." He leaned into his arm more deeply. Cait scrabbled at his skin with her fingers and lashed out with her foot. It connected with his knee, which put him off balance, sending him crashing forward into Cait. While he was there, he punched her in the gut.

Allie screamed, "Leave her alone!" He hit her again. She skidded to where her phone was on the kitchen counter and dialed 911. "I'm calling the cops, Nick, and it's not going to be like Mom and Dad."

"You wouldn't dare." He grunted when Cait tried to knee him in the groin. "That's enough!" He tried to throw her to the ground, but she managed to stay upright. There was no more talking as they engaged in a standing wrestling match, just shatteringly loud barking and gasps and grunts.

Allie wished she could save Cait the way Nick had saved them that last night with their father, but the cords were standing out in his neck, and his face was red under his stubble. He looked homicidal. "Nick, please!" she yelled, willing to give up all her dignity to make this end. She waited to be connected to emergency services, watching as Cait managed to shove Nick half out the door—before he slammed back into her again, sending them both sprawling on the floor. As Cait started to crawl away, the 911 dispatcher picked up and Allie was shouting into the phone, giving her address, and saying, "My brother" and "Assault" and "Hurry."

Nick was on top of Cait now, and one of Cait's hands was against his face, pushing him away. He punched her in the side, and she tried and failed to knee him again. The police weren't going to get here soon enough…

Allie was paralyzed, frozen in place by the same fear that had gripped her as a child. She had to do something more. Cait was in danger. Not her mother, not Nick, and under her fear she discovered a building fury. Anger that Cait was at risk. Anger that Cait had been dragged into Allie's seedy little life. She'd worked so hard to move on, and her past kept showing up like a bad, fucking penny.

When Nick landed a punch to Cait's jaw, Allie's fear suddenly didn't matter anymore. She pushed Pancho out of the way, wound up, and kicked Nick's side as hard as she could. Her bare foot connected with his ribs, and she felt the sharp pain of a toe breaking. He was turning toward her with a murderous expression when Cait reached up, caught his head, and pressed her thumbs against his eyes. He screamed like a little girl and crawled back and away from Cait, shoving her hands away from his face. Allie took the opportunity to kick him again in his soft midsection, which made the air rush out of him in a whoosh. He curled up on his side and groaned, and Allie hissed and hopped around in pain.

When she found some control, she got in his face while Cait sat back against the wall, breathing hard, her fingers soothing her jaw, which had already gone red.

"Are you done, you stupid son of a bitch? Are you finished now? Did you get what you wanted?" He got up on his hands and knees, but before he could do anything more, Allie danced behind him and kicked him in the nuts with her uninjured foot. He crumpled to the floor.

"How dare you?" she shouted at him. "How do you not know better? Didn't you want to be different?"

He was struggling to breathe, but Allie wanted nothing more than to hit him again and again. To knock some sense into him. To pay him back for slapping their mother and for hurting Cait, which was so much worse than when he'd hurt her with that one startling punch. She wanted to see him cry and bleed and shake with the kind of fear she used to feel so often at home.

"Allie." Cait was next to her, one hand on Pancho's collar and the other on Allie's shoulder. "Stop," she said to both of them. Her command worked much better on Pancho than on Allie.

"He deserves to be beaten to within an inch of his life." Allie's voice was distorted by adrenaline: loud, tight, and trembling.

"Maybe, but we're not going to do that."

Allie whirled around. "He hit you. Choked you."

"I'm okay. We're all okay. The police are coming, and he'll be their problem." Cait took Allie's hands in hers and squeezed a little too hard. "Let him be their problem. Please, Allie."

Then Allie started to shake, her teeth chattering with the strength of the emotion gripping her. Her fingertips went numb, and angry tears blurred her vision. "I just—All this time, and—Why'd he have to—" She dissolved and was folded into a firm embrace, pressed against Cait's chest, Nick still rocking back and forth on the floor in her watery peripheral vision. She let Cait hold her while she cried, for herself, for her brother, and for Cait having now seen this ruinous side of her life.

Sirens wailed in the distance.

They'd been to the hospital, which prescribed ice and ibuprofen—and taped two of Allie's toes together. They'd also been to the police station. The cops had taken things seriously, though not without some glances between them that told Allie they weren't on board with the amount of lesbianism in the apartment. Now, they sat next to each other on the couch in a still-shocked aftermath, Cait holding an ice pack to her jaw, her arm wrapped around her chest and the cracked rib there. Nick was stronger than he looked. Cait had called it "man strength" and said it wasn't to be trifled with. She sucked on a protein shake while Allie's stomach still roiled, sour and hate-filled. She knew she should stop, but she couldn't keep her traitorous mouth from apologizing, saying the words "I'm sorry" over and over again. She reached out to touch Cait's forearm with a finger.

"I know you are. I'm sorry, too."

Yeah, sorry she ever got involved with me, Allie thought. Why did it happen then? Right after they'd been so warm and intimate? She sensed a gulf between them now and knew there was no way to make it right.

"I should go."

The look Cait gave to her was sharp with hurt before she closed her eyes and rested her head on the back of the couch in the way that would make her neck seize up after a while. "Do whatever you need to do."

"What I need? Nothing here resembles what I need, Cait."

"I didn't say it did. I'm saying you know best what you need to do now."

Allie's shock morphed into anger and despair in equal measure. "Because I'm an expert in abuse? Because it doesn't matter that you were the one he assaulted? Because you have no use for me now that I don't fit into your neat, quiet life?"

"Hey." Cait sat up, wincing, her warm, brown gaze heavy on Allie. "Can you—I'm not the bad guy here."

"No, it's my brother. My own shitty family. And me, for bringing him into your life."

"Allie, listen. I don't think this has anything to do with you. Or you and me. Nick needs help. He's always needed help and probably has never gotten any."

"Well, he's not going to get it now."

Cait squeezed her temples in the vise of her long fingers, and Allie felt appropriately shamed. "What do you think we should've done?"

"Nothing. Or nothing different, I guess. It's just impossible." Allie's voice went quiet.

"And yet it happened."

She got up. "Why are you being like this?"

"Because my head hurts and my ribs hurt and I couldn't deal with the problem when it was happening. Now I'm apparently saying all the wrong things, so I should just shut up."

"Say it. Say the wrong things."

Cait squinted at her. "That seems like a bad idea. I really don't want to make things worse."

"Say it, Cait." Allie was only vaguely aware of why she was pushing this.

Cait slammed the ice pack down on the coffee table, startling Pancho, who was still clearly unnerved by the earlier altercation and hadn't been more than three feet away from them once they'd gotten back home.

"I hate that you had to hurt him. I hate that you wanted to hurt him. I hate that this beautiful thing we just had was interrupted by such ugliness. I hate that there's no easy explanation for any of it. I hate that you're blaming yourself, and I hate that it feels like you're way across the room even when you're right beside me." She choked up. "I hate that I'm afraid that this is going to take you away from me just when I got you."

Allie slid from the couch and knelt next to Cait's legs, putting her hands on her thighs. Cait looked away from her. Allie rubbed up and down the worn denim. "I hate that you took the brunt of it for me. First Nick did it with my father and then you did it with him. I hate that I seem incapable of fighting my own battles. I hate what you must think of me after this. I hate that I feel like I'm back to having no right to put my arms around you." She shook her head sadly. "I hate that your not being able to look at me feels like this has already taken you away from me."

Tears tracked down Cait's cheeks. She brushed them away, took a shaky breath, and looked at Allie with bloodshot eyes. "God, Allie, being in that house with your father must've been terrifying."

"It was a long time ago."

"Not really, though, right?"

"I'm so sorry." Even now, she couldn't stop saying it, and she wondered a little who she was really apologizing to.

"Hey." The word was sharp. "You have nothing to be sorry for. I'm serious."

"I'm not the person you think I am."

Cait's laugh was low, followed by a soft groan of pain. "No one is. We're all great mysteries to each other."

"You know what I mean."

She looked pained, fresh tears spilling from her eyes. "Don't do this."

"What am I doing?"

"Using this as an excuse to leave me."

That simple statement and the clear anguish behind it knocked the breath out of Allie as surely as if she'd been punched. She picked up the ice pack, climbed carefully onto Cait's lap with her knees on either side of Cait's hips, and pressed the pack gently to Cait's jaw.

"I don't want to leave you. You're pretty heroic, you know? But I don't want to need a hero. I want to be my own hero instead of letting everyone else fight my fights for me."

"How about we just put a moratorium on fighting for now and leave heroes out of it?"

"Hey, it's my turn to be serious."

"I know, and I get it. Is that something you think you need to be alone to work on? Because speaking very selfishly, I don't think that's true." Cait brushed hair back from Allie's face.

Allie kissed Cait, long and slow and soft. She smelled of lemons and antiseptic, and her hair was soft under Allie's free hand.

Cait pulled back. "I like that answer. Feels very correct."

"Doesn't it?" Allie wiped the last remnants of tears from Cait's cheeks. "I want...Can I play for you?"

"Right now?"

"I think you'll like it. I promise it won't be loud."

"I've been waiting weeks for this."

Allie grinned, climbed off Cait's lap, and zipped down to her apartment, coming back with her trumpet, still embellished with the kink in the bell from her previous fight with Nick. She blew some air through it to warm it up as she slowly took the stairs up to the fourth floor, where Cait's door was open a welcome crack. She closed it behind her and locked it, adding the chain for good measure even though Nick was in jail, at least for the night. She'd get her lock changed first thing in the morning.

"Ready?" she asked.

"Lay it on us," Cait said, Pancho's head on her lap.

She raised the trumpet to her lips and started to play "Flamenco Sketches" by Miles Davis from his *Kind of Blue* album, the one that had gotten her interested in jazz in the first place. Learning it was a certain rite of passage for her, and its melancholy but soothing tone and tempo seemed exactly right for this evening and both of their hurts and fears. She played, pacing around the living room, not looking at Cait, closing her eyes when she could, letting the notes pull through her on breath drawn from the tips of her toes. She let her sound ride softly on pillows of air, having no desire to blow Cait out of the room. Instead, she wanted to bring her close and soothe the hurts that Nick had caused. Injuries that Allie had been indirectly responsible for, no matter what Cait said.

Allie wanted to feel again the strange closeness that had permeated Wally's Club when Cait had sat at the bar, nursing a beer, beautiful and solid and undeniable. She wanted to recreate their first kiss in music, rewind time until they were back in the next room, quiet and sated and safe. She let her breath calm her, the oxygen righting so many wrongs in her terror-filled brain. She played to weave a spell between them and bind them together with this kind of magic instead of the trauma that Nick had inflicted on both of them. She wanted to hold Cait here and never let go.

She stopped playing and slowly lowered her instrument. When she turned to Cait, she saw love in her gaze, a love that filled her chest and made her smile in a trembling, brand new way.

CHAPTER SEVENTEEN

Cait squatted next to her bed, getting in Pancho's way and holding a half-full mug of coffee up to the edge of the bed where Allie's head was. Over the last year, this had become routine for them, Cait and Pancho jockeying for position near their favorite person as she rejoined the land of the living. Her blond hair was spread out across the pillow behind her, and a bare shoulder poked out from under the quilt Cait's momma had made for them a couple of months before. It was full of deep blues and greens and looked much more like it was designed for Allie than Cait, which made Cait irrationally happy. She thought of the quilt as being for them, though Momma had expressed no such intention and had specifically asked not to receive any pictures of it in use. Cait had no idea what her father thought. Baby steps.

When Allie didn't stir right away, Cait reached out and ran her fingers back and forth over that creamy shoulder. Her motion was answered with a slow smile and the opening of one blue eye, then the other.

"Morning, babe." Allie's voice was raspy with sleep, and it made Cait melt like it did every morning.

"Moving day," Cait said.

Allie rolled her eyes. "I don't know why you're so excited. I've practically been living here for the last six months, and you're on the hook for getting my couch up here, and it's a heavy son of a bitch."

"First, you've told me how heavy it is before. Second, practically living here isn't the same as officially living here. Until you're officially living here, I need to check two mailboxes instead of just one. Third, since we sold my couch two weeks ago, we've been abjectly couchless, so I'm ready for the replacement."

"It just means we've had to spend more time in bed."

Cait set the coffee on Allie's nightstand, which was absolutely Allie's: big headphones, *Rolling Stones* magazine, and earplugs because, yes, Cait was known to snore. She sat on the edge of the bed after waiting for Allie to scoot her legs over.

"Believe me, I'm not complaining about that, but I also want to stop making trips downstairs to grab things that you forget."

"You could always tell your lazy-ass girlfriend to go get them herself. Does she think she's some kind of a princess just because she wears dresses?" The image of Allie in a pink poufy dress and tiara, surrounded by helpful singing woodland animals, danced through Cait's delighted mind.

Cait went along with Allie, saying, "Probably, especially now that she knows I can't say no to her." She held out her hand, palm up, where Allie could reach it. Her arm snaked out from under the quilt, and she intertwined their fingers. Cait took a breath, but before she could say anything, Allie squeezed her hand and interjected.

"How long have you been up?"

"A couple of hours. You got in late last night, and I wanted to let you sleep. I also needed to get a packet back to a client before I got distracted by moving day."

Allie smiled, rounding out cheeks still flushed from sleep and making her dimples make their first appearance of the day. "I keep seeing those words in my mind as a windswept banner. I guess it goes with the princess thing. I was late because the crew and I went out for drinks. We think this saxophonist is finally going to work out."

"The woman?"

"Yeah, Monica. She's got a startlingly loud laugh, but she knows her stuff."

"And she won't get handsy with you."

She rolled her eyes. "You'd think that would be setting the bar pretty low, but I guess it's not. I'm excited to stop auditioning and letting people go or losing them to other, more lucrative opportunities." She released Cait's hand and ran her fingers through her hair, raking it back from her face and working out some tangles at the ends, all without pulling her head from the pillow. "I mean, what's wrong with suffering together in this terrible stingy business? How are you going to play bluesy jazz if you haven't been through some shit?"

Cait captured her hand again. "Speaking of…are you okay?"

The question was far from idle, and Allie had already dodged it a few times. Sometimes, Cait let things lie with Allie when she wanted her to, but when it mattered, she'd learned to push gently but persistently. It always drew them closer together— once Allie got over being annoyed. She needed to know that Allie was okay because their moving day also happened to be the day Nick was getting out of jail. For the last twelve months, he'd been incarcerated at the Middlesex County Cambridge Jail, not five miles from them. Allie had unwaveringly refused to visit him and was pretty proficient about changing the subject when Cait brought it up.

The only thing that had stopped Cait from worrying about it was that Allie would open up at night before falling asleep. Wrapped tightly in Cait's arms, her back to Cait's front, Allie would talk about her father and Nick. Confusion figured prominently, as well as questioning how these things had happened, but she got resolute about not taking blame for them or thinking she could have changed any of their damning trajectories.

Allie's smile when she answered today was far from sparkling, though, and definitely not princess worthy. "I'm fine."

"Are you worried?"

She sighed. "Sounds like I should ask you the same thing."

"I'm not worried about him, but I'll always worry at least a little about you where he's concerned."

Allie softened and pulled Cait's hand to her lips. "I honestly can't imagine him daring to come back here. He's an opportunist like my dad, and that opportunity ship has sailed. A year in jail was a long time and not long enough, but he's his own problem for once. Mom and I are in agreement about this, in theory at least. I wouldn't put it past her to cave if he went to her." Allie's breath graced Cait's knuckles.

"Your mom's capable of taking care of herself."

"Not really. She's never fought back, and she doesn't have someone like you who will fight for her. That said, I'm not capable of worrying about her anymore." She reached over to grab the mug of coffee but stopped raising it when it was halfway to her mouth and made a face. "I have to brush my teeth first. My mouth tastes like ass. Why did we make moving day the morning after a gig at Wally's?"

"Because it was the only time we could get people to help, and I can't carry that couch on my own."

"Are you sure?" Allie squeezed Cait's bicep, which Cait couldn't help but flex under those fingers. "Because it feels like you can."

"Flattery will get you nowhere."

"Will it get me a make-out session after I brush my teeth?"

"Twist my arm." Cait let Allie out of the bed and lay back in her place, still in her pajamas, a relatively new development. Allie being in her life turned out to be a force that she couldn't— and wasn't interested in—constraining. If Allie wanted an extra twenty minutes in the morning to cuddle, or get even better acquainted, she acquiesced. And Allie's commentary on how Cait pitched herself as a writing coach had been heavily influential in ramping up her client list so quickly. Then there was her expert feedback on Cait's notes to her writing students. That had been helpful but demoralizing in her attempts to actually coach instead of merely edit. With all that had come one more perk: the sound of Allie's trumpet, which now was as familiar to Cait as her voice, even though her practice space had reopened a few months after they'd started dating.

Dating, ha. They'd fallen into each other so quickly and completely they were a lesbian trope. While Cait still valued quiet alone time, she was usually crawling the walls by the time Allie got back from giving lessons or practicing or recording or one of her jazz gigs. Cait used to worry about this irrepressible craving she had for this pint-sized wonder of a woman, but eventually that, too, seemed silly, and she abandoned herself to the ferociously loud pixie—who she'd started calling Pix for short. Cait's outlook, when it came to love and relationships at least, had turned from one of asking why to one of wondering why not.

Allie reappeared in the doorway and shucked off what little she was wearing before worming her way under the covers and on top of Cait.

Cait said, "Oh, this kind of make-out session."

"Anything worth doing is worth doing well. Besides, if we don't look indecently satisfied when our friends get here, we'll have missed quite the opportunity."

Their friends: a phrase that used to be charitable but now was at least mostly true. Allie and Cait had visited Maggie and her family in the hospital after the baby was born and had even babysat the infant one harrowing time despite the fact that neither had childcare experience. They'd found common ground with a couple on the second floor who, they discovered in a chat at the mailboxes, were addicted to seemingly every card game known to man and some Cait was pretty sure they'd made up on the spot. The dog park had coughed up not only a friend for Pancho—a greyhound that teased him with her speed—but one for both of them. Keith, someone who Cait had seen at the gym, was helping her move the heavy stuff from Allie's place up a flight of stairs because, of course, the elevator was out. She'd never talked to him before she'd mentioned him to Allie and was left with her mouth hanging open when Allie stopped in to watch her exercise and walked right up to him and introduced herself.

Cait stopped thinking when Allie took her lower lip between her teeth and bit gently.

"Pay attention," she whispered, and Cait ran her hands from Allie's ass up to her shoulders and back down.

"I'm here," she said, and she was, she truly was. She was here in a way she'd never been present before. She groaned. "I love you, Pix."

Into Cait's neck, Allie mumbled, "My Amazon." Then they were at it again, finding peace and excitement with each other in a way Cait was sure was never going to end.

Bella Books, Inc.
Happy Endings Live Here.
P.O. Box 10543
Tallahassee, FL 32302
Phone: (850) 576-2370
www.BellaBooks.com

More Titles from Bella Books

Hunter's Revenge – Gerri Hill
978-1-64247-447-3 | 276 pgs | paperback: $18.95 | eBook: $9.99
Tori Hunter is back! Don't miss this final chapter in the acclaimed
Tori Hunter series.

Integrity – E. J. Noyes
978-1-64247-465-7 | 28 pgs | paperback: $19.95 | eBook: $9.99
It was supposed to be an ordinary workday...

The Order – TJ O'Shea
978-1-64247-378-0 | 396 pgs | paperback: $19.95 | eBook: $9.99
For two women the battle between new love and old loyalty may prove
more dangerous than the war they're trying to survive.

Under the Stars with You – Jaime Clevenger
978-1-64247-439-8 | 302 pgs | paperback: $19.95 | eBook: $9.99
Sometimes believing in love is the first step. And sometimes it's all
about trusting the stars.

The Missing Piece – Kat Jackson
978-1-64247-445-9 | 250 pgs | paperback: $18.95 | eBook: $9.99
Renee's world collides with possibility and the past, setting off a tidal
wave of changes she could have never predicted.

An Acquired Taste – Cheri Ritz
978-1-64247-462-6 | 206 pgs | paperback: $17.95 | eBook: $9.99
Can Elle and Ashley stand the heat in the *Celebrity Cook Off* kitchen?

Printed in the USA
CPSIA information can be obtained
at www.ICGtesting.com
JSHW020349090724
66105JS00001B/4

9 781642 475920